"This is great erotic fiction! ... Fresh, sexy, and humorous."
—*Romantic Times BOOKreviews*

"Action-packed and ferociously seductive."
—*Romance Reviews Today*

"If you haven't heard of Charlene Teglia, you soon will. ... An absolute winner."
—*Romance Divas*

"A great book full of action and adventure ... Charlene Teglia has a knack for creating wonderful stories with characters that will keep readers coming back for more."
—*Romance Junkies*

"Don't miss out on this incredible new talent."   —*Love Romances*

"A must-read."
—*The Road to Romance*

"A gem of a tale."
—*Fallen Angel Reviews*

"Ms. Teglia is a terrific writer who has penned a story of love and magic that left me sighing at the end."
—*Just Erotic Romance Reviews*

"As usual, Ms. Teglia's sex scenes were small doses of TNT and the tension was perfect."
—*Ecataromance*

"I laughed, then I sighed and had tears in my eyes at the end ... a book I intend to read again and again!"   —*Joyfully Reviewed*

WICKED HOT

CHARLENE TEGLIA

ST. MARTIN'S GRIFFIN
NEW YORK

WICKED HOT. Copyright © 2008 by Charlene Teglia. All rights reserved. Printed in the United States of America. For information, address St. Martin's Press, 175 Fifth Avenue, New York, N.Y. 10010.

www.stmartins.com

Book design by Spring Hoteling

Library of Congress Cataloging-in-Publication Data

Teglia, Charlene.
    Wicked hot / Charlene Teglia.—1st ed.
       p. cm.
    ISBN-13: 978-0-312-36946-0
    ISBN-10: 0-312-36946-8
    1. Demonology—Fiction.   2. Angels—Fiction.   I. Title.
    PS3620.E4357W53 2008
    813'.6—dc22

                                                    2008013016

First Edition: August 2008

10 9 8 7 6 5 4 3 2 1

To my own hero, thank you
for your support and encouragement!

ACKNOWLEDGMENTS

Thanks to Rose and Deidre for being fabulous at their jobs, to the Write Ons for being there, to the Wicked Writers for everything, including comic relief, and to NJ for being my test reader.

WICKED HOT

ONE

I wasn't sure you'd come." He stood in the moonlight with his hands in his pockets, looking almost bashful. Which struck me as laughable, considering our reason for being here.

"I'm here. Whether or not I'll come remains to be seen." I gave him a wide smile and let my trench coat fall open, showing off the black lace bra, panties, and nothing else underneath except my belly button ring winking in the moonlight.

Garrett, if that was really his name, seemed very interested in what wasn't under my coat. I let him get a good long look at ample cleavage and a sleek, bare midriff. Men are visually stimulated, and the more aroused he became, the better my night would be.

The dogging event hadn't drawn too much of a crowd, less than a dozen onlookers. I could easily pick out the ones who'd want to do more than watch.

Ah, dogging, how easy you've made my job, I thought. "Walking the dog" was the popular euphemism for a prearranged meet for one purpose: having sex in a public place. A big draw for voyeurs and exhibitionists alike, dogging events were frequently advertised, recorded, and broadcast on the Internet so the show could be witnessed by the broadest possible audience.

For me it was like shooting fish in a barrel.

I shrugged off my trench coat and let it drop to the grass. I'd agreed to meet Garrett at this park after sunset, and I noted with some pleasure that the lawn offered a lot more room to maneuver than the inside of a car in a public parking lot.

Those cramped encounters so tended to discourage audience participation. The choreography required for front-seat group action gives new meaning to the term cluster-fuck.

I settled my perfect ass on the fabric of my discarded London Fog and smiled all around. "Who's first?"

A tangible rush of lust filled the air, and just like that, I had them all.

Fish in a barrel.

Garrett was first, of course. I let him touch me because it was the best way to hook the ones who liked to watch. They watched his hands unfasten the black lace bra that pushed my cleavage up to heights no mortal woman could aspire to, and there was an almost audible sigh as the lace fell away and nothing but Garrett's hands covered my twin peaks.

Garrett was a little clumsy and had no idea what to do with a body like mine, but he was fully aroused and his sexual energy fed me until I was damn near orgasmic. But far from satiated. Never satiated. The more I fed, the more I hungered, and the circle of men watching us was only going to whet my appetite.

I feasted on their lust, expertly playing them, pulling them into my field and draining them and they never saw what was happening. Garrett's eyes grew glazed and a confused look came over his face as he approached the threshold.

"What—?" he asked. It was an incomplete question, but I answered him anyway.

"You're a pervert, Garrett," I informed him in a matter-of-fact, nonjudgmental voice. "And now you're a damned pervert. Thank you for your soul. Welcome to hell."

You've been a naughty girl, Edana." Nick's voice was deep and approving when I joined him in his office later that night. "Ten men at once. Want a spanking?"

"I'm not that kind of girl." I gave him a wide-eyed innocent look and dropped into the seat across from his desk. I was still wearing the panties, and while I'd put the trench coat back on, I'd left it hanging open to provide a nice peep-show effect.

I wasn't wearing anything else. I'd left my bra in the grass at the park. I like to leave souvenirs, and they're not docked from my pay. Actually, since it counts as littering and could stir impure thoughts in the mind of whoever finds my discards, I get bonuses on top of the amusement factor the habit gives me.

"You're my kind of girl." He patted his lap. "Take off the trench coat and come sit."

"You're the boss." I shrugged out of the trench and strutted around to him, then gave him a little lap-dance action. I got a light spank on my ass for my trouble. I sat down then and heaved an aggrieved sigh. "Is this all the sexual harassment I get? You're not even trying."

"I want you to conserve your energies. I have a special job for you, Edana."

Nick kissed the side of my neck and toyed with my nipples as he spoke so I wouldn't feel ignored. I responded to the gesture, even though I knew I wasn't going to be favored with anything that might feed my need.

"Who?" I asked. I didn't expect an immediate answer. I knew he'd tell me the details when he was good and ready.

"What," he corrected, and I felt something other than my nipples stiffen.

"Not human?"

"Partially."

I swiveled around to face him and hooked my legs over each side of the chair so I straddled his lap. "Tell me more."

He shook his head. "None of your tricks. You've fed well enough tonight." Since my thighs were spread wide, he gave me a light spank on my mound and I hissed at the mixture of arousal and denial. "I want you to seduce a Nephilim."

"A Watcher?" I quit trying to play-seduce Nick and sat

up straight. The Nephilim had once been a widespread race, the half-breed results of intermarriage between human women and angels who'd abandoned both heavenly and hellish realms in favor of life on earth.

The Nephilim had been called many things. *Watcher* was one of the more innocuous terms. They'd also been known more accurately as the Terrors and the Weakeners. "I thought they were extinct. Either they killed each other off fighting or drowned in the Great Flood."

"They're strong. And persistent." Nick flicked my clit, overly hard on purpose, and I scowled at him.

"That wasn't necessary," I protested.

"I'm evil." He shrugged and let his finger travel up to toy with my belly button ring. "This particular Nephilim is a problem. He's giving me headaches. He conjures and binds. He banishes."

At the *b* word, I went ice-cold. "I thought you liked me," I said with a quaver in my voice. "You're sending me out to get banished?"

"I'm sending you because I have confidence in your skill and abilities, darling Edana." He leaned forward and kissed me, filling my mouth with a thrust of his forked tongue and a smoky flavor that was distinctly Nick. "Seduce him. Steal his soul. I want this troublesome Watcher in hell."

I wasn't comforted. I may have large breasts, but words like *bind* and *banish* do stick in my feather head, and while flattery is always nice, I really would have preferred some kind of weapon besides supernatural sex appeal. "You suck as a motivational speaker."

"Nevertheless," he breathed the word against my lips.

"You'll do as I say. Because you're mine and I send you where I will."

Well, he had me there. But that didn't mean I'd just rush off to my doom. "Come on, Nick," I wheedled. "Wouldn't you like a presidential candidate instead? A televangelist? An engineer?"

"I want him," Nick said. He placed three fingertips on my belly, and when he drew them away, three little brands in the shape of his fingertips remained. The burns would heal almost instantaneously, but he'd made his point.

"Fine," I said, getting up. "I'm tired of this afterlife anyway. It's all sex energy and no actual sex."

"Fiendish, some would call that." Nick actually smiled at me when he said it, the smug, evil bastard.

"Whatever. It's like a cosmic joke that in my human life I died a virgin and after centuries as a succubus I can't ever get a human to punch my ticket because my demonic powers drain him before he can do the deed." I felt genuinely aggrieved over that, and let it show in my face. "And now, after all I've done for you, all the souls I've stolen, all the men I've led to their downfall, you're sending me out to be Watcher bait. I hate you."

"Everybody hates me. I'm the devil. It comes with the job description." Nick stood up and patted me on the head. I kicked him in the shins with the pointy toe of my strappy come-fuck-me shoes. He just laughed. "I like your style. I always have." He turned serious then. "You're capable of this, Edana. I am not setting you up to fail. I want him stopped and I want him stopped now, before I lose any more demons to him."

I blinked at that. How many had this bad-ass Nephilim

tagged already? It had to be pretty bad for Nick to get personally involved. He might be the devil, but he didn't micromanage. If he wasn't leaving this matter to one of his lieutenants to handle, if he'd taken on the task of assigning me to deal with it himself, matters were serious.

It was like a bad joke. Hell had a serious problem, and *I* was the one getting sent to deal with it. Armed with my Frederick's of Hollywood wardrobe.

"Do silver bullets work on Nephilim?" I asked.

"No." He tweaked my cheek. "Arm yourself with feminine wiles. They're more powerful and much more lethal. Go shopping."

"Damn."

"That's what you are," Nick agreed in a cheerful voice. "Go damn him, too."

"Right," I said, my lack of enthusiasm palpable. I didn't even wiggle my ass at him as I left the room. I was too depressed. Instead, I peeled out of the panties, kicked off the spike heels and left the items scattered behind me as I headed for my computer terminal. Since the ambient temperature in the office was always measured on the Kelvin scale, clothes were the last thing I needed.

Hell's Internet crashed frequently and without warning, and if that didn't cause me enough aggravation the computer would blue-screen periodically. Shopping for this job could take a while. Which was fine with me. My afterlife as a succubus might not be perfect, but it beat nonexistence. I wasn't in a hurry to cease to be.

Although arguably nonexistence isn't really possible. I've heard enough theologians going on about this one to have heard all the points and counterpoints on that debate. Demons can assume physical form, but in our native state, we're energy. Energy can't be created or destroyed. So how can we cease to exist?

I don't know the answer, but I know nobody's been able to contact a banished demon to find out if they're still self-aware and if they've retained consciousness. My best guess is that energy can be used up, and the prospect of a blast from a powerful Nephilim aimed point-blank at me didn't fill me with positive thoughts.

My best hope was to strike first. Get him before he got me. Do unto others and all that.

Before I started browsing for battle armor in the form of my chosen undress uniform, I did some research to see what I could dig up on the Nephilim. What little I knew wasn't nearly enough to help me spot possible vulnerabilities I could exploit. Still, all men had their weaknesses, and I'd had a lot of experience in using those weaknesses to my advantage.

I learned they'd been known as giants among men, much taller and stronger than their purely human counterparts. Their race had also been credited with bringing the knowledge of magic to humans. The epic of Gilgamesh documented the heroic exploits of one member of this not-so-lost race. Those recorded deeds were enough to make me feel chilly despite my location. Gilgamesh had been one historic badass, and he'd gone after the first succubus, Lilitu. She'd survived and escaped, but he'd come out the clear winner in that contest.

Great. As far as I could tell, I was going up against a sorcerous warrior giant. A powerful being with supernatural abilities and human form with far greater than human strength.

And due to the mixed nature, a soul.

The soul and the human form might make him some-what vulnerable to me, but I didn't like the odds.

"Seduce him," I said out loud. Right. Because he wouldn't see through a succubus and know it was a trap.

Done with my depressing search through the pages of history, I switched my attention to my current files. Nick would have sent me the information on my target, and I wanted to know my enemy.

His name was Eli Moss. His face . . . well, his face would have made me take notice even if I wasn't a being who subsisted on sexual energy. I can't really say he was handsome in the classical sense of the term, but he was certainly compelling. He had animal magnetism, and it showed even through the computer's display.

The mixed heritage altered features in a way that would look exotic to human eyes but not abnormal. Just more rugged, harsher, more beautiful in purely a masculine way. More jaw and cheekbone than your average man, deep-set green eyes that seemed too aware, too knowing. He wore his black hair shoulder length with two small braids on each side and the rest flowing loose, an unusual style in modern times. The hairstyle emphasized his features.

Oh, and he really was big. All over. A giant among men, indeed. I couldn't help it, I felt my nipples tingle and a distinct flare of heat in my midsection as I considered the total package.

And that was just the effect of graphical rendering. What impact would he have in the flesh?

I licked my lips and considered my mission. He was either

going to be a feast for my demonic senses like no other, or my downfall. If I allowed him to distract me, guess which was more likely?

"You seem a decent fellow," I said to his image. "I hate to kill you." The line from *The Princess Bride* earned me a reprimand in the form of Barry Manilow's hit "Mandy" pouring from a hidden speaker. I scowled in the general direction of the source of the music, if you could call it that. I knew better than to complain out loud, though. I'd only get something worse.

I wouldn't actually be killing him, I thought, as I studied Eli's face. He was half angel. The loss of his human soul would mean what, exactly? I couldn't find any precedent in the records. As far as I could tell, angels and demons alike had left the Nephilim alone. I hadn't even known they still existed, which meant at some point they'd passed into the collective realm of myth despite the fact that they demonstrably were still around. Why?

Whatever the reasons, the centuries-long agreement to ignore each other, to live and let live, had ended with this Eli. By binding and banishing demons, he'd forced Nick to take action.

And lucky me, I was the official response. Too bad I wasn't being sent as an ambassador for peace. I didn't think there was enough underwire in the world to distract this man from my nature. He'd see me coming and I'd be toast.

I started shopping for the perfect outfit to wear to my funeral. If I was going out, I planned to go out fighting and dressed to kill.

Two

For reasons possibly known only to him, Eli lived as close to the middle of nowhere as it was possible to get in America, in a tiny Washington town of three thousand people surrounded by Olympic National Park. Oh, and it was also the wettest spot in the continental United States, with an average of 140 inches of rain a year.

I hated rain.

Fortunately, the black leather miniskirt and matching bustier I wore would shed water, and I had a black leather trench coat to help keep me dry. My thigh-high boots would sink up to the heels in mud if I had to do any walking. I made a mental note to avoid that.

I would stand out like a sore thumb among the loggers who made their home in Forks. I also wouldn't pass for a visiting hiker. Tourists might come from all over the world to visit the Olympic Peninsula, but they dressed for camping and fishing, not seduction.

I wasn't trying to blend in, though. I wanted to get Eli's attention. If I couldn't arouse his sex drive, I wanted to arouse his curiosity. He would be smarter than the average human with his mixed heritage, and while that probably meant better physical self-control, it also might mean he'd get overconfident in his ability to put mind over matter, so to speak.

None of the demons who'd fallen to this Watcher had been a succubus. It was actually a smart move on Nick's part. Send a seductress who might slip under his guard instead of a warrior whose presence could only mean a direct challenge.

Besides, he might hesitate to hit a girl. You never could tell.

That's right, think positive. I parked my jeep on the private road that led to Eli's sprawling log cabin retreat in the woods, popped the button that opened the hood, and counted to one hundred. Figuring I'd timed it about right, I shrugged off my trench coat, climbed out, and went around to bend over the hood.

With any luck, Eli would be along right about now. I planted my feet shoulder-width apart and dipped my lower back to emphasize the curve of my ass and make the short skirt ride up higher. I wasn't wearing any underwear. The odds were stacked against me as it was, so I didn't see the point in pulling my punches.

I heard the low growl of an engine coming up behind

me. I resisted the urge to turn around and look. The motor stopped, and booted feet crunched in the gravel. A rough voice that sounded as gravelly as the drive said, "What's a nice girl like you doing in a place like this?"

I suppressed a frisson of fear, turned my head, and gave him a slow, knowing smile over my shoulder. "Who said I was nice?"

Eli Moss was even bigger in person than I'd expected. He was at least seven feet tall, and built to scale. Even with towering heels, I was a shrimp next to him. I wasn't a true demon, after all. I'd started out as human, and in my current form I was still human small.

He tilted his head and considered my answer. He took his time looking over the picture I made, my skirt showing off the lower curve of my ass and the soft flesh between my thighs.

"Naughty girl, are you?"

"Yep." I arched my back to give him a tantalizing display of pussy before I grasped the leather hem and pulled the skirt up higher to bare one side of my butt in invitation. "Very naughty. Want to spank me?"

"You'd like that, wouldn't you?" He smiled at me, and I felt it like a punch in the gut. I actually sucked in a breath. How could he be terrifying and still make me want to get closer at the same time?

"Yes." I figured I might as well be honest. I was lust incarnate, after all. And he was something I'd never expected to encounter. My hunger stirred. He would feed me and feed me, able to last longer than any human male. Unless he destroyed me first.

Eli laughed and walked up to me. Up close his eyes looked more green than hazel. The loose length of his hair with the twin warrior braids framing his face created an effect that was simultaneously sensual and barbaric.

He planted the palm of one large hand on my butt cheek. "Then I'll have to find another way to punish you."

His words sent a shiver of ice through my veins that the heat of his touch couldn't counteract. There were far too many ways he could punish me for me to mistake the threat for a joke. "Wouldn't you rather spank me?" I asked. My voice dropped into a lower register.

"No." He stroked the soft skin of my butt, not lusting, just contemplating the options. His hand felt warm against my skin in contrast to the cold rain. Opposing impulses simultaneously told me to pull away and to press into his touch. I resisted both and held still. "I think maybe I'd better bind you until I figure out what to do with you."

Oh, hell. "If you're not sure what to do with me, I have lots of suggestions." I knew it was hopeless, but I had to try.

"I'm sure you do." He gave my bare ass an almost affectionate pat that didn't comfort me in the least. Then Eli spoke in a language the world hadn't heard since before the time of the Great Flood, when all the earth's languages were one language and the Nephilim lived openly among humans.

The words reverberated through me like a shock wave. When he fell silent, I was bound.

I fought the urge to panic and tried to think, but this was not good. It could only be worse if he knew my true name. Then even if I managed to escape or he let me go, my name would give him the power to conjure me back and banish me. In the meantime, he had me trapped. I couldn't make a move against his command.

He picked me up like I was a doll left out in the rain and carried me to the extended-cab long bed truck he'd parked when he saw me on the road. And then he proceeded to drive the way he'd been headed, toward town, not back to his house. He stopped once to buckle my seatbelt, not because he thought my body would be much hurt by flying through the windshield in an accident but so we wouldn't look suspicious to the humans.

The interior of the pickup was warm and dry and more luxurious than I expected. I might be his prisoner, but at least Eli had put me up in the cab with him instead of tossing me in the back of the truck bed. I tried to be grateful for small mercies.

His next stop was a burger-and-shake joint too small to have a drive-through window. He left me waiting in the truck, went inside, and came back out a few minutes later with a paper bag that smelled divine and two drinks. He placed one that I assumed was mine in the cup holder nearest me.

"I wasn't sure what you liked, so I got chocolate," Eli said.

Chocolate. He'd bought me a chocolate shake, and placed it out of my reach. I cursed him silently as I stared at the cup, my limbs nearly trembling with the effort to move and unable to because he hadn't ordered it.

Eli took a long sip through his straw and then turned his head toward me. He laughed. "Sorry. Go ahead and drink."

I lunged for the cup and filled my mouth with the sweet mixture of cream and chocolate, frozen on my tongue.

"Guess you wouldn't have to watch your weight." Eli settled the paper bag between us and drove back the way he'd come. "How long have you been a succubus?"

"A long time," I mumbled around the straw. I had to answer him, but I didn't intend to give away any information I didn't have to.

"Not good enough." He took the milkshake away from me and when I protested and tried to take it back, he gave my hand a playful slap. "Stop."

And I had to. I subsided in my seat, feeling put out and put upon.

"Answer the question."

I opened my mouth, then closed it again. It wasn't that I was trying to be difficult now that he'd made an issue of it. I just wasn't sure how to answer. My human life was one I'd done my best to forget, and it had ended in a spectacularly bad way. When I passed the threshold, I'd found my soul forfeit and I'd been made a succubus, charged with inciting lust in human men, feeding off their sexual energy, stealing their souls.

How much time had passed between my human death and my new incarnation? I couldn't say. I only knew the world had been different when I'd been sent back out into it.

Eli turned to look at me again and I threw up a hand in self-defense. "I'm not stalling," I said. "I don't know the answer. I didn't exactly have a calendar back then, and time in the nether realm doesn't run the same as it does on earth."

Eli nodded. "Okay. I'll give you that. But you know roughly what year you died in."

Yes, I did. "1066."

That got his attention. It was a well-known date in history. "The Battle of Hastings?"

"I wasn't so much directly involved as I was collateral damage," I said. "But yes."

"Saxon?"

"Does it matter now?" I should've known better than to let him know he'd struck a nerve, but I couldn't keep it out of my voice.

"Answer."

Fine. "I was a Saxon, yes."

"You were a woman. Why'd they kill you?"

"You are fucking relentless." I tried to reach for the shake again and he picked it up.

"You can have it when you tell me why."

"I think it had something to do with the dead Norman I was with," I said.

"You killed a Norman?" Eli handed me the shake. I stuck the straw in my mouth and sucked. Chocolate might not solve everything, but it did make most things better. It was one of the things I loved best about visiting earth.

"Yes," I said after swallowing. It wouldn't be polite to talk with my mouth full. "I killed him."

I wish I could've said *with pleasure,* but it had made me feel sick to my soul, which of course I was, because with that act I'd damned myself. An act of hatred, of rage, and I'd died unrepentant a few seconds later when three more Normans rushed on the scene and ran me through.

"It was a mortal sin," I added. "Hence my afterlife."

Talking about it made me feel a little ill even now. I put the shake back in the cup holder and turned my head to look out the window.

Everything was so green, everywhere I looked, lush with growth. Evergreens and deciduous trees, flowering bushes, rhododendrons as tall as Eli, ferns and salal tangling together. The rain fell steadily, and a cool mist hung in the air. Something inside me responded to the setting, as if remembering the past had brought back the memory of the girl I'd once been, on a wet and wooded island far away from here.

Dangerous territory. The last thing I needed to bring into a fight for my afterlife was baggage from the past. I turned my attention to the present and used the icy beverage Eli had so thoughtfully provided to ground myself in the now.

Of course, he might not have done it to be thoughtful. He might've been trying to soften me up. I didn't know enough about his race or him to make assumptions. Still, I wasn't about to look a gift shake in the mouth. I'd learned to take my pleasures where and as I could, because there was always more torment waiting.

As if to confirm this, Eli switched on the radio and the strains of "Mandy" filled the truck. I groaned. "Can you change the station?"

"Nope," he said. "Unless you want to hear gospel. Those are our only two choices out here."

I shuddered. Listening to gospel music would be worse than Barry, but only just. I consoled myself with the knowledge that the song had to end, and in the meantime, I had ice cream.

The song ended. "Copacabana" began. I turned pleading eyes to Eli. "Make it stop. Turn it off."

He slanted a look at me. The corners of his lips curled up. "Is it bothering you?"

"If you don't turn it off, I will beg you to banish me before we get wherever we're going."

"How do you know I won't do that anyway?"

"Because you haven't yet," I answered. "You said yourself you were binding me until you figured out what to do with me. If you'd just wanted me banished, you would have done it already."

"You seem awfully nonchalant about being in my power."

I shrugged. "I knew the odds going in. And it's not like I have a choice in where I go and what I do." Maybe that would make him feel sorry for me. Not likely, from a race with well-deserved nicknames like Terrors and Weakeners, but a girl could always hope.

He didn't turn off the radio. On the bright side, he didn't switch it to the gospel station. I endured Barry Manilow and being bound by a member of a race that should've been extinct and wondered if I'd been punished enough yet for my sins.

I did know better than to blame my problems on heaven. I'd put myself in this situation by my own actions. Nobody had forced me to kill that man. And I did have an out. It was impossible, but it did exist.

All I had to do to be free from eternal torment and service as a succubus was to win a mortal's love and be given a soul freely.

The rub, of course, is that no mortal could ever get close enough to love me without being destroyed by my demonic powers, and if one did, who would willingly give up a soul? It was insane. But hey, the out clause existed, and I couldn't say my afterlife wasn't fair.

"Copacabana" finally ended. The commercial break came as a relief.

"Are you hungry?"

Eli's voice startled me. "Yes."

I was famished, in fact. Food wasn't what sustained me, but it helped a lot. I needed to feed, one way or another, and calories were a form of energy.

"You can start eating if you need to."

Well, damn. The way he'd worded it, I couldn't. I *could* wait until we got back to his place, assuming we were heading there. It just wouldn't be very enjoyable. And since I didn't need to, by his wording I didn't have permission to start early.

It never hurt to ask, though.

"I can wait, but I'd rather not. Can I eat?"

Eli shook his head. "If you can wait, wait."

I sat back in my seat and tried to ignore the scents teasing my nose. Cheeseburger. Fries. My mouth watered.

I needed a distraction, and Eli could provide it.

"Why are you here?" I figured I might as well just get to the point.

"I was hungry. I wanted a Rainy Day special," Eli said.

I rolled my eyes at him. "Why are you *here*? Nephilim were supposedly wiped from the face of the earth by the time the Great Flood ended. So my question is actually twofold.

Why does a Nephilim exist, and why here in Forks, where it rains all the damn time?"

"It's actually very sunny in the summer," Eli said.

I ground my teeth together. "Fine. Don't tell me."

"And it's no longer possible for enough rain to fall to flood the entire planet, so a little drizzle isn't worrisome."

Eli sounded thoughtful as he maneuvered the truck along the driveway. He parked next to the sprawling farmhouse. I noted the weathered siding, the encroaching moss on the roof's shingles, and the general air of age. This place had been here for a while. Long enough for the trees surrounding the house to have grown to towering heights.

Eli picked up the bag of food and got out of the truck. "Come on."

And like a pet dog, I had to follow him.

THREE

E li opened the front door and waved a hand, inviting me inside. Okay, ordering me. But he was polite about it, I had to give him that. I brushed my leather-clad body against his when I passed him, but he didn't react at all.

I chalked it up to angelic immunity to demonic charms. The idea that I just didn't do it for him was too depressing to contemplate, and defeatist to boot.

I, on the other hand, didn't have any immunity to his charms. Seducing Eli really wasn't going to be a hardship for me. The face, all jutting angles and planes. The eyes, as deep and unreadable as the ocean, full of who knew what hidden threats beneath the surface. The body, a smorgasbord of sinful possibilities in one tall, muscular package with a distinctive scent that made me want to get closer. A hint of cedar, an edge of musk.

"You could at least pretend you're happy to see me," I said as he joined me inside and shut the door behind us. "A big guy like you has to have a big . . . smile."

He did grin at me then, flashing white teeth and a dimple I hadn't suspected. "And you called me relentless."

"Hey, if the very large shoe fits . . ." I let my voice trail off and shrugged a bare shoulder. Goosebumps danced over my skin and I missed my leather trench, back inside the jeep. The air had a damp chill I wasn't used to.

"Hello. Who's our new friend?"

I turned toward a new male voice. The voice belonged to another very tall and well-muscled man, late twenties I guessed, with bright blue eyes and brown hair worn in a crew cut that gave him a military look. He also had presence and an undercurrent of power. If I hadn't seen Eli first, I might've embarrassed myself by staring or drooling. The two of them in the same room? Succubus delight. "Hello," I answered, giving him a wide smile.

He shook his head at Eli. "You go out for burgers and come back with a hot blonde?"

"Ignore the hot blonde," Eli said. He turned to me. "Don't seduce him."

I gave him a look of disbelief. "I seduce, therefore I am. If you don't want me to seduce him, send him away or put me in a closet."

I wanted to kick myself as soon as I said it. I did not want to take up residence in some dark, small, closed-in space that

smelled of must and dust, and where he'd find it easier to ignore me. I'd also find it really hard to make any progress with
him if he shut me up somewhere. I didn't like being bound,
but if it kept me close to him, I could still use the proximity
to try to wear him down.

"Practice self-control," Eli advised me. "Especially if you
want me to let you have any fries with your burger."

"Succubus?" the new man asked Eli.

"Yep. Found her lying in wait for me at the road."

"Well, she's a lot more decorative than the last demon who
showed up here," the man said, giving me an appreciative
look. "No cloven hoofs. No horns."

"I might be horny," I said, wiggling my eyebrows at
him.

"No fries," Eli said, and I let my shoulders sag and my
lower lip tremble. "Cut it out. You know you don't deserve
them."

"I'm Dal," Dal said, still smiling at me. The smile showed
off two deep dimples in addition to giving his mouth a tempting curve. "You can have my fries."

"No, she can't." Eli put his hand on the small of my back
and propelled me down the hallway, toward the kitchen. The
point of contact felt warm, but totally devoid of lust.

Dal wasn't giving off any lust, either, which made me
wonder if Eli was the only Nephilim in the house. It was either that, or I was losing my touch.

"Are you a Nephilim, too?" I asked him.

"Yes." He hooked a finger into the soft leather of my bustier, brushing the cleft between my breasts in the process. "I'm
immune to your charms, so it's okay to let me see them."

"Dal," Eli's voice rumbled in a low warning.

"I just wanted to see if she had scales or something." Dal gave Eli an innocent look before turning his attention back to me. "Do you have scales? Or a tail?"

"The kitchen's through here," Eli said, pushing me forward and stepping so that his body forced Dal away from mine. Dal released his playful finger hold on my bustier and allowed Eli to muscle him out.

I watched him and wondered how deep I was in, here. Dal might seem like the more playful of the two, but if he'd wanted to crowd Eli out, I thought it might've been a close match. Neither of these guys struck me as a pushover. Eli was taller, but Dal wasn't far behind, and I suspected that what he lacked in height he made up in muscle and hustle. The two were built on the same frame: heavy musculature, long bones. The Nephilim had been renowned fighters. How many of them were there? These two hadn't sprung from nowhere.

Eli pulled out a straight-backed wooden chair with his foot and pushed me into it with his hand. I sat, partly because he hadn't left me a choice and partly because I was hungry.

"Inviting demons to lunch," Dal said, taking a chair for himself. "What would Mom say?"

"You two are brothers?" I asked Eli, not Dal, which was dumb because Dal seemed a lot more inclined to give me information. But it was Eli I'd turned to automatically. As if I saw him as the senior, the one in authority. Or maybe it was just because he'd bound me.

"Lunch," Eli said, ignoring us both and settling the bag in the middle of the table. The wood surface bore the scratches, scars, and dings that came with time and use, but it was clean.

The whole house was neat with a surprising lack of dust, from what I could see. Not the typical bachelor dwelling. Or maybe they had a housekeeper. The kitchen had a glass-paned back door, and the way the linoleum floor was worn in front of it, I suspected it was the main entry.

Eli sat beside me and passed out paper-wrapped sandwiches. He placed the fries in front of himself and Dal. Oh well, at least I'd gotten a shake on the way.

Dal saw me looking and slid a French fry across the table to me. I couldn't pick it up, though. I stared at it, then at Eli. He picked up the fry and ate it himself. "Don't encourage her," he said to Dal.

"She's hungry," Dal said.

"Demons are always hungry." Eli tore into his Rainy Day burger, and I did the same. Delicious.

"Look who's talking," I said when I'd finished chewing and swallowing.

"I have a big . . . appetite." Eli smiled at me, flashing that dimple again. It made my stomach lurch. Or maybe that was just hunger. I took another bite of burger.

"She's the tenth one this month," Dal said to Eli. "I'd say they're escalating, except sending us a stacked blonde in a miniskirt seems more like lying down on the job."

"I like lying down on the job," I said, winking at Dal. "But sitting, standing, and kneeling all work for me, too."

"She's a succubus," Eli reminded Dal. "She's more dangerous than she looks. They're not lying down on the job, they're switching tactics."

"She doesn't look all that dangerous," Dal said, munching his fries. I gave him my best dangerous look. He should've been scared. He had fries and I didn't. "Then again, who knows what she's hiding under the leather? I think she should take it off and let us frisk her for weapons. We probably need to do a full cavity search to make sure we don't miss anything."

"You don't give up easily, do you?" Eli finished his burger and crumpled the empty wrapper in one big hand.

"I'm just saying, we owe it to ourselves to take a closer look. Investigate." Dal nodded toward me. "And think of her. How bad must she feel if we won't even give her a chance to work her wicked wiles? One demon, two Nephilim. It's an unfair fight. She ought to at least feel like we took her seriously."

"I take her very seriously." Eli chased his burger with the last of the fries. "Which is why I've got her bound."

I was starting to feel left out of the conversation. I was definitely out of the loop. If they'd already defeated nine demons this month alone, how long had this conflict been going on and how big a problem was it? How many Nephilim were running around? I'd been surprised enough by the existence of one. I hadn't expected two, but now it seemed shortsighted not to envision more.

"How many of you are there?" I asked.

"Two," Dal said, giving Eli a sad look. "She's cute, but she can't count."

"I can count." I stuck my tongue out at Dal. "But since you think I'm cute I will ignore the insult to my intelligence."

"I think you're hot." Dal scooted back and patted his lap in invitation. "Come on over here and show me your dangerous arsenal of feminine weapons."

"I can't seduce you. I'm bound and Eli's forbidden it."

"I'm not bound. Nobody says I can't seduce you." Dal grinned at me, daring me.

Eli didn't tell me to stay put. And while he wasn't giving off any lust, Dal might be willing to answer my questions if I played along. I did not like my odds of success when I was so in the dark. I went to him and settled myself on his thighs. He wrapped an arm around me and pulled me closer, his hand trailing down so that his fingertips rested on the bare upper curve of my breast.

"There are two of you," I prompted. "Are any other Nephilim going to pop out and surprise me?"

"Think you could handle more than two of us at a time?" Dal countered. "I'd hate to see you overworked."

I snorted.

Dal began stroking my thighs with his free hand. "There's just the two of us. The warrior and the teacher. And one of you. Hungry for a sandwich?"

I couldn't help grinning at the image of myself as the filling of a Dal and Eli sandwich. Two for one. Nick would be thrilled. "Why two? Why not two hundred?"

"Two hundred? Mom probably would have killed Dad at three," Dal said. "Even as babies, we were large."

Two Nephilim, brothers. Human mother.

"You *were* extinct," I said. "Your father's an angel and he decided to start a new batch."

"Not a batch. Two. The warrior and the teacher, one complete set." Dal didn't exactly confirm my guess, but he didn't deny it, either. He ran a finger along the outline of my bustier. "Want to show me your complete set?"

"Will you tell me what's going on if I do?" Although I couldn't really do it. Eli's direct order not to seduce Dal kept my hands frozen when I tried to reach for the zipper that would split the leather open and spill my set out for his viewing pleasure.

"Nothing you need to worry about." Dal undid the zipper that ran up the side of my ribs and I was suddenly bare from the waist up. Dal covered my breasts with his hands, and I felt nothing. Not even a spark of desire. Was I that easy to resist?

Then the kitchen door swung open and a young brunette came through it. I tried to place her age. Not a child, but no older than twenty, at a guess.

Her hair had the sheen of true black that no dye reproduced correctly, and it swept back behind her like raven's wings. Her eyes settled on Dal's hands. Her face didn't show any expression, but the eyes turned a midnight shade of blue and a tinge of white showed around her mouth.

"Am I early?" She aimed the question at Dal, ignoring both Eli and me. "I can come back when you're finished if I am."

A bolt of white-hot lust swept over me as Dal's hands tightened on my flesh, giving me a nice squeeze. It wasn't for me. It was for her. Interesting. Dal had the hots for Mystery Guest and was putting on this show for her benefit. He'd timed it perfectly, too. I couldn't help wondering why.

Equally interesting, the lust was contained and controlled before I could drain more than a little of his life-force.

"I wouldn't want to keep you waiting that long," he said. "Eli won't mind keeping this sweet thing busy while you and I have our lesson."

He helped me up and turned me toward Eli, sending me in the right direction with a helpful pat on the ass. His hand lingered on my backside overlong enough to make it clear he liked it where it was. Just in case fondling my bare tits in front of her was too subtle.

I went back to Eli and left my top on the kitchen floor where it fell when I stood up.

"Trying to seduce me?" Eli pitched his voice low, for my ears only.

"You didn't forbid me to." I came closer, until my nipples brushed against the soft fabric of his shirt.

"No, I didn't." His face didn't give anything away, but since he wasn't pushing me back, I put my palms on his chest, smoothing his shirt. I moved against him in a suggestive wiggle, projecting a confidence I didn't feel.

"Then I can try," I said.

Behind us, the brunette said something in a flat tone and Dal answered with a hint of command in his voice. Underneath the teasing exterior lay a well of power. I filed that away for future reference. It wouldn't do to underestimate him.

The warrior and the teacher, he'd said. And the brunette had come for her lesson, so it was obvious which was which. Eli was the warrior, the one I'd been sent for. But I couldn't help thinking about the kind of curriculum a Nephilim teacher specialized in.

Their race had taught magic to humans once. Now they were back, and Dal had a student. Coincidence? I thought not. And I wondered which of the warrior-and-teacher pair posed the greater long-term threat to demonic goals.

Two pairs of footsteps receded and the kitchen door swung shut behind them. The sounds derailed my train of thought and brought me sharply back to the present.

"Alone at last." I peeked up at Eli, giving him my best come-hither smile.

"You won't succeed." His voice was even and neutral, giving nothing away.

"Are you sure?" I trailed a hand down his front and then raked him lightly with my nails. I couldn't feel any reaction, but I held onto my image of seductive confidence and smiled wider. Ninety percent of success in anything is attitude, and I really didn't want to lose.

"I'm sure." He covered my hand with one of his, pinning it in place. "I won't forbid you to try, though."

"Very sporting of you." I thought about dropping my skirt and giving him full frontal nudity, but I didn't think it would get to him. Sometimes less is more. Eli struck me as the type who would find the most direct approach easiest to sidestep. Too bad. Subtle was not my strong suit. "Do you want to frisk me for weapons?"

"I think Dal already did that."

"He might have missed something."

"If it's important, he doesn't miss it."

"I'm missing something." I abandoned seduction and scowled up at Eli, letting him see my frustration and exasperation. "I'm the tenth demon this month? Nephilim are alive in the world again, and your brother couldn't think of a better way to tell a girl he isn't gay than to grope another one in front of her?" Eli's lips twitched in reaction on that last one. "I don't suppose you're going to enlighten me about any of this."

"Dal isn't gay," Eli said, his face straight.

I rolled my eyes. "Thank you. That's helpful."

"Did you expect help? You're the enemy."

"Maybe, but I'm not much of a threat," I pointed out. "I'm helpless in your power. You're probably going to kill me anyway. So what would it hurt to tell me a few things?"

"I'm not gay, either." He offered the information deadpan.

I ground my teeth together.

"Love to stay and chat, but I have things to do and demons to kill." Eli curled a finger under my chin and looked into my eyes.

He didn't do anything but breathe. As he did, a cold beyond anything I'd imagined, the opposite of hell's flames that still somehow managed to burn with arctic agony, pierced me with a thousand jagged edges. Then he said a phrase that sent me away into the icy emptiness of space, leaving me falling in the dark void while I screamed soundlessly.

FOUR

Rematerializing hurt like a son of a bitch. But at least I wasn't falling anymore, and though it was dark when I opened my eyes, it wasn't the empty blackness of space. Wherever Eli's words had sent me had been a place of such cold and endless dark that the memory of it made me shudder.

That point had clearly gone to his side of the scoreboard. I was so not off to a good start.

"Hungry?"

I recognized Eli's voice, although it took a minute for my ears to process the sound and make sense of it. I'd been blind and deaf in that dark place. Or maybe it just seemed like that due to an absolute absence of sound or anything to see.

"Cold." I forced the word out through frozen lips. I wanted my trench coat, left behind because it didn't show enough skin and I was supposed to tempt this inhuman beast into lusting after me.

I doubted that I made a very seductive picture right now, huddled on the plank floor, aching with cold, my face undoubtedly smeared with tears.

"That's because you're hungry."

No, you sadistic bastard, it's because you sent me into the void, I wanted to scream. I didn't, for two reasons. One, I didn't think I had enough air in my starved lungs to waste on screaming. And two, if I missed this opportunity he might not feed me and that would be worse than the cold.

"You're right," I said, doing my best to sound cooperative and agreeable. I said the words through gritted teeth, but he'd probably put that down to trying to stop the chattering. I could hope, anyway.

"Get up, then. Unless you want to eat down there?"

I felt his foot prod my ribs as he spoke, a nudge to get me moving, and wondered if it was a good sign that he'd chosen to touch me or if it was just proof that I didn't tempt him at all. Although he was scrutinizing me with an intent expression. Was that his concerned look?

I shook my head. Too complicated. Eat first, size up the situation and strategize after. "I'm getting up."

It was harder than I expected to scramble to my feet. Eli didn't offer to help, but he didn't laugh at me while I scrabbled for purchase on the smooth wood floor before I got my feet under me, either.

I took stock of my surroundings at the same time. We

were in the living room, which contained a couple of large, well-padded reclining chairs, a wood-burning stove, a wood-box, and a low bookcase along one wall. Given Eli and Dal's scale, I guessed the oversized chairs would fit them better than a couch.

I wondered if Eli would start a fire soon. A lingering scent of woodsmoke told me that the stove was probably getting used overnight as summer faded into autumn and the nighttime temperatures dropped.

Some heat would be nice. My little trip had left me cold in more ways than one. I now knew where banished demons went. I imagined falling in the dark forever, the absolute nothingness of it, and the torment of knowing it would never end. A violent shudder racked me.

"Did you have to do that?" I asked Eli through numb lips. "I was already bound. You could've just told me to sit in the corner or something if you wanted me out of the way for a while."

"I'm sure you would have preferred to hear and see everything I was doing." Eli stared down at me, no remorse at all on his stern face.

"Of course," I said. "If I can't seduce you, at least I could spy on you. A demon's got to make herself useful." I shivered again. Then I realized I was naked. Somehow I'd lost the rest of my clothes. Eli's doing? On purpose, or accidental? Hard to say, and he wasn't giving me any clues.

"Make yourself useful in the kitchen."

My jaw dropped. Then snapped shut. "You want me to cook for you?"

"No. You can clean up after, do the dishes."

I nodded, struck silent by incredulity. When was the last time I'd been given kitchen chores? Most men, when presented with a succubus, did not think of using her to scrub pots.

The living room opened onto the hall. I headed toward the kitchen and then came to an abrupt and awkward halt when Eli told me to stop and my body obeyed his command before my brain had a chance to send the order. Being bound was going to take some getting used to. Although hopefully I wouldn't be in this state long enough to grow accustomed to it. All I had to do was seduce him, drain him, and bring back his soul. Free myself and avoid a fate worse than death: banishment that didn't end in a reprieve for dinner and dishwashing.

Eli put something over my shoulders. It felt a little rough, but warm, and I shrugged into it, fast, before he changed his mind. It was a heavy plaid shirt, wool by the itchy feel of the fabric against my bare skin, but I wasn't going to complain.

"Thank you."

"I'm the one who forbid you to seduce Dal," Eli said with a shrug. "Can't contradict myself by sending you out there naked."

I nodded. Then wondered if he would bother to forbid me to do something that wasn't possible. If I could seduce Dal, then a Nephilim could be tempted. Eli could be tempted. I kept my thoughts to myself, though, and simply noted, "You didn't seem concerned when he wanted to get me half-naked and grope me."

"I didn't forbid Dal to seduce you." Eli gave me a slight shove between the shoulder blades, pushing me forward.

I snorted at that, but I went. I was cold and hungry and I needed energy of some sort. Since Eli wasn't giving me the kind I was made to subsist on, I needed a substitute. There would come a point when a substitute wouldn't be enough, but I wasn't there yet.

Dinner turned out to be some sort of casserole, noodles and meat and sauce. With vegetables. The food pyramid was well represented.

Neither Eli nor Dal seemed to be in much of a mood for small talk. I wasn't feeling terribly chatty myself, so silence reigned over the table. I sat and ate and tried to take in as many details as I could.

Dal's posture and facial expressions were both considerably more closed-down than before he'd left to tutor his student. Eli was unreadable, too. He seemed both relaxed and alert, ready for action but not keyed-up. I wondered how quickly he could react if a threat appeared. Fast, I suspected.

I wondered why Eli had brought me back. Not out of the goodness of his heart, and probably not because he found my body irresistible, either. So maybe he thought I could be useful to him in some way. If so, I'd do anything I could to encourage that line of thinking. Not only would it maybe keep me out of the void, it might let me get close enough for him to let down his guard, and maybe I could find a weakness I could use.

If I'd had any doubt that Eli was my enemy, today's events had settled the question. This wasn't just a matter of doing my job. My survival was at stake. If one of us was going down, I didn't want it to be me.

I looked around the kitchen and noted the lack of modern

amenities. Dishwashers were standard in most places by now. But I saw only a plain row of cupboards below and beside the sink. An ancient stove that might be gas-burning instead of electric. A refrigerator that was either a retro model or so old it was amazing it still worked.

I didn't see any vents for a furnace, which told me they probably relied on the woodstove for heat. No vents also meant no central air conditioning. Not that it'd be needed in this area. Even at the height of summer it didn't often get above the seventies.

I'd seen gas lamps here and there throughout the house, and I wondered if these two liked to live simply or if power outages happened so often in this remote setting that they just stayed prepared. The house had electricity, at least. But it felt very much like a place out of time, a relic of older days.

Somewhat like the house's inhabitants. They were very out of place in this modern era, yet here they sat. It was easy to picture them in different clothing, wielding swords or axes, coming back from a hunt with a dead animal in tow.

Of course, for all I knew they did that now. This area was a popular destination for hunting and fishing. It was still hard to picture either of them using modern weapons. But bow hunting? That fit.

"Do you hunt?" I asked Dal, tired of the silence.

"What, demons?" He leaned back and gave me a wink, flashing a dimple in the process. "Don't have to look far if I want one."

"I was thinking more like rabbits or elk." I waved a hand around the kitchen. "Eli said I had kitchen duties. I was worried about them stretching to cover skinning dead animals."

As soon as I said it, I wanted to kick myself for giving Eli ideas. If I had to gut fish or dress out a carcass, I was going to find a way to escape and get back to hell. Screw this job. Somebody else could deal with the Nephilim.

"We take care of our own kills," Dal said in a tone of voice that would have sent ice down my spine if it hadn't been frozen already. Something in his eyes reminded me that Eli wasn't the only dangerous one. And Dal was obviously in a rotten mood after dealing with his pupil.

"Good. That's good," I mumbled, and put another forkful of casserole in my mouth so there wouldn't be any room for my foot. I did my best to project cute, harmless, and helpful. Not somebody a Nephilim who was feeling combative might see as a target.

It wasn't hard to guess at the source of Dal's crankiness. He had the hots for his student witch. Given the performance he'd put on for her benefit with me earlier, he didn't want her to know it, didn't intend to act on it, or both.

If I hadn't been forbidden to seduce him, I could use that to tempt him into seeing me as an outlet for all that delicious pent-up lust. A surge of hunger swept over me at the very thought. I channeled it toward my dinner and went after the noodles with an intensity that really wasn't ladylike.

I wanted to sigh at the wasted opportunity. I'd uncovered a weakness I could exploit on the wrong brother. I was still hoping to find any chink in Eli's armor. I had to believe one existed. Nobody was perfect, and nobody was above temptation.

Everybody wants something, I reminded myself. Find out what Eli wants.

I did wonder why Dal was denying himself the thing he obviously wanted, though. The last time his race had multiplied on the earth, they'd gone through women with the same eager lust they had for battle. Of course, I didn't know that he wasn't going through women. Just that he wasn't acting on his desire for one woman.

More questions, more unexplained mysteries. The two of them kept giving me more pieces to the puzzle, and I wasn't getting any closer to putting it together.

I didn't have to make sense of it all, though, did I? I just needed to solve one mystery: how to get to Eli. I wasn't here to figure out the rest of it. I was only here to do what I did best, use sex to lead a man to his downfall.

I snuck a look at him and found him staring at me. I swallowed hard and the casserole lodged in my throat. I swallowed again and asked, "Time to do the dishes?"

"You're very curious about us," Eli said. Not exactly the answer I was looking for.

I shrugged. "Who wouldn't be? Your race hasn't been seen for thousands of years. At least, not that I know of. Your return is bound to stir up gossip. If there was a supernatural version of tabloids, the paparazzi would be all over both of you."

"That explains it," Dal said, joining the conversation. "All those demons popping up just want an interview."

"I can't speak for the others, but I was sent here to sleep with you," I volunteered. Even if I couldn't seduce him, it wouldn't hurt to plant a seed of lust in his head.

"Very hospitable. Except you don't actually sleep with your assignments, do you?" Eli's voice had a husky overtone that sounded like sex and drew me like a magnet.

"No." I set my fork down.

"What would happen if you did?"

I blinked. "It's really not possible," I said. "Any man who gets close enough for action gives in to lust, which I feed off. Which drains his life-force to critical levels, and then his soul belongs to the boss. Kind of brings the whole thing to a dead stop."

Honesty wasn't always the best policy, but they knew what I was, so I wasn't telling them anything they didn't already know. And my bad pun made Dal's mouth crook into a little smile. For some reason, that made me feel warmer. As if distracting him from his problems gave me some inner satisfaction. That was a little unsettling because Dal wasn't my friend, and I couldn't afford to start thinking of him that way.

"What if your intended victim didn't give in to lust?" Eli asked, his eyes unfathomable.

"Then he'd hardly be in the mood," I pointed out.

Although if that same man had a far greater than normal life-force, he could possibly have the strength to feed a demon without being drained to critical levels. If, say, that man wasn't human. Dal had lusted and then regained control before he was in any danger.

I drew in a breath at the realization, and Eli caught my reaction. He looked at me like a lion about to pounce on his prey, but I didn't feel like running. I wondered, instead, who was tempting who. If I couldn't afford to feel friendship for a Nephilim, I really couldn't afford to think of one as a lover.

Nevertheless, the idea had been implanted. It was far too easy to imagine having the endless hunger of centuries appeased, to know satiation even once. Knowing it was impossible didn't stop me from longing for it. Knowing it was stupid didn't help much, either.

Lust makes everybody stupid. And as a creature of lust maybe I was more prone to stupidity than average, because I couldn't bring myself to stop entertaining the dangerous temptation Eli presented, of having my cake and eating it, too.

FIVE

I stood with my hands plunged into hot water, which struck me as appropriate since I was in it metaphorically up to my neck. I scrubbed at the plates with more energy than expertise. The task gave me something to focus on, and it helped chase the last of the lingering chill away.

Part of me was trying to think. Why had Eli spared me? Why was he tempting me with the prospect of gaining a chance to succeed in my mission?

The other part simply hungered for sensation. Eli's hands on my body. Eli's desire, going to my head like fine wine. I imagined feasting on his lust and trembled.

Could I really make this formidable adversary want me?

I certainly had motivation to do my damnedest. If he wanted me, he'd hesitate to speak the words that would end my existence.

"I think that one's clean."

Dal's voice came from very close behind me and made me jump, but he did provide a welcome distraction. I latched onto it gratefully.

"Want to rinse?" I asked.

He came to stand beside me for an answer, took the plate from my soap-slippery hand. He rinsed the plate and positioned it in the drying rack with efficient precision that made me raise an eyebrow.

"It's a dish, not a military campaign," I said.

"The two aren't necessarily mutually exclusive." Dal gave me a leisurely and thorough once-over. "You, for instance, are both a dish and a military campaign."

"I don't know that hell's organized enough for military maneuvers," I said. "We kind of specialize in chaos. And there's only one of me. I don't think I can qualify as a campaign by myself."

"I bet you could overthrow an army." Dal's face was serious, although his eyes had a teasing light. The mood his student had left him in was lifting, but there was still an edge to his words and an undercurrent I felt from him that told me he was feeling far from genial.

"I hope you're not looking for a fight about the nature of women and how we've all been the downfall of man since Eve and Lilith," I said, handing him another plate. "Sure, I seduce men. But nobody makes them stay in my path. That's a choice they're all responsible for."

"Interesting way to look at it."

"Nobody made you come and help me with the dishes."
I scrubbed at another plate that had been clean for the last five minutes.

"But your outfit looked so inviting." Now his voice sounded more relaxed and I relaxed with the shift in tone.

"Eli doesn't wear my size. It's warm, though."

I looked down at the shirt and wondered if I'd been missing something in my approach to fashion. This big, shapeless, ugly shirt might do something to stir the masculine imagination that was more subtle than the leather and lace lingerie approach.

For starters, it was so ugly that conceivably any man with even a shred of taste would be offended enough to mentally rip it off me. And then he could take the short step from picturing me naked to picturing sex.

It also probably advertised, "Nothing underneath!" as if the words were written on my back in neon letters.

I wondered if it was having any effect on Eli. Hard to say, since he'd left the kitchen after dropping his loaded question on my head. If he'd intended to leave me stewing, he'd succeeded.

"Eli doesn't do what you do for that shirt."

I handed over the very clean plate with more force than was strictly necessary and gave Dal an exasperated look along with the dish. "You don't have to pretend. I know who you want and it isn't me. I'm a succubus. We notice those things."

"It doesn't mean anything."

I frowned at him and tried to decipher the meaning.

"What, your teasing or what you not-so-secretly want to teach your student?"

"Wanting. It doesn't mean anything." He rinsed and placed the plate with the others as if the open space was a target and he was hitting his mark.

"Well, I'm glad you're not leading me on." I groped in the bottom of the sink for the stopper and pulled it to allow the soapy water to swirl down the drain.

"I think it'd be difficult to lead you anywhere."

Dal's voice sounded genuinely complimentary. My head snapped up in disbelief. "Careful, Nephilim, somebody might start to think you like me. I'd hate to think of you grieving after your brother casts me into outer darkness to spend eternity wailing and gnashing my teeth."

"How exactly does one gnash?" He screwed up his face as if pondering the question.

"Like this, I think." I bared my teeth and tapped them together a couple of times to demonstrate.

"It's not your best look." Dal shook his head. "Smiling is much more attractive."

"I do try to present myself in the most attractive light." I fluttered my lashes at him. It didn't cross the line into the realm of forbidden attempted seduction, apparently, because I was able to do it.

"Even if you presented yourself in total darkness, you'd be attractive." Dal smoothed back my hair and gave me a sexy wink.

"I do some of my best work under cover of darkness," I said, reminiscing. "You'd be amazed how many men won't kick a strange woman out of bed if she's naked. Or how few questions they ask about how she came to be there."

"They probably think it's bad manners to question a miracle." He flicked one of my nipples with a playful gesture. I felt it harden in response and wondered if I was going to get into trouble for letting Dal flirt with me. Eli hadn't forbidden him to, but he might banish me for allowing it. That thought chased away the warmth that had been slowing building inside me like a dash of cold water.

"You probably shouldn't do that," I said.

"But you like it." He grinned at me.

I smiled back, but I did it shaking my head in exasperation. "I'm a succubus. Of course I like it. But let's talk about why you're not flirting with teacher's pet. I see a lot of lust in my line of work. I don't come across a lot of self-denial."

"Some things are more important than the desire of the moment."

"Like not distracting your student from the lesson plan," I guessed. "Sex magic probably isn't on the syllabus."

He made a faint choking sound. "No."

"It's a valid branch, you know." I raised a brow at him. "Surely you aren't withholding knowledge from your student. Doesn't she deserve to be fully instructed in all forms?"

He stepped back and let out a whistle. "You really are temptation on two feet. You make it sound not only rational but responsible. If I'm a caring teacher, I should give in to the urge to fuck her blind for her own good, out of the sincere motivation to provide her with the most complete education possible. Nicely done, demon."

"Thank you," I said, my voice humble. "I thought it was inspired. I made you think about it, too, didn't I?"

"Maybe." Dal's face went impassive.

I wondered again if I was crossing a line, but Eli hadn't forbid me to tempt Dal with the thing he really wanted. He'd just forbidden me to tempt him directly with myself. It was probably cheating or exploiting a loophole, but he couldn't really expect a demon to play fair or fail to take advantage of any opening. As long as I didn't do anything that infringed on the obedience I was bound to, it seemed I had some wiggle room.

That was unexpected. I wasn't going to question my good fortune, though. I needed any advantage I could find because Eli had the upper hand and was doing a good job of tying both of mine behind my back.

I thought about humming a few bars of "Teacher's Pet," but decided not to rub it into the ground. I'd given Dal something to think about, and I knew from experience the thought would come back to haunt him. Temptation's like that. It's easy to plant a seductive idea. Not so easy to get rid of it, or to fight it when it keeps returning like a boomerang. So I'd let the power of suggestion do my dirty work.

Dal was teaching magic, and that had some strategic importance. It mattered enough that he wouldn't risk losing his student by taking what he wanted. If I could blur the student-teacher lines and get them both screwed, well, one less witch who understood the rules of conjuring would suit Nick fine.

It was a tiny taste of success, but it boosted my mood and my confidence. Nephilim weren't immune to temptation. I wasn't doomed. True, Eli had used some of my own best tactics against me and left me to wrestle with temptation, but even that could work for me. I'd been assigned to seduce him. Who would know or care if I enjoyed it a little too much?

Nobody said I couldn't take pleasure in my job. And there had been little enough of that over the centuries. I deserved a little taste of the sexual pleasure I gave, didn't I?

That was rationalizing, a little voice in my head pointed out.

Maybe, I told the voice that couldn't be conscience, but as a demon, selfishness *was* my nature. Why fight it?

"I see you had help," Eli said. I looked up to see him framed in the doorway looking more like a military man at parade rest than a man comfortably at home. I fought the urge to salute, since it probably wouldn't endear me to him.

"I washed," I pointed out. "Dal rinsed. You said to do the dishes, you didn't say I couldn't have help."

"True." Eli studied me, then his gaze flicked to his brother. "Thank you for your help." The dismissal was clear. Dal raised a brow but made to leave. Eli stood aside to let him go past and down the hall. And then it was just the two of us.

"Here we are, alone again." I smiled at Eli and hoped my expression looked sexy and inviting instead of sick with fear. The last time we'd been alone together had not ended in a pleasant experience for me. Actually, we were zero for three if I counted the first time I'd been alone with him, when he bound me.

Eli inclined his head, acknowledging my words but not gifting me with a response beyond that. I stood there for a minute while he watched me, and I knew that if it was a contest to see who'd break the silence I was already the loser. Letting him wait me out would just make me nervous.

"Any other tasks you'd like me to perform?" I made the offer in a suggestive tone, my voice pitched low and husky.

"And you called me relentless."

I shrugged. "So you're the pot, I'm the kettle. I never claimed to be any better than you."

"You think we're well matched, then."

If possible, he became even harder to read. I searched his face and posture for clues, found none, and shrugged again. "I find you a worthy adversary."

"And a worthy lover?"

I did a slow blink. "If any man could be, I believe it would be you."

"Then you aren't afraid to put it to the test."

I held his eyes with a steady gaze and unbuttoned the shirt I wore for an answer. I took my time with each button, working my way from top to bottom with an air of grace and poise I was far from feeling. When I reached the last one, I shifted it off my shoulders and let the fabric fall. It made a slow, soft slide down my body before it puddled around my feet.

Eli didn't react with overt lust, but his eyes took on a more intent expression as he focused on my body. He made a leisurely study of every feature I'd uncovered. Whether he was trying to intimidate me or just give me the compliment of paying attention to the expanse of bare flesh decorated only by the gleam of my belly button ring, I couldn't say, but I stood still and let him look me over, prepared to wait for his next move however long it might take. The ball was in his court, so to speak.

"Impressive body," he finally said.

"I'm glad you think so." My voice was demure enough to suit a novitiate, while my eyes issued a courtesan's invitation.

"Flashy design, but I wonder how it rates for performance."

I felt my lips quirk and wondered if he meant to be funny or if I was supposed to take that as an insult. Or challenge? Probably a challenge, I decided.

"There's only one way to find out." I walked toward him, making my steps measured and deliberate, letting my body undulate as I moved. I kept coming until my naked flesh brushed up against his clothes, then took another half-step to bring myself into full contact with him.

I tilted my head back to look up into his eyes. Then I ran my hands up the breadth of his chest, framed his face, and drew him down for a kiss.

He consented to let me and inclined his head, lowering it until our lips brushed once, twice, before making firm contact. His lips were hard, unmoving. Mine clung to the shape of his mouth, soft and giving, enticing.

"Is that the best you can do?" Eli asked the question against my mouth, his voice dispassionate, no give in his posture.

Fire burned in my veins. I forgot fear in the hot rush of anger and pride. No man dismissed me. No man remained unmoved when I wanted him to react.

"No. This is." I sank my teeth into his lower lip with a feral growl.

Six

I released the flesh I'd nipped and then ground my mouth hard against his, bruising the small bite. I tasted a coppery hint of blood and felt a surge of triumph. I leaned into him, raked his chest lightly with my nails before gripping the fabric of his shirt in my fists and jerking it tight.

I kissed him like I hated him and wanted to make him suffer, and he laughed, a low, dark sound. It sent a shiver down my spine and made my sex contract, and that pissed me off even more.

"Promising." Eli spoke against my lips.

"Promise this." I released his shirt and went for the thin braids that framed his face winding them around my hands and giving them a sharp tug. He laughed again and I thrust my tongue into his mouth while I bucked my pelvis against his. I poured all my frustrated fury into action and it felt good but it wasn't enough.

I loosened my hold on Eli's braids and let them slide through my hands. Then I gripped his shirt just inside the collar, above the top button, and pulled hard. The button popped off. I tore his shirt open by stages while I ate at his mouth. The buttons rained across the kitchen's linoleum floor, each one adding its soft percussive rhythm to the others, making a sound like encouragement. Once I had the shirt open, I jerked it down his shoulders. Then I wound my legs around Eli's thighs and clung, all lips and hands and angry heat.

The icy blade at the back of my neck stopped me. I let out a low hiss and let Eli's lower lip slide free of my mouth. "You could've just said stop."

"Get off my son." The voice wasn't Eli's. It was deep, masculine, and coming from behind me.

I shut my eyes and groaned. "You have got to be kidding me." The interruption was not welcome. Maybe I hadn't found a crack in Eli's control, but any kiss that ended in missing or damaged clothing and skin-to-skin contact couldn't be considered a failure.

The blade bit into the skin, a sharper warning, and I yelped. "Okay, okay." I stayed as still as I could to avoid hurting myself by moving into the weapon I couldn't see but damn well felt. "Please move whatever that is far enough back that I can let go without beheading myself in the process."

"One less demon in the world." I didn't hear any regret or hesitation in the voice over the prospect.

"So I don't get any points for being polite and cooperative? How is that fair?" I heaved a sigh and very slowly let my legs slide down Eli's, one at a time, more from a desire to prolong my afterlife than to prolong the contact.

When my feet touched the floor I carefully loosened my grip on what was left of his shirt and put my empty hands out to the sides, palms up. The cold sharp object went away, but it left a chill behind. I wanted to rub my arms to chase it away but didn't dare make a move.

"Eli, please tell your dad that I'm in your power," I said. "Bound demon. No threat."

"You were a threat to my shirt," Eli pointed out. "I think you broke some of those buttons."

"It's possible. I don't know my own strength sometimes." I tried to make my voice humble while I resisted the urge to kick him. Next he'd tell me to find them all and sew them back on. Although if it kept me in one piece and unbanished, I couldn't really complain.

"Pick them up."

I knew it. I clenched my jaw and nodded. I didn't make any attempt to get started on the job, though.

Eli picked me up and set me behind him. "Trouble?"

"Yes. If you're done playing with your prey, your sword is needed."

I resisted the urge to point out that I wasn't Eli's prey, he was mine, but I had to know about the swords.

"What are you planning to do, run around acting out scenes from *Highlander*?" I asked Eli. "Call me crazy, but I think the humans might notice a couple of huge guys waving giant weapons with sharp edges around."

"They won't see us," Eli answered.

"Maybe not, but they'll notice the disembodied swords."

"You can't see them."

I decided to test this. I peered around Eli and tried to focus on his dad. It wasn't easy to do. It was like trying to see something made of light. Or maybe more like an absence of light that the waves bent around, confusing my eyes. I squinted and the place where light followed some strange rules became a shape like a man, but I couldn't see any sword. It was real enough, though. The sting at the back of my neck told me that.

"Okay, the shimmery spot there probably won't be noticed, but you're hard to miss," I told Eli.

"Does that mean you'll miss me?"

"Ha. Ha." I blinked at the light again and sucked in a breath when I suddenly saw the man made of light or maybe something more elemental. The face, the form, the hand gripping what had to be a sword's hilt began to materialize.

The reality of the angel in Eli's kitchen staggered me. I understood why they weren't seen. This was something entirely too real for the eye or the mind to grasp, too different, too, well, scary. The sight of the angel made everything else around it seem insubstantial and false, as shimmery and unreal as he'd first looked to me, and it brought back the visceral memory of falling into nothingness. I took an involuntary step closer to Eli. Call it cowardice or survival instinct.

I had a new respect for Eli and Dal's mother, whoever she

was. It would take a braver female than me to get close enough to a creature like that to procreate. How could a human even survive touching something so elementally real that its very existence threatened to unmake everything around it?

If hell was the realm of chaos, then heaven was the realm of order that so superseded the material universe that every particle in existence must conform to its will. Simply by standing there, this angel posed a bigger danger to the house that had withstood time and countless coastal storms than a hurricane-force wind. I had the strong impression that if he grew any more real here, all the matter in his vicinity would be unable to occupy the same space.

No wonder Sodom and Gomorrah had vanished from the face of the earth. Angels visited.

"Behave while I'm gone," Eli said.

"No problem. I'll find all the buttons. I'll clean the kitchen."

I knew I was babbling but I didn't care. The only answer came in the form of a rush of wind that filled the room. Then the air stilled, and I was alone in the kitchen.

"Nice to meet you, Eli's dad," I mumbled through numb lips. "So glad we had this chance to get to know each other."

I wondered where they were going, what the swords were for, and felt cold all over again. I retrieved the thick wool shirt I'd been wearing and burrowed into it, hugging the scratchy fabric to myself and welcoming the irritating rasp on my bare skin as proof that I still stood there.

Then I got down on the floor and started picking up the

loose buttons. Each one felt cool and slick in my hand, so small but so tangible. And so very three-dimensional.

I felt ridiculously grateful for their simplicity. No need to grapple with impossible geometries that bent reality like a wire coat hanger to grasp a button. The mundane world of matter seemed so reasonable and safe when you considered the alternatives. No wonder the Nephilim chose this realm and shared it with humanity. I envied Dal and Eli, although not the complications of their family get-togethers. At Thanksgiving, their dad could carve the turkey by molecules.

"Did Eli tell you to scrub the floor on your knees next?"

I held my hand out in Dal's direction, palm turned up so he could see the buttons I'd collected. "No. And I'll thank you not to give him any helpful suggestions like that."

The sound of Dal's footsteps came closer and closer in an unhurried rhythm until they stopped beside me. "Were those from his shirt or yours?"

"His." I tipped my head up and tried to look smug but it probably just came off as miserable.

"Rough day on the job?" Dal squatted down beside me and retrieved a stray button, which he placed in my hand, taking the opportunity to trail his finger along my palm in the process.

"Are you offering to make it better?" I let out a dramatic sigh. "Two Nephilim. One I can kiss, one I can't. Guess which one I'm alone with. I'd say I suck at this succubus gig, but until recently I had an excellent track record."

"I believe you." Dal patted my head. "The torn-off buttons scattered all over the kitchen floor? Very suggestive. I may be having impure thoughts right now."

He wasn't, but I appreciated the support. "Thank you."

I consoled myself with the thought that I had been kissing Eli, until his dad and business interrupted. That was progress. Next time I might even get his pants off.

Yes, and at this rate, Eli might have an impure thought or a lusty impulse sometime in the next month. By then I'd probably be a raisin from long-term exposure to humidity and heavy rainfall. Could I inspire lust if my hair frizzed?

"You're welcome." Dal winked at me. He found the last button and tossed it my way. I caught it.

"Your dad was here," I said, wondering if that would trigger any revelations. "He arrived just when things were getting interesting."

Dal tried to look sympathetic but the grin splitting his face ruined the effect. "No wonder you look depressed. There you were, doing your worst, buttons flying in all directions. And then somebody interrupts."

"I think the timing was deliberate." I stood up and carefully placed the handful of buttons on the table. "But I am not discouraged."

"You don't seem like the type to give up easily," Dal agreed.

"You don't seem very upset over the possibility that I'll seduce your brother." I raised a brow at him. "Are you that sure I don't have a chance in hell?"

"Maybe I'm just paying attention to his test and taking notes."

I wondered what sort of test I could represent while I gave in to the urge to rub my arms. Between the damp, the trip to Voidville, and my close encounter with the here-but-not-here angel sword, I was starting to feel like I'd never be warm again. "It's cold in here. Could you start a fire?"

Dal waved me toward the hall for an answer, and I realized it maybe wasn't just my charming company that had drawn him to the kitchen. "You're guarding me," I said.

"I thought I was being subtle about it." Dal put a hand to the small of my back and prodded me forward. "And yes, because I'm a nice guy, I will start a fire."

"You were subtle. I didn't catch on until just now."

We reached the living room and I curled up in the big chair nearest the woodstove. Dal did things with kindling, paper, and a strategic arrangement of logs that told me he had a lot of experience starting fires the nonmagical way. It kind of boggled my mind that the two of them really did live here, playing human. Doing normal, everyday things like bringing in wood and washing the dishes. In between magic lessons and fights involving demons and invisible swords.

"Thank you," I said, as Dal poked at the fire, made adjustments, and closed the stove door. "You're a very humane guard."

"You're a pretty well-behaved prisoner."

"I am? Damn. I need to work on that."

Dal's lips twitched in a smile. "Feel free to show me your worst."

"You really do like me, don't you?" I asked as I scooted deeper into the chair and held my feet out to better feel the heat radiating from the stove.

"I can trust myself around you."

That was unexpected. Very. I tried hard not to stare, but

really, what did he expect if he went around dropping state-ments like that? "I don't suppose you'd care to explain that," I said finally. I made it more of an invitation than a direct question and waited for a response.

I didn't have to wait very long.

"I'm surprised you need me to spell it out for you," Dal said, turning his face toward me. Something glittered in his eyes and I remembered all over again that this wasn't a man, wasn't anything in my experience. "If I lose control of my lust, you probably won't get hurt."

SEVEN

Oh. That." I tried for a light tone while inside I went very still. Lust for battle and women, and a voracious appetite for both, that was the history of his race. "Is this why you're oh-so-careful around your student witch?"

It would explain his restraint, and his attempt to use me to discourage her.

Dal gave an abrupt nod. "She's human. Fragile."

"Mmm." I made a neutral noise that could be taken for agreement. "You know, human women have been surviving male lust for centuries. Some even enjoy it."

The fire popped and a log settled inside the stove. The sounds made Dal turn away from me again. He was quiet long enough for me to wonder what would happen if the twin lusts for sex and violence ran together. Maybe they had, in the past. Gilgamesh *had* taken an axe to Lilitu.

I did a surreptitious sweep for potential weapons in the room. I didn't see any. Then again, if he had one of those invisible swords I wouldn't know it was there until I felt it. At which point it would be kind of late to duck.

I spotted a baseball pennant tacked up on one wall and latched onto it for a change of topic. "So. How about those Mariners?"

Dal let out a short, surprised laugh. "Unless your boss made a deal we don't know about, I don't think they're going to win this year."

"Never can tell," I said, remembering the time I'd been sent to seduce a major league pitcher at a critical time. "Divine intervention, deals with the devil, interference happens." Although mostly games were won and lost by human effort and human error. Like all human endeavors and experiences, the supernatural got blamed or credited more than events warranted.

"You've done a lot of interfering." Dal's face wasn't easy to read in the low light. No clues there.

"Some."

"You came here to interfere."

"I guess I did." I wanted to scrunch deeper into the chair and made myself move forward instead, scooting to the edge to lean toward Dal. "Although not with you. At least, not directly."

"Any interference is directly with us." Dal stood up slowly, stretching to his full height. Which meant he towered over me. "We guard the balance."

"Guard the balance?" I echoed the words and wondered what exactly he meant. Maybe if I asked outright he'd enlighten me. "What balance?"

"The balance." Dal planted his hands on his hips and stared down at me. "Did they train you at all, or just put you in a push-up bra and send you out into the world?"

Now that stung. "Hey. It takes training to adjust a push-up bra for maximum effect."

"I'm sure you aced the test. Did you learn anything at all about the balance between good and evil?"

I frowned at him. "Is this a trick question? What, do you think there's actually some sort of balancing scale and if it goes too far in one direction the universe is out of whack? And if so, isn't that a problem for somebody else? Like human scientists, maybe?"

"There is some sort of balancing scale. Humanity. And yes, if it goes too far in one direction or another, there's a problem, but not one science can address."

I opened and closed my mouth. Then I tried again. "Okay, consider me uneducated, untrained, and ignorant. How is this balance thing a problem?"

"What would happen to you if there were no humans?"

"Um. I'd be unemployed?" I thought a little further ahead and realized I'd also be starving without any human lust to feed on. Would I die? Again?

"For starters." Dal nodded. "Do you realize there's a danger of that happening? Demons are overrunning humans."

Now that was an interesting statement. I turned it over and thought about how it fit with my experience. It was true that demon ranks had grown and activity was at an all-time high in my unlifetime. But were we really overrunning humans?

"I'll give you that there's sort of a boom economy going on," I told Dal. "But if it's true that demons are threatening the balance, why now? And what does it have to do with you?"

"It has everything to do with me. It's why we're here. For millennia there's been a balance. Even with the Nephilim gone, humanity retained our legacy."

I nodded. "Magic."

"Yes." Dal smiled at me as if he wanted to give me a gold star for catching on. "Magic gave humans a defense against demons, a way to keep them in check. Until mankind abandoned magic for science and belief in a rational universe and the old knowledge died out."

It did make sense. We had been gaining in numbers, and it did seem to have happened in proportion to the developing technologies that made drastic changes in the human world. "So now you guys are back to restore the balance and teach humans magic again."

No wonder Dal considered his student witch too important to trifle with. He wouldn't risk her when her abilities were his reason for being here. If he lost control of himself and damaged her, she'd be no good to him. He'd have to find another pupil and start over.

I had to wonder if it had crossed his mind yet that she might get so pissed off at him for sleeping around and ignoring her that she'd quit. I hadn't missed the look in her eyes when he'd put on his little show for her. Either I was no judge of human nature or Dal was playing with fire. It looked to me like he was damned if he did, and damned if he didn't. I could almost feel sorry for him.

"You said something about a test," I prompted Dal and hoped for more insights. So far, my day had been overflowing with them.

"I did. You're Eli's test. Claire is mine."

I frowned. "I don't get it. What are you guys, on probation?"

Dal blew out a breath. "In a word, yes. The last time angels and humans intermixed, the resulting half-breeds were a big threat to the balance. They didn't control their human lusts, they were driven by them. With their supernatural powers that made them too dangerous. They eventually had to be removed from this realm."

That sounded like the old "who will guard the guardians" problem, the supernatural version. Once the Nephilim fought off the encroaching demons, who else was left to fight? Humanity. Each other. And the way they'd gone through women had probably further threatened mankind as more half-breeds than humans were born. It made sense that the returned Nephilim would be kept on a tight leash, to make sure they didn't create a bigger problem than the one they were supposed to solve.

"So that's why Eli's keeping me around," I said slowly. "If he can handle a succubus without going lust-crazed, it's proof that he's in control of himself and he can be trusted with humans." One mystery solved. I had wondered why he hadn't banished me on sight. Now I knew.

"Go to the head of the class." Dal reached over and tousled my hair. "He's also probably tired of washing the dishes."

I made a rude sound in response. "I'll be the only demon with dishpan hands. I'm never going to live it down." I stretched and then curled up in a more comfortable position as I settled myself deeper into the chair. "I have to say, it all sounds a little unfair for you two. 'Come and save the world, but don't screw up or it's all over for you.' So Eli fights demons and you train witches and both of you behave yourselves like good little Nephilim while restoring the balance for the good of mankind. What do you get out of it?"

Dal reached down and scooped me up, took my place in the chair and dumped me on his lap. The chair's frame creaked as it adjusted to hold our combined weight. I breathed in and caught the trace of woodsmoke that clung to his clothes. "Besides a second chance for our race? Life. We get life, here and now, and all that the world has to offer."

I elbowed him in the ribs. "Yes, you two are really living it up. I bet you can't even get pizza delivered out here."

"Delivery pizza from a fast-food chain is not a peak experience. The world has more interesting things to offer." Dal's voice was a low rumble. The sound was soothing. I curled into him and closed my eyes to listen better. I felt warm and sleepy. Part of me registered that I was low on energy, but doing something about that would mean getting up and going back to the kitchen. The kitchen was a lot further from the source of heat.

"Tell me about the interesting things the world has to

offer," I said. For a surreal moment I felt like a child asking for a story, but I was too drowsy to do anything else.

"Rainbows. Sunrises. Sunsets. High tide and low tide. Meteor showers. Moon cycles. That hour of light in the late afternoon that turns everything golden. The sound of the surf and the wind in the trees. The smell of cedar forest."

"How very nature loving." I yawned.

"Climbing a mountain is a peak experience," Dal said, ignoring me. "Hiking around a wilderness coastline at dawn, feeling like the only living being in the world, that's an experience. An alpine meadow full of flowers in the middle of winter."

I grew warmer when he said that and somnolence slipped away as I was fed a sudden spike of lust. "You're lusting after flowers," I said. "Ewww. That's taking a love of nature too far."

But while I said the words I realized it wasn't right. Not flowers, but what they reminded him of. I wondered if a certain witch had been with him in that winter meadow turned to summer. I could almost see them, the young woman with the dark blue eyes and the midnight hair and towering beside her, a little closer than teaching required, the sorcerer who transformed the world around them with a word of power.

"How cozy." Eli's voice was soft but it carried an edge that had me reaching up to cover the back of my neck, the same spot the invisible sword had touched. "Am I interrupting?"

He filled the doorway, and in that frame his unnatural height really struck me. How could he be passing for human outside of professional basketball? The height alone didn't do it, though. The clincher was the shape. Too large, musculature too heavy. Even weight training and steroids couldn't duplicate that build on a human male. To my eyes he was unmistakably alien, other, not of this world. The jeans, boots, and sweater he now wore didn't disguise the warrior's body underneath.

"Not really," I said. "Dal has been filling me in on all sorts of interesting items. Such as why you didn't banish my butt on sight. Did you have a good time with your dad?"

"I did my duty." Eli took a step into the room. The warrior braids on either side of his face swung with the movement while the rest of the loose length flowed behind him. His long hair emphasized his stark features and his deep-set eyes. In the low light, they almost seemed to shine with a faint glow of power. Then again, maybe it wasn't a trick of the light.

"I'm sure you always do." My voice was neutral but I couldn't help thinking about what his duty involved. Well, both of us had our roles to fulfill and our duties to perform. I was bound to seduce him. He was bound to withstand me and banish me when he passed his test. It'd be nice if he could prove himself worthy without consigning me to a nasty fate in the process. Then again, if I succeeded in seducing him, would his fate be any better?

"I wonder if I could ask a favor."

Eli didn't exactly give me an encouraging look in response to my segue, but he waited long enough for me to ask my question, which was probably about as much encouragement as I could hope for.

I patted Dal's chest. "Nature boy here has been telling me about the appeal of the great outdoors. Hiking along the coast, feeling like the only people in the world. I wanted to experience that. Would you take me?"

Eli stared at me in silence for a minute. I guessed that wasn't the request he'd expected.

"You want the Pacific wilderness coast as the scene to stage your supernatural seduction?"

I shrugged. "I'm sure it's going to be cold and damp and uncomfortable, but unless you were planning to get right to business here with Dal watching, we have to go somewhere."

And if an alpine meadow had led to his brother's moment of weakness, maybe the key to Eli's lust was equally isolated and elemental. Maybe I could tempt him, the way Dal had been tempted. Dal was resisting, but Claire wasn't a determined and experienced seducer of men. If I could catch Eli in a weak moment, I might have a fighting chance.

"No," Eli said after another moment of silence. "I wasn't planning to get right to business here, with Dal watching."

Dal heaved an exaggerated sigh of disappointment. "And here I was hoping I'd get to see the show."

"So you could pick up some pointers?" I grinned at him. "I'd be happy to pass on a few little tips. Eli could help me demonstrate."

"I'll demonstrate how to control a demonic female," Eli offered. He didn't sound like he was joking. He snapped his fingers. "Come here. Now."

I jerked upright and went to him like a marionette whose strings had been pulled. I came to an abrupt halt right up against him.

"Useful," Dal said. "But not very graceful. And you couldn't do it in public without causing comment."

"Good thing we're unlikely to encounter any humans where we're going."

"So we are going to the beach? Oh, goody." I leaned fractionally closer and breathed in the hint of cedar that clung to Eli. "Can we have a picnic?"

"Were you this impossible when you were human?" Eli asked the question in an expressionless voice that made me want to goad him.

"When I was human, I killed the last man I met," I reminded him. "I earned my afterlife and I've had a lot of time to reinforce my bad habits."

"You've earned a lot of repentance, then."

"Are you going to make me do penance, Eli?" I asked him the question in throaty murmur. "Do you want me on my knees?"

I slid down as I spoke, my lips moving along his chest and down his belly, my intent clear despite the layer of clothing that kept me from making contact with bare skin. He caught me and held me in an unbreakable grip, checking me before my mouth reached his groin.

"The area is clear," Eli said to Dal over my head. "Keep a close eye on things. I'll be back."

"You sound so Terminator when you say that," I piped up. "It's hot."

"Without her," Eli added.

"Spoilsport."

Dal's voice was the last thing I heard before a rush of wind filled my ears. And then Eli and I were standing together at the edge of the world.

Cold and salt stung my cheeks. The surf made a rhythmic

roar that rose and fell but never quieted. I thought I might actually have to shout to be heard over it, even with Eli standing close beside me.

The sea and its heavy surf stretched out in front of us until it vanished into mist. The view made it easy to remember why people once believed you could sail off the edge of the world.

Driftwood littered the beach. Some of the scattered logs stood as wide as I was tall, bleached by sun and sea to a grayish white. The beach was rugged and rocky, a narrow shelf between forest and ocean that was largely submerged at high tide when the sea reclaimed all the land below the wooded cliffs.

No footprints appeared on the rocky stretch of sand we stood on. No signs of human habitation, as far as I could see. This area seemed entirely overlooked in a century of power lines and utility poles. We really might have been alone in the world, the only two people alive.

Eight

"You take me to the best places," I said to Eli, raising my voice to be audible over the surf.

"You picked the location."

"Where exactly are we?"

"Third beach." Eli gestured to a point behind us. "There's a trail through the forest that descends to the shore."

I couldn't see a trail but the way the heights rose above us, I imagined anybody climbing back up that way would be feeling the burn.

The wind blew Eli's long hair back and teased his braids. Maybe it was an illusion, but he looked more relaxed in this wild setting than he had in his house. What did it say about him if he was more at home away from civilization? That I had good instincts and I'd made a good choice getting him out here. I congratulated myself for doing something right.

Not only did he look more relaxed, more approachable, he looked more than ever like a man out of time despite the modern clothes. He would have fit in on the set of *Highlander,* although I'm not sure he would have liked to hear that he resembled the bad guy more than the hero of that movie.

"Is the tide coming in?" I measured the height of the cliffs with my eye and wondered what would happen to a hiker trapped on the beach when the water rose.

"Going out. We're just past high tide."

"Oh. Good." I kicked at a rock and realized I was wearing boots. Not the boots I'd worn to meet Eli in. These were made for hiking. I looked down at myself and saw that along with some travel hocus-pocus, Eli had outfitted me for the outdoors. I now wore jeans below the flannel shirt, and a heavy fleece vest over it.

"Thank you." I indicated my warmly clad body and gave Eli a genuine smile. "It's cold by the water."

"You wouldn't be used to the cold." Eli pointed downward as if indicating the direction I'd come from.

"No," I agreed. I linked my arm through his. To my surprise, he allowed it. "Let's walk."

We set off at a steady pace. The rocky ground meant I had to pay attention to my footing. The loose gravel slid underneath my boots and Eli didn't shorten his stride for my benefit, so I had to work harder to keep up. If that was a sign of things to come, I couldn't expect any concessions. Although Eli had a habit of throwing in a pleasant surprise when I least expected it. The chocolate shake. The warm clothes. Giving me a fair shot at seducing him.

Then again, maybe he was just trying to keep me off balance, so I'd never be able to predict what he'd do next. The chocolate shake had been followed by the void. And the last time I'd kissed him . . .

I found myself rubbing the back of my neck again and made myself stop. Either an angel with a sword was nearby and ready to use it, or we were alone here. Either way, I had to make the most of my opportunity while it lasted.

"So how do you like it here, really?" I asked him. "You made jokes about the rain before, but did you pick this location, or did you just get stuck here?"

"Here is where Dal needed to be," Eli answered. "We had to live near his student. And it's worked to our advantage. We have an effect on humans. Living in relative isolation, the effect is minimal."

An effect. I thought about the way Claire had looked at Dal, the impact Eli had on me, and it wasn't hard to connect the dots. "Is it pheromones? Animal magnetism? What?"

"Something like that." Eli turned his face toward me as we walked. "We . . . stir people up."

"So all that legendary fighting and fucking wasn't entirely your doing," I observed.

He stopped and scowled at me. I gave him wide eyes and an innocent shrug. "Hey, just saying. It wasn't one-sided. Not just Nephilim going after people, but humans coming after you." I tilted my head as if thinking it over. "Doesn't that seem unfair? For your race to get sent away when humans were just as much at fault?"

"Life isn't fair." Eli bent forward until his lips touched my forehead. "That's why it pays to fight dirty."

I couldn't stop a surprised laugh. "You aren't what I expected."

"But I am what you want. Despite yourself."

His words made a shiver run along my spine. "I want all men."

"And yet, you can't have any of them. That seems unfair to me, to give you a craving no man can satisfy." Eli's lips seemed to burn against my skin as he spoke. "Except me. I could hold you down right here and fuck you until the tide came back in."

That would take hours. And I had the sure sense that he meant it literally, not just as an expression to indicate that he'd last a long time. "You really think you can do it without me draining you," I said. "How do you think you can go that far without giving in to lust and putting yourself in my power?"

"I'm not human." Eli said it as if it should have been obvious.

"You don't seem very concerned about the possibility of losing your mortal soul." I took a half-step forward, bringing my body into contact with his. "You think you can have me and not lose control?"

"I think if you can make me lose control, I deserve the penalty." His arms came around me and his hands closed on my ass in a hard grip.

"You're a bit of a daredevil, aren't you?" I closed my eyes and pressed closer, rocking my hips into him.

"I admit you do give new appeal to playing with fire."

Eli let out a low laugh. It sounded dark and sexual and harsh. His fingers dug into the soft flesh he held, and I realized that despite his actions and our proximity, he was in control. Lust wasn't driving him.

"When you play with fire, you risk singed fingers." I ran my hands along his arms, tracing the outline of his muscles. He didn't encourage my touch. He didn't shrug it off, either. "I think it's your turn to kiss me. I went first."

"A kiss." He rasped out the word.

"Yes."

I waited to see what he'd do next. I didn't have to wait long. He used his hold on my butt to lift me until my mouth was level with his. I wound my legs around his waist for additional support and because it gave me a good opportunity to get closer. I dug my hands into his biceps, hard and taut under his sweater.

Then Eli lowered his mouth to mine and kissed me as if it was a prelude to battle and a sensual declaration of war. His lips ravaged mine, payback for the brutal kiss I'd given him. I tilted my head back to offer him a better angle and opened my lips under the bruising pressure of his. He made a low, growling sound and sent his tongue probing in search of mine.

We circled, tested, and parried with our tongues, the actions more reminiscent of a duel than a kiss. Opponents feeling each other out, taking each other's measure, gauging skill and style. Each searching for an opening in the other's guard.

Eli ended the skirmish of lips and tongues and drew back, his forehead touching mine, our mouths the smallest space apart. A gap either of us could close easily. "You're not an amateur."

"Neither are you." My voice was a little breathless, and it wasn't done for deliberate effect. Eli had made me work to keep up with him in the kiss, just like he had walking, and I hadn't expected it.

"I didn't have to hold back with you." Eli stated this as if I shouldn't have had to have it explained. It was like an echo of my conversation with Dal.

Here was a being with enough sex drive to go through a hundred women: I thought about the implications of his not holding back and felt almost dizzy with sexual greed. Maybe the experience would be worth the risk. Almost immediately I wanted to smack myself. Worth risking eternal banishment? Lust makes everybody stupid.

On the other hand, Eli was treating me almost like an equal and that was . . . interesting. Unique in my experience. I had the funny sense that it was the closest thing I'd get to a compliment for him to spar with me on my field of battle. Like he thought I could give him a challenging fight.

"Do you really want me here, on this beach?" I asked Eli. "All those rocks under us, digging in and making things un-comfortable?"

"You wanted to come here," Eli reminded me.

"Yeah, well, there's historical precedent to temptation in the wilderness," I said. "Also, I thought the beach would be softer. Sandy."

"There's sand when the tide's further out." Eli looked dead serious, but I had the distinct impression he was laugh-ing at me inside.

Rolling around on the beach sounded sexy, but not if it included hitting my head on a rock. Of course, having my skin scoured off by sand probably wouldn't be much more fun. A job was a job, though. I steeled myself for it. "Fine. Let's do it, then. I get to be on top."

"I'm not scraping my ass on these rocks for you."

I bit back a laugh that turned to a gasp as we transitioned, from the beach below to the forested cliff above in a blink.

"This is more like it," Eli said. "A soft bed of moss and ferns."

I clutched at him and looked around. It was like being in a primeval forest, the trees were so ancient, tall, and moss-covered. Soft, filtered light came from the canopy high above us, making our little spot seem dim and intimate. The roar of the surf below filled the air with a surging rhythm, and the air had a tang of salt that mixed with the green scent of forest. A place out of time. Out of the modern world. A place that sat just on the cusp of two realms, the world of water and the world of woods.

"Yes," I agreed. My voice sounded hushed to my own ears. "This is more like it."

Eli lowered me to the forest floor. The moss under us felt surprisingly soft and springy. It beat being backed up against a nearby tree, especially since the ones I could see had a tendency to sprout shelf lichen all around their trunks. He arranged us side by side, facing each other. One of his large hands rested on my hip. The other arm went under me, making a sort of pillow for me. His long hair spilled over my shoulder, and somehow that felt more intimate than the kisses we'd exchanged.

Eli looked into my eyes, and I felt my breath stop. "Lying down, we're the same height," he said, his voice rasping with an edge of hunger that called to my own.

"So we are." I put the palm of one hand on his chest, stroked down, slid it under his sweater to touch his bare skin. Heat seared my hand and I gasped at the reminder that Eli wasn't the only one playing with fire. "Did you do that on purpose? Magic?"

"Do what?" Eli pressed into my touch and I realized the heat was just him. Once I got used to it, it wasn't painful. In fact, it felt really good. I found myself wanting to touch more of him, all of him, to burn the imprint of his body into mine and absorb all that fire inside him.

"Nothing." I hooked a leg over his thigh, bringing us closer.

Eli squeezed my hip. "In a hurry?"

"Maybe." I wanted more of his heat. I rocked my pelvis into him and arched my back to crush my breasts into the hard wall of his chest.

"You're a greedy little creature." Eli's hand released my hip and moved to the zipper of my jeans, easing it open. Then instead of sliding his hand down to cup my sex, he spread his fingers over my belly, reaching up to toy with the ring in my navel.

"You say that like it's a bad thing." My voice sounded breathless. Eli manipulated the ring, flicking, twisting and tugging at it. The resulting movement sent waves of sensation dancing through my nerve endings and along my skin in a rush of heat.

"You want me to touch you, don't you?" Eli's chin scraped my cheek, a rough caress that made me shudder.

"Yes." Hunger rose, sharp, sweet. He would touch me and I would feed. I trembled with anticipation and want.

Eli released my navel ring and kneaded the soft flesh of my belly. He slid his hand up under my shirt to cup my breast. His fingers searched out my nipple and pinched at it, hard. He stopped just short of the edge of true pain and the stimulation sent a jolting shock through my body that came to rest in my clit, making it throb in sympathy with the pressure on my nipple.

I wanted him to use both hands so he could pinch both points simultaneously. He didn't. He released my nipple and then settled his hand between my open thighs, just resting over my sex, the barrier of my jeans between the heat of his touch and my flesh. I arched into his hand. He laughed, a dark, low sound that made shivers rush along my spine. Then he took his hand away, not hurrying, letting his fingers trail along the center seam of my jeans in the process. I hissed in frustration.

"Greedy." Eli made a fist in the open fabric at my belly and tugged upward so that the thick seam bit into the sensitive flesh he'd been teasing. I hissed again, this time at being caught on the edge of pleasure and pain. It almost hurt, but then again . . . the unexpected sensation made my clit throb harder.

I made a restless, helpless movement with my hips, not quite protest or plea, and found myself almost wanting to laugh. Eli had turned the tables on me.

I was the practiced seducer, and with a few touches he

had me dangling on the brink of coming in my pants. He'd done it so quickly, so easily. And it wasn't like my body had a lot of practice in finding pleasure. It brought pleasure to others, certainly, but my own came from feeding the hunger that ached like a knot inside me. Never from sexual release. I wasn't sure it was even possible.

Fear that this moment might slip away and I'd never find out gripped me. I moved again, this time with more purpose, trying to get enough pressure in the right place. It eluded me and I made a sound of frustration.

Eli gave a low laugh and released his grip on my jeans. The tension on the fabric went slack.

Dammit, dammit, dammit. I cursed silently and pushed my pelvis into Eli, trying to replace the contact I'd lost and now craved.

"Need something?" Eli's voice was rough and knowing. I wanted to hit him for being so damn smug, but I was too distracted by the coiling ache centered in my sex.

"Maybe." I ran my hand down until it found a very masculine tumescence that Eli's jeans did nothing to disguise. He jerked in reaction and I grinned.

"Uh-uh." Eli captured my wrist and pulled my exploring hand away. "I didn't say you could touch that."

"You didn't say I couldn't." I flopped back on the moss and stared up at the green roof high overhead. It beat looking into Eli's otherworldly eyes and seeing an expression of smug victory there. I glanced over at him, unable to stop myself from checking now that I'd thought of it. He was watching me, but with that dark, glittering edge I'd caught in Dal's gaze. Not lust, but something.

If I'd been a human woman, I might've taken it as the look of a wild beast preparing to pounce on its prey. I might have been afraid. I should have been afraid, but instead I found it exciting.

My nipple throbbed in reaction to Eli's ungentle touch, and my clit ached for the same sensual punishment. Holding his gaze with my own, I reached down and worked the jeans over my hips. I lifted up enough to shimmy them down my thighs, leaving my pussy bared in invitation, my legs trapped together by the pants enough to prevent Eli from easily opening my thighs for full access.

NINE

"Hmmm." Eli's gaze swept down my bared abdomen to the nest of curls between my legs. "I think I smell sulfur."

"Bastard." I undid the zip on my fleece outwear and began to work on loosening the buttons that went up the front of the wool shirt.

"Planning to show me your tits, too?" His voice sounded disinterested but his eyes still had that dangerous glitter.

"Yes. Men worship them." I took my time with the buttons, dragging out the little chore, uncovering one inch of flesh at a time. Finally I undid the last one, and then opened the shirt to bare my torso to view. My tits were impressive, full and round. My nipples pulled into hard buds from the cool air and excitement and Eli's ministrations.

"What do you want me to touch?" Eli asked.

"Anything you like," I purred.

Eli made a show of studying me as if the decision of where and what to handle first was a monumental matter. I had to make an effort not to press my thighs together harder in an attempt to get some relief. When he finally reached a hand out, though, he didn't touch me anywhere. He took ahold of my jeans and tugged them further down. I raised my knees to help. When he got them down to my ankles, he stopped.

"Spread your thighs."

I did, pointing my knees out to the sides. With the jeans binding my ankles, my legs could only spread in an open diamond shape that displayed my pussy to full view.

He struck faster than my eye could follow. His open palm smacked my sex and I gasped in shock at the stinging sensation that made more blood rush to his target. My sex grew more swollen, more sensitized. He smacked me again with his open palm and this time I arched up into the strike, an involuntary response. A third time his hand came down to spank my pussy and my clit throbbed hard. A fourth and I felt the coiling inside my abdomen tighten. A fifth and I again bucked my hips up to meet the light smack, trying for more pressure, trying to keep his hand there, between my legs, where I needed it.

"If you come while I'm doing this, I'll turn you over and spank your ass pink," Eli informed me. His hand descended again. I writhed and bit my lip. I wasn't going to give him the satisfaction of coming while he spanked my bare pussy with his open palm and I damn well wasn't going to invite him to paddle my ass when he was finished. Was I?

I could feel my sex responding as his palm made contact again. Then again. Just when I was on the brink of something that felt unstoppable, he stopped. I bit back a curse and concentrated on breathing. My chest rose and fell fast enough to betray my level of arousal if the slickness between my thighs wasn't enough of a clue.

"You didn't come." Eli placed his hand over the soft curls at the top of my thighs and petted me as if in approval. One finger traced down through the curls, searched out and stroked over my swollen, exposed clit. I moaned. "You wanted to though, didn't you?"

"Yes." I admitted it freely. No point lying when he had his hand right where he could feel for himself how close I was. I was hot, slick, and swollen. He drew his fingertip along my nether lips and gathered a coating of moisture that he stroked over my clit.

"You still want to." Eli sounded amused. I wanted to kill him. I glared at him, but the effect was probably ruined by the way I rocked into his hand.

His fingertips captured my clit and pinched the way I'd wanted him to when he was giving the same treatment to my nipple. He released me just when I thought the top of my head might blow off, stroked lightly over the flesh he'd just pinched. His fingertip was slick with my own lubrication and the touch was so gentle after the just-short-of-painful pinch that the combination broke me. I came, arching and moaning, all the while aware that he'd used the lightest touch to push me off the edge.

Then I lay there panting and trying to recover from the first orgasm of my existence, at the hand of a creature that shouldn't exist.

"I think that round went to you," I said when I was finally able to trust myself to speak.

"You think?" Eli stroked his hand over my belly and toyed with my ring again.

"Well, it's hard to feel like the loser when that's the consolation prize," I pointed out.

"Good one, was it?" Eli's hand skimmed up my ribs, around my breasts.

"Hard to say." I frowned as if thinking it over. "No basis for comparison. That kind of gives you the edge. I might think you're a genius in the sack when in reality you're barely average."

"I'm not average." Eli cupped a breast and stroked my nipple with one finger, a gesture I might have taken for lazy and idle if I didn't know better. I doubted he did anything without prior calculation.

"So you say. You still haven't shown me yours." I didn't expect him to unzip and introduce me to his little warrior, but I figured it didn't hurt to bring it up.

"I'd show you mine, but you might faint." Eli settled onto his back beside me with a little space between us. He stacked his hands under his head and looked up at the sky.

"That big?" I rolled over and shifted myself on top of him. His clothes felt rough against my bare skin. My ankles were still trapped by my jeans so I stretched out with my legs together. "I did assume you were built to scale."

I could feel against my belly the bulge in question, hard,

rounded, and very warm even though the fabric. I resisted the urge to rub against him.

He gave a low laugh that vibrated against my chest. "You sound like you're really hoping I've got an anaconda in my shorts." His hands came around to settle on my bare ass, cupping my cheeks.

"Maybe not that long," I said, giving in to the urge to rock my body into his. "But it is thick. And hard. I'm pretty sure snakes don't feel like tree trunks."

Eli snorted. "Just don't make any cracks about my bark."

"I won't. Only your bite." I nipped at his chest.

"You're not a sore loser. I appreciate that." His hands squeezed my butt, then smoothed down the backs of my thighs.

"I might be sore tomorrow," I said suggestively. "Besides, it's not over until it's over."

"Cocky."

"No, that would be you."

Eli delivered a light slap to my backside in response. I squirmed against him and didn't know if I should hope he'd do it again or hope he wouldn't. The unexpected foreplay of his palm spanking my sex had me wondering what other surprises he had in store for me.

I closed my eyes and listened to the sounds around us. The ocean surging below, birds high above, and the rustling of wind through leaves made a soothing combination. Not quiet, but restful. Eli's heart thudded under my ear and the rhythm marked time to the beat of our hidden corner of the world.

When Eli spoke, it startled me out of the reverie I'd fallen into. "When you said you had no basis for comparison, you meant in this form, didn't you?"

"Does it matter?" I kept my eyes closed, but the moment was gone. Which was for the best. Relaxing and letting my guard down was the last thing I should be doing.

"Answer the question."

And of course I couldn't evade. It was an order, so I was bound to answer. That didn't mean I'd volunteer any information I didn't have to, though. "Not in this form."

"And in your other?"

I sighed and levered myself up and off Eli. "Not in my other form, either. Happy now?"

He didn't look happy. He frowned at me. I reached down and yanked my jeans up. It just didn't seem like the moment to try to seduce him in return.

"Why not?"

I stopped adjusting the pants to stare back at Eli. "What do you mean, why not? I died a virgin. Yes, it is ironic. I believe the devil has a twisted sense of humor. End of story."

Eli continued to frown. I finished with the zipper and snap and started buttoning my shirt. Nick was probably laughing his ass off right now, and the idea made me grit my teeth.

"This could be a problem," Eli finally said.

I flopped onto my back on the ground. "Funny. That's exactly what I thought when you put your hand on my butt and bound me to you."

I didn't really see the issue, but then again, if I was complicating matters for him in any way, that was probably a good thing. I was pretty much striking out on our scorecard so far. First bound, then sent to the void, and now the loser of the who-can-seduce-whom contest. Although thinking back on that last item, I wasn't sure I'd put up much of a fight at all.

It was entirely outside my experience, being the one who was tempted instead of doing the tempting. I hadn't expected to feel desire for anything beyond the need to feed, and it had sort of blindsided me. Also, Eli's approach to foreplay wasn't exactly conventional. How could I have known it would affect me like it had?

I couldn't, I decided. But now I was forewarned, and that meant forearmed. Next time I wouldn't be taken by surprise.

"I'm not going to release you," Eli informed me.

I swung around to look at him. "Well, duh. I didn't think you would. I'm pretty sure you'd only unbind me if you knew my name and could summon me back."

He sat up and the movement brought him closer to me. "You would be right about that."

I shrugged. "It's good strategy. I mean, it sucks for me, but it's good strategy. Besides, if you send me back, Nick will just send something worse after you. If I were you, I'd stick with the demon you know. Especially since you're kicking my ass."

Eli's mouth twitched at that. I noticed he didn't disagree, though.

Well, so, we both knew he was winning. But I meant what I'd said to him earlier. It wasn't over until it was over. I might be losing so far, but that didn't mean I planned to go down without a fight.

"Time to go back." Eli stood and curled an arm around me, pulling me into his side.

I nodded. I wanted to stay, to walk on that isolated stretch of beach and listen to the waves hitting the shore, but it was better not to get too attached to any place in the world. It wasn't my world, not anymore.

I still felt a pang of loss when we transitioned back to the house in the woods. I told myself it was for the lonely coast I'd only seen briefly and would probably never see again.

We landed back in the living room, where we'd started. Dal had left, but the fire still burned and gave off a drying heat that countered the perpetual damp chill in the air. Eli left me there without a word, which I took to mean I was on my own for entertainment and at least temporarily considered safe to leave unguarded.

I huddled up to the stove for a few minutes until I realized heat wasn't doing it for me. I needed energy. Despite what had happened between us, Eli hadn't given in to lust. Aside from the little snack Dal had provided with his wayward longing for a certain witch, it had been long enough since I'd fed that I was going to be affected soon.

It was easy enough to make my way down the hall to the kitchen. I foraged in the refrigerator for sandwich makings. Except for bread, I came up short. The guys needed to go grocery shopping. I opened the freezer and discovered what they were really living on. Frozen meals in a variety of sizes and brands.

I found frozen calzones, grabbed two, and followed the directions for heating. The Spartan kitchen did at least include a microwave. Within a few minutes I had my meal. I started to sit at the kitchen table, but the room felt cold and empty. So I took my plate back to the living room and perched in the chair nearest the stove.

Once my stomach was full, I set the plate on a nearby table and curled up, eyes closed. I could pretend I was plotting my next move, but really I just wanted a nap.

A creaking floorboard told me I wasn't alone anymore

just before Dal spoke. "I hope you're not waiting for a bed-
time story and a blankie."

I squinted up at him. "Are you offering?"

"No." He held a hand out to me. "Come on, I'll show
you where you can sleep."

"Guess it isn't with you." I sighed as if crushed by the
unfairness of it.

He laughed. "No. You probably hog the covers and steal
all the pillows."

I spread my hands. "I *am* a demon."

"See?"

Dal led me to a room that I took to be Eli's. Mostly by
the glowing symbol on the door, which I saw after I tried to
go inside and bounced off an invisible barrier instead.

"Very funny." I stood just short of the threshold and
scowled at Dal. "I can't go in there."

Dal passed his hand over the symbol. When he finished,
it wasn't gone but changed in some subtle way. I frowned,
trying to pinpoint the difference. Had that squiggle been
there before? Or was a line missing?

"There." He waved me inside. I stepped forward and found
that the barrier that had repelled me before now gave way
and let me pass.

"Thank you." I closed the door in his face to express my
gratitude. Then I turned around and examined my surroundings, taking inventory.

A thick, faded quilt covered a king-sized bed. No surprise,
given Eli's proportions. A table that held books and a lamp.
An armoire I suspected I wouldn't be able to open. All the
furniture was some dark wood that showed the patina of age.

In the middle of the room the wood floor shone with a faint gleam as if recently mopped clean. I stepped forward and touched my toe into the center of the room, testing. I found what I expected, a tingle of residual magic. Not very long ago a circle had been drawn here.

I walked over to the armoire and tried the doors, then the drawers. They stuck shut. Eli probably kept his warrior gear and magical implements inside. "Warrior and teacher," I snorted.

Dal was the one devoted to sorcery and Eli to the fighting arts. It was still clear to me that while each had his specialty in opposite areas, they had trained in both. I didn't doubt that Dal was a formidable fighter and Eli had already demonstrated his prowess for sorcery.

If he was a better fighter than sorcerer, I was screwed. I couldn't match him for either physical or magical power. I had one area of strength and skill, and so far he hadn't shown any weakness for my only weapon: seduction.

I gave up on the armoire and flung myself on the bed. I went over the kiss in the kitchen, then replayed the kiss in the wilderness. Had Eli betrayed himself in some small way? Was there some cue I'd missed?

He hadn't, as far as I could remember. I, however, had betrayed myself repeatedly. I swore out loud, rolled up in the quilt, and pulled a pillow over my head. As if that could shut out the memory of my body reacting to Eli's manipulation while I enthusiastically cooperated in my own doom. Kind of like what I'd done to how many mortals?

Payback is such a bitch.

Ten

"Somebody's been sleeping in my bed." It was Eli's voice, not one of the three bears, but the quote almost made me smile. Almost. The thoughts Eli interrupted were a little too dark to give way to good cheer. I was grateful for the interruption anyway. Listening to my own brain racing like a hyperactive hamster trapped on a wheel wasn't getting me anywhere.

"I'm not sleeping. I'm thinking. And I'd say something about finding the bed too soft, but I don't want to give you a complex," I said, feigning a yawn.

"You'd better worry about finding something too hard." Eli ran a hand down my body, ending with a firm squeeze to my crotch. That made my eyes fly open.

"Hello. Did you want to see if Goldilocks is a natural blonde?"

"I already know." Eli gave me a wicked half-smile.

"Still. Seeing *is* believing." I undid my pants, raised my hips, and shimmied the fabric down my thighs.

"You don't need much encouragement to drop trou, do you?"

If I'd been human, I might have been insulted by Eli's tone of voice. Then again, I might've been turned on. There was something proprietary and very sexy about the way he said it.

I sat up and finished stripping off my lower body, then got to work on the upper half. "I am what I am, to quote Popeye."

"So you'd whip your pants off for any man."

I tilted my head back and gave Eli a wicked smile. "Why? Did you want to watch me with somebody? Is that what does it for you?"

He studied me, his eyes narrow. "What if I said yes?"

I finished getting naked and made myself comfortable before I answered him. I fluffed up the pillows, leaned back, and arranged my legs in a flattering line that would draw his eye upward. "Unless I'm missing something, the only other male here is your brother, and you forbade me to seduce him."

"Suppose I changed my mind?"

I studied his face and posture carefully for clues. He wasn't giving much away, but Eli did seem perfectly sincere. Maybe, just maybe, my luck was turning.

"Did you?" I asked the question directly.

"Suppose I did." Eli answered without answering. He reached down and gripped my knees, pulling them apart. "Suppose I told you I was going to bring him in here and watch while he made you come. Would you be just as willing to spread your legs for him as you were for me?"

For some reason, the question struck me as double-edged. If I said no, then I would be pretty much challenging him to make it a direct order, which we both knew I couldn't disobey. But if I said yes, would I be undermining any tenuous connection we might have established already? Or strengthening it?

One thing I knew for certain: if there was any possibility that he did in fact want to watch, I couldn't afford to miss any chance at unlocking the key to his lust.

"I'm willing to do as you command," I said, trying to match him for caginess.

"You're willing to give in to my brother the way you gave in to me. To get a basis for comparison?" Eli's voice sounded flat and a little hard as he asked the question, and again he gave me no clues.

I wanted to grind my teeth. Most times when a threesome opportunity came my way, it wasn't this complicated. Of course, most times making that threesome a fully realized event wasn't in the realm of possibility, so neither were any consequences beyond my would-be partners falling victim to lust. This conversation was like tap-dancing over landmines.

"I'm a succubus," I pointed out. "Your brother is welcome to try to seduce me, but I can't promise it won't backfire. Are you going to take it out on me if it does?"

"I won't take it out on you if Dal is consumed by lust."

"That's a relief."

"It shouldn't be." That hard edge was glittering in Eli's eyes again. "If he gives in to lust, he'll take it out on you. Anything I did would be superfluous."

"Wow." I batted my lashes at Eli. "You do know how to offer a girl a good time. If he's consumed by lust, I'll consume him."

"So you're willing."

Oh, hell, yes. I licked my lips and half-lowered my eyes, looking at Eli through my lashes. "I think your brother might have an opinion or two of his own about this, but yes. I'll play."

"Thought so." Eli ran his hands up my thighs and brushed his fingertips along my outer labia. "You realize you present us with a unique opportunity."

"Likewise." My voice came out husky and I didn't even have to try to do it on purpose.

"If Dal is able to rule his passions, it may allow him to pursue other opportunities." Eli petted my pussy while he spoke, his touch as casual as his tone of voice.

I nodded. Dal was at an impasse with his witch. If he couldn't trust himself, he'd never risk approaching her. I was one female he might be willing to test himself against. I was expendable, and if he destroyed me, well, he was just doing his job. The Nephilim were here to check demonic incursions into the world, and I was a demon.

I liked Dal. Under different circumstances we might truly have been friends. I wasn't exactly altruistic in my motives, though. He'd fed me an appetizer or two of his lust, and when it came to feeding, I was always hungry for more. If he put his hands on me, he'd be thinking of her. And he'd feel delicious desire.

I also wanted to explore any possibility that might tempt Eli. Some men like to watch. Some like it a lot. Some especially like watching a female in their power perform sex acts with another man, as the man in power commands. Making the acts more about the man in charge and his submissive female than the other man.

Eli might really get off on ordering me to fuck his brother. Or suck Dal's cock. Or sit on his face. There were multiple possibilities and no limits. Whatever Eli told me to do, I'd do it. Now that I had his assurance that he wasn't setting me up for punishment if I drained his brother to the point of no return, it was pretty much a win-win-win scenario.

I could be a friend to Dal. I could have a chance to feed the way I needed to. I could ingratiate myself with Eli and maybe finally spark some lust, make some progress on achieving my mission to seduce him.

Maybe, greed whispered, I could feed on both of them at once. I felt almost drunk at the very idea.

Eli gave my sex a final stroke, his finger dipping just between my nether lips to test the moisture gathered there. His touch had readied me, plumping my labia and drawing the dew that now coated his fingertip. He placed his finger in his mouth, tasted me on it, and gave me an approving nod. He reached up to pinch one of my nipples with his other hand. "Let's see what Dalen has to say, then."

Dalen. I rolled the sound of his full name around and

liked it. Dal was more familiar, unassuming. Dalen was for-mal and hinted at power. Dal would be fun in the sack. Dalen, formidable.

Eli took the hand he'd used to taste me and traced some-thing in the air. Dalen appeared beside the bed.

"You called?" He quirked a brow at Eli, then turned to give me an appreciative look. "Looking hot, babe."

"Thanks." I smiled at him, legs open, my well-stroked and slick pussy an obvious invitation.

He smiled back at me. "Now I feel overdressed."

"Then maybe you should undress." Eli looked at Dal and waved toward me, as if he was giving his brother direction and granting permission at the same time.

"Is somebody in the mood for a sandwich?" Dal's brows shot up, twin arcs of surprise. "Or did you plan to watch while I do all the work?"

Eli's mouth curved in a half-smile. "I doubt you'll have to do all the work. She'll help. Won't you?" He directed the last question at me.

I skimmed my hands along my body. "Whatever you say."

Dal's eyes followed my hands. Then they returned to Eli. "If you decide you want to join in too late, I may not leave any for you."

He sounded dead serious. I mentally kicked myself for even thinking the word *dead. No time to chicken out now, Edana. This is a golden opportunity. A double golden opportunity.*

"I wouldn't underestimate her." Eli reached down to fon-dle my breast while he spoke. "Or yourself."

For an answer, Dal stripped. I liked that he did it the

manual way instead of waving his clothes away by magic. I got to watch the show, watch his body unveiled by steps and stages. When he got to his shorts, I looked at Eli. "I still haven't seen yours."

Eli rubbed his thumb over my nipple. "I haven't decided whether or not I'm going to show it to you. Maybe if you prove yourself worthy of Dal's cock, I'll let you see mine."

"A challenge." I smiled at him, all seductive confidence. "You're on."

"Hey. I'm getting naked over here. Eyes on me." Dal peeled off his shorts and I got an eyeful. I didn't have to work at looking appreciative of the sight. Dal naked was really something. Dal naked and sporting the biggest hard-on I'd ever seen was the stuff succubus dreams are made of.

"Dal." I let my eyes go wide. "Did you answer one of those penis-enlargement ads on the Internet?"

Dal laughed and wrapped his hand around his shaft, showing off his equipment for me. "Didn't have to. I am a factory-ready fun machine."

I slicked the tip of my tongue along my lower lip. "Is there any particular use that voids the warranty?"

"No. But there is a risk I'll void you." Dal's face went sober.

I sat forward and moved closer to him. I placed one hand on his chest and used the other to reach between his legs and cup his balls. They were taut and firm, and warm. He was hot to the touch like Eli, and I felt the same compulsion to let his heat sear me.

"I won't say I'm indestructible," I told Dal. I lowered my face to his penis so that when I spoke again, my lips just brushed the sensitive skin on his head. "But I am the closest thing to it you're going to come across." Then I licked the tip of his cock, a lazy, lingering lap of my tongue, dipping against the slit which produced a bead of pre-come.

Dal threaded the fingers of his free hand into my hair and used his other hand to draw his cock along my lips. "Are you really willing to take that risk?"

I parted my lips just a little, tasting more of Dal as he teased my mouth. The heat seemed to be coming off him in a wave now and I felt dizzy from it. "Yes." I licked at him as if he was an irresistible treat that I had to taste more of. "Are you?" I ran my tongue around the sensitive head and felt him react by growing harder, something I would have said was impossible.

"You think this is a solution." Dal spoke to Eli, not to me. So I gave my mouth permission to do something other than speak, stretching it around Dal's cock and inviting him to feed me more of his length.

"It's an option." Eli ran his hand down my back. "One I think you owe it to yourself to explore."

"And you'll watch, in case I need a spotter." Dal thrust into my mouth, just a little but enough to make me angle my head in encouragement. I couldn't deep-throat him, but I could take a lot more. And I wanted to take as much as I could get. Knowing that Eli wanted me to, and was watching me do it, maybe even imagining me giving his cock the same treatment, made me want to get on my knees and give Dal the best head of his lifetime.

"I'll watch." Eli stroked my back again. I rose onto my knees to get into the best position and wrapped my mouth and tongue around Dal's shaft.

"If you decide you want to do more than watch, I'll try not to get greedy." Dal fed me another inch and I took it, already hungering for more.

"I think two of us are a match for her." Eli caressed the curve of my bare ass. "Even if we both succumbed to lust, I don't believe she could drain us to critical levels. Not if she was feeding on both of us at the same time."

"Balance." Dal rocked into my mouth. I accepted more of his length, opening my throat, laving him with my tongue.

"I believe we can maintain it, yes." Eli cupped my butt, then traced a finger down the line that separated the twin cheeks. I moved one knee out to the side and arched my back in invitation. From behind me, Eli now had access to my pussy. Or my ass. Or both. In front of me, I had Dal filling my mouth with his cock.

"For either of us alone, maybe too great a risk." Eli palmed my sex. "Together, there may still be risk but it's minimal. I believe the opportunity outweighs the potential risk."

Dal was probably willing to risk a lot more than a no-strings-attached blow job from a naked blonde to find out if he could ever get to first base with the woman he wanted without going bestial on her ass.

For myself, the risk was no different than it had ever been since I got this assignment. I had known from the beginning there was a good chance I wouldn't be coming back from this one. The chance to take something for myself along the way, a moment of satiation in an eternity of denial—that, I couldn't pass up. Wouldn't pass up.

"You're sure you won't mind if I come down her throat?"

Dal flexed his fingers on the back of my head, urging me to take more of him.

"I'm sure I can have that pleasure myself if I decide I want it." Eli planted both of his hands on my ass and squeezed, a steady exertion of pressure that somehow made a tingle of heat grow between my legs. "We can take turns thrusting our cocks between those full lips of hers and coating the back of her throat with come."

Dal rocked a little harder into my mouth. "I think she likes that idea."

"Do you want Dal to coat the back of your throat with his hot come?" Eli pinched my bottom as he asked the question as if he thought he might have to do something to draw my attention away from the organ I was busy wrapping my lips around.

"Mmmm," I answered, sucking harder. I felt my throat work convulsively at the idea. Dal's heat, filling my mouth. Spilling into my mouth for me to swallow down . . .

"Work for it." Eli delivered a light slap to my ass. "Suck him. Show me why I should let you have a taste of my cock."

I loved a challenge. I proceeded to put on the best performance of my afterlife.

ELEVEN

I finally let Dal's deliciously salty cock pop free from my mouth after I'd lapped up every trace of his come and swallowed every drop. If that didn't tempt Eli into letting me perform the same service for him, I didn't know what would.

He'd been entertained enough by the show I'd put on for him to give me his unwavering attention. He'd stroked and caressed my body while I went down on Dal, then filled my hungry sheath with his fingers, stroking them in and out of my delighted pussy to match the rhythm of my head bobbing up and down on Dalen's cock.

Now that I'd experienced it, I thought getting banged by

one man while I blew another rated as one of those peak experiences Dal found in nature. Just thinking about it made me want to gloat.

Positioned between two hot men, I thought I might never be cold again. They radiated heat and I absorbed it readily. Dal didn't seem in any danger of losing control of himself, and neither did Eli. Despite the lack of lust on their part, I felt pretty much like a cat in catnip. I wanted to roll in both of them.

"Two hot men," I said out loud, and giggled at the pun. They were hot, and *hot*. Two gorgeous guys who gave off rays I could tan in.

"She sounds drunk." Dal addressed his statement to Eli, his voice half-amused, half-perplexed. He threaded his fingers into my hair and used the hold to tug my face up to look at him. "Hey. Demon. Beelzebabe. You okay?"

I let out a throaty laugh. Beelzebabe? I hadn't told either of them my name, and I guess they had to call me something. It beat *Yo, demon* or *devil spawn*. I felt a new surge of affection for Dal. He'd given me a nickname. "Never better. Did you like your blow job?"

"Yeah." His eyes crinkled in the corners, and that made me feel strangely happy. "Thanks, Babe."

"Any time." I licked at the taut skin of his abdomen and then rubbed my cheek against it like a feline. "I like you."

"What about me?" Eli pulled me back against his chest. "Do you like me?"

"Sometimes." I made the admission in a cheerful voice and frowned at myself. I did sound drunk. Did Nephilim produce something intoxicating, or something that induced a similar effect? Some substance I might have taken in by swallowing Dal's ejaculation or by physical contact with them? Or simply by breathing the air, if it was airborne, like pheromones?

No, airborne wouldn't account for it. I struggled to think, remembering eating with the two of them, and both of them together in the kitchen before that first kiss with Eli. I'd been with the two of them in fairly close quarters several times and hadn't felt like this. But only one of them had touched me at a time. It had to be the physical contact, and the effect probably grew as more touch reinforced it.

Not that I wanted the touching to stop. I felt starved for touch, and the glide of Eli's palms over my flesh fed a hunger I was unfamiliar with—my own.

It was too much of a struggle to reason with heat fogging my brain. Did it really matter why getting naked with two Nephilim gave me a buzz? I decided that thinking was over-rated and surrendered to feeling.

"Only sometimes?" Eli caressed my breasts and I closed my eyes with a smile.

"I like you right now." His hands were making my flesh happy. His warmth glowed against my back like banked coals and I luxuriated in the heat. "You're so warm."

"A minute ago I was hot," Eli pointed out. He teased my nipples with his talented fingers. "Now I'm just warm?"

"*Hot* was a play on words," I said and my voice slurred. I frowned again. Maybe it wasn't just their proximity and the bliss of physical contact that was going to my head. "Is this a spell?"

"I told you we have an effect." Eli kissed the nape of my neck. I shuddered as a ripple of sheer wanting went through me. "It seems the effect isn't limited to humans. Interesting."

He sounded almost scientifically detached. Not the way a male who had his hands full of my bare breasts ought to sound.

"You sound like Spock," I said. My voice sounded petulant even to me, but what did he expect? He could at least act enthusiastic out of politeness. Then again, this was Eli.

I opened my eyes and peered up at Dal. "Any second now he'll say, 'Fascinating.'" I quoted the character's signature word in my best impersonation. "Do you think he'll give me another orgasm in the interests of scientific discovery?"

"He gave you an orgasm?" Dal grinned at me. "Was it a good one?"

"Yep." I beamed, happy again at the memory. I hadn't had Eli's hand between my legs long enough during the blow job to come a second time, but it had felt excellent all the same. Then I frowned. "At least, I think it was a good one. It was my first and only one. Maybe it was only average and I don't know better."

"I'll give you an orgasm," Dal offered. "It's the least I can do after you sucked me off. I should return the favor. Then you can decide whose was better, mine or his."

"Maybe you'll both be average." I giggled at the very idea of these two only performing the sexual equivalent of a C grade. I'd probably have another orgasm without any help if I just stayed between them long enough. Drunk on essence of Nephilim.

"Do I look average?" Dal put a hand to his equipment. It was not average. It was porn star material.

"You are hung," I informed him. "And you're still hard when I just made you come. That's so not average."

"I'm hung." Eli murmured the words at the curve of my neck and pressed his sadly still clothed cock against my ass to prove it.

"I know." I wiggled my hips, grinding his very well-hung and heavily engorged cock into the snug crevice between my butt cheeks. If he'd been as naked as I was, it would've felt so much better. Just thinking of him without the barriers and restrictions clothing posed made me imagine the sensual possibilities.

I wondered if he'd like to pleasure himself by gliding back and forth in that soft cleft, my ass making a cushion for his turgid flesh. Or maybe he liked a little sodomy. Would he want to work his hard length into my puckered anus? Or would he rather plunge into my slick, ready sex? Maybe he'd like both. Maybe they'd both like to take turns, tandem fucking me and trading positions. . . .

Focus, I told myself and turned my attention back to the topic of conversation. Eli and his cruelty in withholding his joystick from me.

"Not that you're letting me play with it," I complained, picking up the thread again. "You're so selfish. You should share your toys."

"I'm sharing you."

Yeah, he was. "Am I a toy?"

"Well, we're playing with you," Dal pointed out.

True. "Wanna toy with me, big guy? Let's play a game called 'give a girl an orgasm.'"

"She *is* drunk." Dal frowned at Eli. "Is this taking advantage?"

"Hello? Demon. *Succubus.*" I prompted his memory since

it seemed to need a jog and then wrapped my hands around Dal's jutting penis and stroked his shaft up and down. "Lives for sex. Literally. How is giving me an orgasm taking advantage of me? I'm taking advantage of you."

I wanted another orgasm, dammit. Only one, in how many centuries of sexual servitude? It was so unfair. I deserved orgasms.

"You are taking liberties with my person," Dal said. His lips twitched with humor. "You really want me to make you come?"

"Oh, hell, yes." I rose up and rubbed the breasts Eli was no longer caressing against his chest. "Do me with your hands, your mouth. Your choice. Just do me."

"Eli?" I wanted to shriek with frustration as Dal looked over my shoulder to confer with big brother. What, he didn't think he'd been given adequate permission already? Was he trying to get out of returning the favor?

"I'll hold her."

Oh. Then again, maybe they just needed to coordinate positions. Three people in a bed, two of them very large men, it could take a little effort to synchronize activity. I let them arrange me between them. They settled on Eli sitting back on the bed with me reclined against his chest and seated between his thighs. Dal kneeled between my open legs. I held my breath, wondering what he'd choose. Hands? Mouth? Both?

He went with his mouth. I let out my breath in a rush as his lips closed over my clit and sucked. Good choice, I thought, feeling dizzy with pleasure.

Dal devoured me, and their dual heat had me writhing in

delight. My hips bucked as he took me with his mouth, alternating between suction on my clit, lapping at my sensitized labia, thrusting his tongue into me. It felt fantastic. It felt incredible. Dal was clearly a genius, and I said so in a drunken slur. Or at least I tried to. Maybe it only came out as inarticulate moaning.

My rocking and squirming pushed me back against Eli. He cradled me, supported me, and while Dal focused on my sex, Eli cupped my breasts in his palms. His hands stroked, squeezed, teased. His fingers played my nipples, and the stimulation combined with Dal's oral skills had me nearly delirious with sensation.

Eli pinched my nipples, steadily increasing the pressure until he reached a point that nearly made my eyes roll back. My sex clenched in reaction. Dal closed his mouth over my clit and sucked hard. And I came, my back bowing, head arched back, wrenched by the power of my release.

It left me spent and shuddering, gasping for air. I fell back against Eli, grateful for his arms around me. He wrapped me in a snugger embrace, one hand going down to cup my belly as Dal cupped a hand over my sex, pressing his palm into me. I wondered if he could feel my pussy quivering with aftershocks.

"How was that, Babe?" Dal asked the question, a teasing lilt combined with masculine smugness in his voice. "Better than average?"

"That was world-class," I said. "Although it's hard to say how your performance would rate solo."

"Hey. Was there anybody else between your legs?" He gave me a challenging look.

"Eli helped. The nipple stimulation. Sorry. I can't overlook that in scoring your performance." I grinned, feeling sated and smug and so warm I could've happily stayed right where I was for the rest of eternity.

"Babe. You look flushed." Dal was frowning at me. Why frowning? This was a happy moment. Other than the fact that he wanted full credit for my second orgasm, which really wasn't fair to Eli so I couldn't go along with it.

Although why I wanted to be fair to Eli, I couldn't say. He'd bound me. He'd parked me in cold storage without a word of warning or apology. Was that fair to me?

"We're overheating her." Eli sounded more stern than usual and I wanted to roll my eyes at him for it, but I was too tired. Must've been the orgasm, wringing me out. "Help me. Lift her."

Dal's hands closed on my waist, pulled me forward. Eli released me and slid out from behind me. Both of them drew back, leaving me alone on the bed.

"Hey." I wanted to protest my abandonment, but all that came out was a weak *Hey*. Dammit. Without their warmth I was going to be cold again. A shiver racked me, right on cue, but then I realized I wasn't shaking with cold. Heat baked me. Waves of it were coming off me. Suddenly I didn't feel so great. I felt sick and shocky and desperate for air.

"Open the window," Eli said to Dal, as if he'd read my mind. Dal nodded and had cold air swirling into the bedroom in the blink of an eye. They both stood over me, looking down at me, while I shook and panted and wondered if I was going to throw up. Demons don't throw up, but tell that to the nausea that boiled in my belly and twisted my abdomen.

"I'll go." Dal stared down at me, worry on his face. "The effect is multiplied by us being together, not just doubled. She should be okay if I keep my distance for a little while."

I could tell he didn't want to do it, that he felt guilty and didn't want to abandon me after unintentionally harming me. Too bad I didn't feed on guilt. I tried to tell him it was okay, but I couldn't seem to get any words past my chattering teeth. How could I be so hot and shake like I was freezing?

Eli nodded. Dal receded, and then there was just me and the cold, damp air flowing over my naked body. I tried to focus, but couldn't see Eli. Had he left, too? No, there he was, drawing strange symbols on the floor. He came back and scooped me up, holding me away from his torso to keep space between us. He lowered me onto the floor, stepped back, and spoke a word.

Snow fell. I blinked and tried to understand it. Was this illusion? Was I still in Eli's bedroom, or somewhere else?

Snowflakes drifted over my belly, tickled my nose, clung to my lashes and blurred my vision. It felt good, so unbelievably good. I rolled in an unbroken expanse of snow under a glittering canopy of stars, and the heat inside me dissipated, leaving melted patches where I'd rolled or rested. My head cleared. My vision cleared. My stomach relaxed.

Ah. Better.

I lay back in the hushed field of snow and admired the way moonlight and starlight made it glitter like a field of diamonds. The snow felt like a velvety blanket under me that crunched just a little when I moved.

I scooped some up and made a ball with my hands, enjoying the way it packed and clung. I threw my impossible snowball and laughed as it vanished from sight.

Then the laughter died away. Where was I? Had Eli sent me to the North Pole? Was he going to leave me here?

As if conjured by my thought, I heard his voice. Distant at first, then louder, stronger, chanting words that pulled me back to him.

I blinked and I was on the floor of his bedroom again. No snow. But my skin glowed from rolling naked in that cold, crystalline field.

"Did that really happen?" I asked him.

"Did what happen?" He reached down and picked me up, but this time he cradled me against his chest.

"I was someplace with snow. Or maybe I dreamed it."

"Not a dream." Eli carried me to the bed, settled me on it, covered me with the quilt.

"You're so informative." I gripped the quilt and snugged it up around my shoulder. "I could fill a book with the things I've learned from you."

He laughed, a short, abrupt sound. As if I amused him against his will. His lips brushed my forehead. Then he was gone, leaving me curled in his bed. I decided to be glad he wasn't making me sleep on the floor. Still, part of me felt peeved that they could so easily resist me and so readily walk away from me. Like a naked succubus posed no temptation.

I was really going to have to work on that.

TWELVE

There was a dragon outside the kitchen door. I rubbed my eyes and blinked, but it was still there. I'd woken up alone and made my way to the source of sustenance, since my hosts were not sustaining me with their lust, and the first thing I saw when I stumbled naked and bleary-eyed into the kitchen was a dragon.

Its great head was lowered to peer through the glass. I debated the etiquette of answering the door in my birthday suit, then shrugged. It was a dragon, not a Girl Scout selling cookies.

I opened the door. "Hello."

"Hello." The dragon emitted a breath of flame as it spoke.

I jumped back to avoid getting my hair burned. I already had bedhead. On top of that, my hair was frizzy from the humidity. I didn't need to add singed to the list of things making me less attractive to my target.

"Hey. Watch it. I'm not sure where the kitchen fire extinguisher is." I frowned at the dragon, who regarded me with multifaceted eyes and blatant curiosity.

"I apologize," the scaly and serpentine winged visitor on the back porch finally said. "I came for a progress report."

A familiar scent of sulfur came with the words. I cocked my head and stared. "Nick? Is that you?"

"Ah. You like me in this form." The dragon grinned, an odd expression to see on that inhuman face. It showed a lot of teeth, all of them glittering and sharp. "I had no idea it would delight you to talk to a giant man-eating reptile who could scorch you with a breath."

"I've already been scorched." I scuffed the floor with my foot at the memory of last night's shake and bake. I'd been having such a good time up until then, too. "How come getting sandwiched between two Nephilim cooked me?"

"You were sandwiched between them?" A tiny flame flickered from the dragon's mouth as Nick spoke, but it was controlled this time and didn't come close to burning me. Light played over the beast's body, making a rainbow of color. Smoke curled from his nostrils.

I'd never seen the boss look so cool.

"Can you blow smoke rings or little animal shapes?" I asked, fascinated.

"I can do anything. Tell me more about the Nephilim."

Right. Business. "Dalen's got the hots for a witch, so he's

using me for practice. To see if he can control his lust without endangering his partner. This may either get me a Nephilim feast and you a new soul, or I may get incinerated. Is there any chance he can do that? Give off so much lust that I can't handle it and end up a pile of formerly blond ashes?"

The beast drummed its fore nails on the porch, clearly impatient. "What of Eli?"

Nick didn't answer my question. I was used to him answering questions with questions, but that didn't mean I liked it, and right now it was more than annoying. I thought anything that could end in *Edana goes bye-bye* damn well constituted a need-to-know basis.

I ground my teeth and narrowed my eyes at him. "Fucking Socratic method."

"Temper, temper."

"I'm a demon. And it's first thing in the morning after I did not get any lust the night before." I scowled at Nick the dragon. "I am not in a good mood."

"Report." A warning flame erupted with the demand.

"Go to hell." I stepped back and slammed the door. If he wasn't going to help me, why should I help him? I went to the fridge and searched out bread for toast. I ignored the ominous roaring and rattling sounds Nick made outside and popped two slices in. What else? Protein. I found peanut butter in a cabinet, a knife in a drawer, and I had everything I needed for breakfast.

I was spreading a thick layer of the extra crunchy variety on my toast when Dal came in. I smiled at him. "Hey."

"Hey." He crossed the room to tousle my hair. "Did I hear the back door slam?"

"Jehovah's Witnesses," I said. "They're relentless. They'll probably be back." I knew without looking that Nick was gone.

"If a naked hottie answered the door, I know I'd be back." Humor gleamed in his eyes. I found myself smiling in response. It was so easy to like Dal. So hard to hold onto a bad mood in his presence.

"Want some toast?" I waved a smeary knife at the bread and jar of peanut butter on the counter.

"Sure. You're really taking your kitchen duties to heart." Dal patted my butt as he went to make coffee.

"I'm here. Might as well make the most of it." I dropped more bread in for Dal.

"You seem to have bounced back from last night."

"Yep. That's me. I bounce." I turned and jiggled my breasts to demonstrate. Dal gave me an appreciative look. "Eli did something with snow that made it all better."

It had felt surprisingly good to roll naked in the snow. Maybe those people who jumped out of saunas into snowbanks in the dead of winter weren't entirely crazy. Of course, a few more minutes of it and the experience probably would have lost its charm.

What a night I'd had. From blow job to snow job. But hey, I'd gotten a second orgasm, and Eli had not been unmoved by the sight of me getting Dalen off. I was making progress. Sort of. Maybe.

"Where is Eli?"

I shrugged. "Out playing with his sword, for all I know."

"I take it you didn't get to play with his sword."

The sexual meaning in Dal's voice made me grin. "Not yet, but I plan to get my hand on the hilt."

Dal snorted. "Hand, my ass. You want to be his sheath."

Oh, yeah. I pictured Eli, hard and demanding between my thighs. The broad head of his cock probing the slick folds of my pussy. The full, glorious length of him thrusting into me, filling me, ending my ridiculous token virginity . . . I wanted that, all right.

"Nothing wrong with enjoying your work," I said in a bright voice. "Here's your toast." I put it on a plate and handed it to him.

"Come and sit on my lap so I can grope you while I eat it."

Worked for me. I waited while he hit the brew button on the coffeemaker and settled himself at the table with his plate in front of him. I carried my breakfast over and placed it beside his, then did a little bump and grind as I took a seat on him. I wiggled my butt into his groin and smiled when he reacted with a trouser salute.

He reached around and squeezed one of my breasts in retaliation. Or maybe it was a reward. Then I wondered if he was setting up for a repeat of yesterday's performance. "Are you expecting your student witch?"

"If I was, would you squirm naked on my lap in front of her while I played with you?"

"Depends." I thought it over. "You did give off a hefty jolt of lust when she saw you touching me. That was nice. Also, you have good hands. Getting fondled by you is not a hardship. That said, I'm not sure it's in my best interests to play along. She might decide I'm standing in the way of getting what she wants. I don't think I'd like being turned into a newt."

"Turning a babe like you into a newt would be a crime against men everywhere."

"Flatterer." I ate my toast while Dal munched his. In between bites he tweaked my nipples and flicked my navel ring. When we'd both finished, he worked a hand between my legs and cupped my sex.

"Mmm. That's nice." I felt the warmth of his palm pressing against my labia, subtly stimulating me. My flesh responded with liquid heat.

"Claire's going to be here in a minute," he said, nuzzling my neck while he gave my pussy a little squeeze that massaged my clit and teased my nether lips with his fingertips as they curled in. Not quite penetrating, but a clear prelude. "If you don't want me to toy with you in front of her, get up."

I snuggled into his heat and thought it over. I knew he'd pleasure me with his hand while he lusted after the one he didn't dare touch, making me a surrogate recipient of his passions. I wouldn't mind getting the benefit of all the pent-up desire he wouldn't slake on her, not to mention a much-needed infusion of lust, but . . .

"I don't object to having an audience, but I'm allergic to newt." I rocked into his hand once, gave a regretful sigh, and hopped off his lap. I put an extra swing in my hips for him, knowing he'd watch as I left the kitchen.

Fooling around with Dal had brightened my mood. Having a full tummy didn't hurt, either. Now all I needed to make my morning complete was a little hint of lust from Eli.

Of course, I couldn't get him to lust after me if I couldn't find him. I wandered through the various rooms in the house, except Dal's, which was barred to me the way Eli's had been until the symbol on the door had been altered to let me pass. Too bad. I would've liked the chance to appease my curiosity.

None of the rooms yielded Eli, so I went back to his room and raided his drawers. Since they opened, I figured he didn't mind. I couldn't stay naked all day. Well, I could, but it might be awkward if any humans came around. Or if Eli's dad came back. Or if I met up with Dal's witch. Yep, lots of reasons to get dressed.

Eli and I wore vastly different sizes, but I found a pair of plaid cotton boxers I could pass off as shorts, especially when teamed with a loose sweatshirt that came down to my thighs. The shorts were huge on me, but I made them work by pulling the spare fabric forward, then folding and tucking it into the waistband.

There was still no sign of Eli by the time I'd made myself presentable, if not a fashion maven. Dal and his witch were no doubt off doing magic studies. I went to the back door, then hesitated before going out. Had Eli told me to stay inside? I didn't think so, but if I was going out of bounds, his binding would keep me from going through the door.

I walked out onto the porch. That answered that question. I wandered around the yard, taking in my surroundings. There was a lack of urban noise that took some getting used to. Earth was such a loud place in the modern age. Not here.

This place was filled with the chatter of birds and chipmunks, the sound of wind in the trees, distant animal noises. But the roar of traffic and wail of sirens and the general din that a few million people living on top of each other created, that was absent. It felt odd.

I sniffed and didn't breathe exhaust or factory fumes. I smelled rain and earth and evergreen.

It was unnatural.

I decided I'd had enough of nature and turned to go back inside. What I saw changed my mind.

Eli, bare to the waist, running through a series of stances and forms with his angel sword, moving sometimes too fast for my eye to follow, pausing, lunging, twirling. It was like a dance. A deadly dance where a misstep would cost you a limb or worse, but nevertheless Eli made violence beautiful.

I'd never seen anything like it. I'd seen fighting men over the centuries. I'd seen martial arts. But Eli was in a class by himself. "The warrior," I murmured out loud.

He was just that. A warrior. Born to wield the sword, lethal and powerful and unhesitating. No wonder he was mowing down demons. No wonder Nick was worried. How did you fight a force like that?

You didn't. Not directly. Nick's plan made more sense to me all the time. I couldn't engage Eli directly. Even if I was bigger, stronger, had a different set of abilities, I wouldn't have a prayer. But slipping under his guard, that might be the way to find a vulnerability.

Not that it mattered. At the rate I was going, I'd get under his guard in about a hundred years, by which point I'd be long dead from lust starvation. But I liked watching him practice, so I stayed and admired the play of his muscles and the physical strength and mental focus evident his every move. No wasted effort, no mistakes, no mercy.

I'm toast.

Eli must've seen me, because he turned and began walking toward me, sword slashing through the air. A smart person would've run. I stood my ground. If Eli wanted to take me out, running wouldn't save me.

He came to a halt inches from me and drove the sword into the ground between my feet. I'd seen the blur of motion it made in his hands, but now that it was still I found it impossible to fix my eyes on. I knew it was very real, though. And very sharp.

"Can I hope that's sexually symbolic?" I asked him, trying to make my voice light and teasing instead of going high in panic.

He regarded me in silence that stretched out until I had to fight to keep from shifting my balance from one foot to the other in awkward fidgeting. Then his hands went to the waistband of his pants. He unfastened them with jerky movements and yanked them open to free his cock.

If I thought he'd made an arresting image half-clothed and wielding a deadly supernatural weapon, this topped it. The open fabric of his pants framed his aroused member, setting it off in a way that drew more attention to it than if he'd been naked. His chest gleamed from exertion, every muscle defined and clearly outlined. His cock jutted toward me like a divining rod, and I felt moisture coat my sex in response.

"Suck." That one word broke from his lips, his tone harsh and guttural, his expression fierce and forbidding.

Yum. I didn't need the compulsion of the bond to bend me to his will. Obeying Eli's command would be my pleasure. I licked my lips in anticipation, then considered the sword between us. "We'll have to move. There's something in the way."

Eli made a motion with his hand and the sword I couldn't quite see was gone. I tested the space where it had been, moving slowly and cautiously, but it was really gone. I knelt in front of him and touched the tip of my tongue to the broad head of his shaft. He tasted of salt and musk and he made my mouth water.

I reached up to cup his balls with one hand. They were warm and firm in my palm, the skin drawn tight from his erection. I stroked them and felt him react to my touch. I drew my tongue down the length of him until I reached my hand. Then I opened wide and took his balls into my mouth, carefully, one at a time. After giving each a little gentle suction, I began to kiss my way back up his shaft.

My fingertips searched out the secret spot between the sac and his anus, and stroked there. The right amount of pressure applied just at that point could stave off orgasm, and it was also wonderfully receptive to stimulation.

My lips reached his head again. I lapped at him, drawing my tongue around and over the sensitive skin while I caressed his balls and that spot between his legs. Then I stretched my lips around the width of him and sucked his cock into my mouth.

THIRTEEN

Eli filled my mouth and his scent, cedar and musk, filled my nostrils. I used both hands to caress him and to grip and stroke the base of his shaft. He was fully engorged, hard with arousal, and yet the skin was velvety soft. I licked and sucked and stroked his cock, my movements leisurely and languid.

I wanted to enjoy this. I wanted to make it last. I wanted to feel him pulse in my mouth when his orgasm hit, to feel the salty liquid heat of him spilling onto my tongue, to drink him down, greedily swallowing every drop as he fucked my mouth until he'd pumped his balls empty.

I was lost in the taste and texture of him, my head bobbing

up and down on him, when a sharp female voice cut through the haze of desire.

"What's she still doing here?"

"I think that's obvious." Dal's voice answered the witch.

I didn't allow the fact that I'd gathered an audience to distract me. I deep-throated Eli, taking as much of his length and width as I could.

"They couldn't get a room?" Claire's disapproval was clear. I guess she wasn't destined to be my new best friend for life.

"You don't like to watch?"

Dal was teasing her. If she turned him into a newt, he'd deserve it.

"Do you?" She turned the tables back on him. Or at least thought she had.

"Sure." I heard him coming toward me, felt his hands cup and squeeze my ass as he offered earthy encouragement. "Suck him hard, Babe. Give it to him good."

I laved Eli with my tongue as I sucked and felt his balls tighten in my hand. He was getting close. Drawing a crowd obviously didn't bother him, either.

Dal slid his hands into the waist of my borrowed boxers. They unfolded under the pressure and fell off with almost no help. He left them around my knees and stood back to admire his handiwork. "Nice ass. It's damn cute the way you wiggle it when you're giving head."

I hear Claire's sharply indrawn breath and then her rapidly receding footsteps and figured he'd gotten the reaction he was trying for. She was leaving.

I arched my lower back for Dal, undulating my hips to let

him know I'd heard. He gave my bared butt an appreciative pat. "Show-off. Spread your knees further apart. Show me your pussy."

That sounded interesting. And promising. I shifted so that my legs were spread wider. Knowing Dal could see every detail of my exposed sex made me grow warmer and added a wicked thrill to my erotic labor.

Eli's cock jerked in my mouth. I felt the telltale contraction in his balls, and then he was coming in a hot, liquid jet. I pulled back so that my lips enclosed him just below the head, sucking and swallowing while he rocked his hips in urgent rhythm. When he was finished, he jerked himself free and left me kneeling there in the grass, panting, my lips swollen, the taste of him in my mouth.

Then he looked over my head and addressed Dal as if I wasn't still at his feet, one hand cupping his balls and the other encircling his cock, engorged and erect despite the orgasm I'd just given him. "How's she doing?"

"Looked like she was doing really good from where I stood," Dal said. He ran a hand over my ass.

"Not the demon. Your witch."

"She's doing better than I expected. She's harnessing her power and gaining control rapidly. She's almost ready."

No wonder he was trying so hard to drive her away. When he no longer had the safe roles of teacher and student to hide behind, when he had to deal with her as an equal, what would happen? I had a feeling he was going to find out. I'd had a lot of time to observe human nature, and his student seemed like the type who'd fight for what she wanted.

I gave Eli a little squeeze and pumped my hand up and

down his shaft to remind him I was still down there. Then I licked him like a lollipop. Not that I expected him to be overwhelmed with lust right after he'd come down my throat, but the tactile memory might come back to haunt him later, and the size of his hard-on told me he hadn't lost interest.

I wondered what might have happened if Dal hadn't interrupted, hadn't provided a distraction with his witch trainee while I was servicing Eli's cock with my mouth. I hoped I'd have another chance to find out.

"Enough." Eli stepped back and fastened his pants. I grinned at the sight. He might've put it away, but there was still a very visible ridge straining against the fabric. If he kept getting erect around me, sooner or later that would have to lead to some lust. I could hope, anyway.

I found it very interesting that the two of them could exert such tight control that they were able to respond physically while they resisted my demonic pull. And I knew from my experience at Dal's hands that they could give off lust in small amounts without surrendering that control and without weakening to the point of falling under my power.

Of course, there was the risk that if I finally unleashed Eli's lust, it wouldn't just feed me. It would overrun me. I really wished Nick had settled that niggling little concern. What if the full lust of a Nephilim was more than a succubus could channel?

The more time I spent around the two of them, the more questions I had, and the one thing I was crystal-clear on was that my ignorance where they were concerned was about the size of the Grand Canyon.

"If you say so," I said with a regretful sigh. I gave Eli a

bold caress, despite the fact that he was once again clothed from the waist down. If I felt less than fully confident, I could at least fake it for his benefit.

Eli reached down to grasp my hand and pull me to my feet. "I say so."

"Well, I'll just have to be content until next time, then." I licked my lips as if savoring the taste of him and smiled.

His eyes darkened in reaction and I felt my stomach tighten. The breeze teased the curls that were all that covered my sex. The boxers tangled around my ankles, having slid all the way down as I stood up. For a moment I thought he might say something, might pull me closer, touch me. Then he turned away and headed toward the house and the moment was lost.

I bent over to pull up my boxers. Dal let out a low whistle behind me. "Babe, there's no man in the world who could watch you do that without wanting to nail you where you stand."

I grinned, even though he couldn't see my face. "I know." My confidence crept up a notch to match the sassy note of self-assurance in my voice.

"If you weren't saving yourself for Eli, I'd be tempted to give it to you right now," Dal said. He came closer behind me and ran his hands down my front, teasing me from breast to belly.

I arched into his hands and pressed the soft globes of my ass back against the hard bulge of his cock. "How do you know I'm saving myself for Eli?"

"I just do." He slid a hand down inside the boxers I was still holding up and searched out my core, testing me with his fingers and finding me soft and slick and ready. "Uh-huh. I can feel how hot and bothered you are. You got this way going down on him."

"I got this way going down on you, too," I said. I tilted my pelvis, sending the tip of his finger into me with the shift in position.

"Yeah. Because you knew he was enjoying watching you do it. And while you were sucking me off, he was stuffing your little muffin with his fingers."

Laughter bubbled up from my belly and spilled out my lips. "Stuffing my muffin?"

"You don't like the description?" Dal found my clit and stroked it, his finger gliding easily over the sensitive little bud of flesh now that it was coated with my own moisture. "But you did like it." His voice was knowing.

"Yes, I did." I admitted the truth freely. I'd loved filling my mouth with Dal while Eli filled me with his fingers. I'd gotten Dal's mouth between my legs afterward as a reward. And if I hadn't given Dal head at Eli's command, would he have fed me his cock this morning?

"I bet it wasn't easy for him to walk away just now."

"Ah, but he did walk away." I sighed and Dal laughed at my blatant disappointment.

"You'll get him next time." He gave my sex an encouraging squeeze before turning me loose. I finished tucking the boxer shorts back together so they'd stay up.

"I'm not sure whose side you're on." I turned to face him. "Is this brotherly loyalty? Egging on the seductress who's come to feed on his lust and steal his soul?"

Dal wiggled his brows at me. "I thought you just liked to come."

I blinked at the unexpected way he'd twisted my own words. But he did have a point. I'd already had two orgasms and I'd been hoping for a third while I was on my knees in front of Eli. Was I losing sight of my objective? I made myself give a careless shrug. "Maybe I do like to come. It's a new discovery. And not one I'm ever likely to get to repeat after this assignment."

"You're not in a hurry for it to be over, then, are you?"

I gave Dal a long look, but couldn't see anything underneath the light surface he wanted me to see. "No," I finally said. "I'm not in a hurry for it to be over."

And I wasn't.

The realization sobered me. I kept up my end of the conversation, responding to Dal's teasing, but in the back of my mind a nagging worry began to grow. It whispered that I didn't need to wonder whose side Dal was on.

He'd interrupted my oral assault on Eli, distracted us both, then stayed on in case he was needed as a spotter. He'd kept me busy while Eli walked away afterward. The timing struck me as far too convenient for coincidence. If I'd tried to follow Eli, would Dal have stopped me?

It was clear where Dalen's loyalties rested. With his brother, and with his mission to reintroduce magic and preserve the balance. He also found me useful for driving a wedge between himself and the object of his desire while giving himself a safe outlet for his sex drive. He wasn't my friend, and I needed to quit letting him lull me into thinking he was. There was nobody on my side but me.

I'd been alone long enough that I should have been used to it by now. The only people who'd ever cared about me had fallen to Norman swords, one after another, that bloody and horrible day. Then I'd grabbed a weapon and swung it in retaliation, only to find that I'd fallen, too. And I'd fallen further than my family, having damned myself with my final act, fallen all the way to the pit.

"I said, are you coming in?"

Dal's tone of voice told me that he'd repeated himself at least once. I shook off the past and told myself to focus on the present. "In a minute."

"You'll get cold." He indicated my bare legs and feet. "Come in and I'll make a fire for you. If you're good, I'll even make you hot cocoa. With marshmallows."

"I'm not good." There was a bitter tone to my voice and I smiled brightly to counteract it. "But since Eli is, you don't have to worry about me getting him alone and coming on to him."

"I thought you didn't mind me guarding you." Dal's smile disappeared and I actually felt churlish for spoiling his enjoyment of the easy camaraderie we'd fallen into.

"I just want a minute." I waved a hand toward a nearby grouping of trees. "I think I hear something. A bird, maybe."

I did hear something just out of range, something I couldn't quite identify although it seemed like I should know it. "I'll be right in."

"All right." Dal gave me a searching look, then went in. The door shut behind him. I didn't imagine that he trusted me, though. If I didn't follow him into the house within minutes I was willing to bet he'd be right on my tail, and if he couldn't tease and cajole me into letting him herd me around, he'd change tactics and strong-arm me.

It wouldn't take me long to satisfy my curiosity about that sound, so familiar and yet faint enough that full recognition eluded me. I walked toward the stand of trees. The sound grew stronger. When I could hear it clearly, I stopped dead and swore out loud. Then I looked for the source, running my foot through the grass until my toes bumped a small plastic unit.

Barry Manilow's disembodied voice wailed about memories in the moonlight from a tiny speaker.

I picked it up. Then I drop-kicked it, hard, and felt a deep sense of satisfaction when the plastic radio struck a tree trunk and splintered into pieces that were mercifully silent.

FOURTEEN

Destroying the radio didn't entirely relieve my bad mood, so I was glad to find the kitchen empty when I came in the back door. I needed something to do to work off the urge to snarl and snap and stomp. If I snarled at Eli, how would that help further my cause?

I rummaged under the kitchen sink and found a bucket, a bottle of cleaner, and rags. I dumped in a generous measure of the liquid detergent, filled the bucket with hot water, and got busy scouring. The countertops were first. Then the appliances, followed by the cabinet fronts. When I'd scrubbed the last one clean, I rinsed out the cloth and started on the floor. I'd almost finished when a masculine voice broke the near-silence.

"When I said you had kitchen duties, I didn't expect you to embrace the assignment so enthusiastically."

Great. I didn't have to turn my head to know Eli was lounging in the door frame, looking down at me. And what did I look like? A frizzy-haired, dirty, badly dressed wreck. Yeah, that would inspire some lust.

I felt a tear trickle down my cheek and brushed it away. Then I bore down harder, scouring the floor into submission.

"It looks . . . very clean." Eli actually seemed to be trying to think of something nice to say. I sniffled and tossed the rag into the bucket.

"Thank you."

"Would you turn around, please? I don't care to talk to the back of your head."

"Yeah, it's so inconvenient to have to wait for me to turn around if you want to order me to give you head again." Despite my complaint, I turned around anyway. He'd told me to, and he'd bound me, so he got what he wanted. One dirty-faced, tear-streaked, unsexy succubus with a surly-looking expression.

Eli regarded me in silence for a minute. "If I was that impatient for physical release, I wouldn't need you to turn around. I could simply come up behind you and use the most convenient orifice available."

I really hated that the idea of him doing that turned me on. I sighed and sat back so I didn't have to get a crick in my neck from looking up at him. "Did you want something?"

"Dal said you objected to him guarding you."

I shrugged. "He's just doing his job."

"And you're just doing yours."

"That's right." I stood up and carried the bucket of dirty water to the sink. I emptied it and watched the water swirl down the drain. "I'm just doing my job." So why did I still want to break something?

Because it wasn't just a job. Because I wasn't objective. Because everything about this situation was messing with my head. Being Eli's prisoner was turning me into a victim of Stockholm syndrome or something.

I put the emptied bucket away, wrung out the cloth to dry, and washed my hands thoroughly.

"Do you resent your job?"

"No." I rinsed and dried my hands. "I'm going to lure you into lusting for me, feed on you, and deliver your soul. Along the way I might get a few orgasms. What is there to resent?"

"Maybe you resent giving me satisfaction without receiving yours in turn." Eli walked up behind me and settled his hands on my shoulders. His fingers dug in and kneaded the tension-knotted muscles.

"Maybe I do." I realized that I'd been on edge ever since Eli pulled out of my mouth and walked away from me. Was I just suffering from my own unrelieved sexual frustration? "Although to be fair, it was your turn. You made me come by the beach. You didn't get yours then."

"Yes, but that was a contest I wanted to win." His hands smoothed their way over my collarbone, paused there to tease the sensitive hollows, then stroked the upper curves of my breasts. "You came. I didn't. I won."

"Hmm." I didn't agree or disagree. I held my breath, waiting for him to slide his hands down further, cup the aching mounds of my flesh, stroke my nipples.

"Today, you were watching me and I wanted your mouth around my cock. I took what I wanted. But I left you wanting, didn't I?" His voice was deep and dark and it made me tremble.

"Yes." Dammit.

His hands glided down, fingertips teasing the tight buds of my nipples that poked out against the thick fabric of the sweatshirt. He stroked down to my waist, gathered up folds of sweatshirt until he gripped the hem, lifted it up. Cool air rushed over my bare torso and made my nipples grow even harder in reaction.

I raised my arms to help as Eli pulled the sweatshirt up and over my head. He let it fall to the floor, then filled his hands with my naked breasts. The heat of his touch burned me like a brand and sent an answering heat curling through me. I could feel the hard ridge of his erection pressing into me. I rubbed back against it like a cat.

He toyed with me, squeezing and kneading my tits with his strong palms, circling my nipples, tugging at them until my sex reacted, growing swollen and liquid, inviting. His warrior braids tickled my bare shoulders, and I reveled in the sensual experience of being intimately touched by a man with long hair.

"What do you want now?" Eli asked me. He released my breasts and smoothed his hands down my sides until they cupped and gripped my hips.

"An automatic dishwasher," I said, fighting to keep my voice even.

He laughed and rocked his pelvis forward, grinding his cock into me. "I think you want something else."

"Well, you already have a microwave." I spoiled the flippant statement by gasping when he scored the sensitive area just inside my hipbones with his short nails, raking lightly across the thin cotton.

"These look familiar." Eli fisted his hands in the loose fabric of the boxers I wore.

"They're yours. I borrowed them. I didn't think you'd mind."

"I mind. I want them back." He'd pulled the fold that secured the oversized boxers free in the process of tugging at them, so it took very little effort for him to work them down my hips. He kept hold of the fabric and slid down my body as he drew the shorts down my legs, and I closed my eyes at the contact rush he gave me. His teeth raked the exposed curve of my ass as he settled the boxers around my ankles.

"Step out."

I obeyed, shifting my weight onto first one foot, then the other, while Eli freed his boxers. He stayed low and stroked his hands up the insides of my bare legs until he was touching the soft skin of my inner thighs, his fingertips just brushing against my sex.

It took an effort not to bend my knees and sink down, just a little, just enough to get a more intimate touch, a deeper caress. I let out a hissing breath of disappointment when he took his hands away without probing further.

"Turn around."

That would put me crotch to face with Eli. I turned obediently and waited to see what he'd do next. He looked pagan and fierce crouched on the floor in front of me, backing me up against the kitchen sink so that I was trapped between him and the lower cabinets.

"Spread your legs wider apart."

I moved my feet until they were shoulder width and turned the toes out to open myself a little more.

"Very good." Eli's voice was soft with approval and sensual promise. He reached up between my legs, inserted a fingertip into my slick folds, and drew it forward in a long, lingering stroke. He ended the motion by bringing the finger to his mouth and sucking it, tasting me on himself.

I wanted his tongue to replace his finger. I wanted him to lap at my folds, to work his tongue between them, to bury his face between my thighs and explore and taste and nibble and suckle. He knew it, too. The knowledge glimmered in his eyes. He drew his fingertip out of his mouth and stroked it over my clit. I moaned.

He leaned forward until his long hair tickled my bare legs and his breath warmed my labia. He let his finger trail from my clit and drew it the length of my sex in reverse motion, gathering moisture from my cleft that he used to coat the puckered opening of my anus, easing the entry of his finger as he slowly inserted it until he had it buried all the way inside me.

He held it still while I strove to relax the clenched muscles of my untried ass, but it was a tight fit. His tongue swirled around my clit, licked lower, lapped at my pussy until another moan broke from my lips and I opened my thighs wider, inadvertently seating myself harder onto his hand and deepening the penetration.

Eli rewarded me by sliding his tongue into me, a deep, slow thrust that he repeated until my legs started to shake. Then he licked the length of my sex, tongued my clit again, and closed his mouth over that sensitive flesh and sucked while he slowly began to move the finger he'd wedged into my ass.

My hips moved in helpless reaction, arching into the sweet pressure of his mouth on my clit, inadvertently giving him a better angle to continue his sensual invasion of my anus.

The skin felt incredibly sensitive, gripping his finger as it slid in and out, and the unfamiliar pressure became a raw kind of pleasure.

He released my clit and licked at my slit, tasting me, teasing me with his tongue. "I think you like that," he murmured as he sent his finger in a deeper, harder thrust.

"It's . . . interesting," I managed.

"Merely interesting?" Eli licked at me again, and again, drawing his tongue along my folds until I wanted to scream for release.

"Enjoyable," I gasped out.

"I think you'll learn to enjoy it more," Eli said. He suckled my clit until I whimpered. He continued to work his thick finger in and out of my ass while he varied his oral assault on my sex, licking, lapping, suckling, thrusting his tongue deeply into me, then retreating to lick lightly along my slick, swollen folds.

"It's growing on me," I said as I felt a spiraling coil of need building low in my body.

"I want you to come like this," Eli informed me. "I want you to give in to me and come for me while I lick your soft little pussy and make your tight ass burn for more."

I might have whimpered. I definitely ground my pussy into his face and reamed his finger harder into my anus as the coil drew tighter and my hips bucked wildly.

Eli claimed me with his mouth and penetrated me with his index finger and I knew without being told that he intended me to take his cock in that tight entry.

He fucked me with his tongue and drew little mewling sounds of need from me until I was nearly sobbing for release. Then he simultaneously thrust a second finger into my ass and closed his mouth over my clit, sucking hard. The twin demands of his fingers and his mouth sent me shooting over the edge, coming hard in waves of rapid succession, until gradually the intensity diminished and I was only trembling and shuddering while he raked my clit lightly with his teeth and scissored his fingers deep inside my anal passage.

Eli was slow to release me, kissing and licking at my sex as if savoring the taste of me while he worked his fingers free of my ass. He gave me a last deep thrust of his tongue that made my world a very happy place, then stood up to tower over me, his body so close to mine I could feel the heat of him but not quite touching.

"Now we're even."

I gulped and nodded. "Oh. Yeah. Thanks."

He leaned his body into mine as he reached around me to soap and rinse his hands. He took his time about it, and I took the opportunity to bury my nose in his chest and inhale that musky, masculine, woodsy smell that was uniquely his.

My body hummed with the pleasurable buzz of afterglow, my sex throbbed and tingled from the attentions of his mouth and tongue, and my ass reported a slight ache from muscles unused to activity. Eli's hard-on pressing into me made me wonder dizzily if there was more ahead. I wanted more. His heat drew me like a magnet.

"It doesn't seem very fair to you, though," I finally said, sliding my body along his.

"All's fair in love and war." Eli turned off the water and

dried his hands on my breasts. The unexpected liquid shock made my nipples harden almost painfully.

"Oh. Well, then, here's to war." I reached for his cock and caressed the hard ridge that jutted against his pants. "Want to engage the enemy some more?"

"No." He lowered his head and kissed the curve of my neck, moved lower to close his mouth over one tight nipple and suck for one eye-rolling, blissful moment before he let it slide free of his lips. "I want to fuck."

"Ah."

He claimed my other nipple, enclosed it in the moist heat of his mouth and gave a hard suck that made my womb clench.

"Is this a party for two, or three?" I asked.

"That's what I was wondering."

Dal's voice made my head turn toward the source of the sound. He filled the doorway, watching us with an expression I couldn't read. I wondered how long he'd been there. Long enough, apparently. I wasn't too surprised that I hadn't heard him come in. I'd been so enthralled by what Eli was doing to me that I might have missed a parade with elephants passing through the kitchen.

Eli turned his face toward his brother. He spoke to Dal while he palmed my sex in a caress that made my muscles quiver deep inside. "There's plenty of her to go around."

That sounded fun. Oh, wait. It had been really fun last night, too. Right up until the point where I got sick.

"Is that a good idea?" I rocked my pelvis into Eli's hand, trying to encourage him to spear a finger into my aching flesh.

"You want me to slide my cock into you for the first time without him here?" Eli asked me, his eyes glittering with that hot edge of warning. "You want to trust that I can take your virgin flesh and retain my control? If I lose it, you'll suffer more than overheating."

He drove a finger into my sex while he spoke, hard, demanding, without warning, and I made a small sound of protest.

"Would you rather get a little too warm? Or have your sweet little pussy ravaged and savaged, your untried backside reamed without mercy, your body used up and spent while I go on fucking every hole you have because he isn't here to stop me?"

I blew out a shaky breath. "When you put it like that."

But one very disquieting thought crossed my mind. What would I do if both of them went lust-crazed on me? Would I be able to feed on them simultaneously, draining them until they were under my control? Or was I going to find myself a victim of lust—after spending centuries perfecting the art of inciting it?

Dal sniffed and gave us both an odd look. "Why does it smell like a chemical forest of pine trees in here?"

For a minute, I just stared, speechless. I'd been so caught up in the moment with Eli that I'd forgotten what I was doing when he found me in the kitchen. I started to laugh, thinking how wrong that was. When staging a seduction, the overpowering, acrid scent of pine cleaner was not the standard key to unlocking a man's libido. Unless you happened to be seducing a man with a bizarre evergreen fetish.

"I was cleaning," I admitted to Dal. "I know the smell's awful."

"You were cleaning?"

This was clearly not the answer he expected. "Yes."

His lips twitched. "I'm seeing the logic, here. Behavioral reinforcement. If scrubbing the kitchen got you some satisfaction, next you'll be motivated to make a clean sweep of the whole house. We get better housekeeping than we've ever had, and you get multiple o's."

Put that way, I could really learn to like the harsh smell of chemical pine.

I looked up at Eli, wondering why he'd approached me when I looked awful, smelled worse, and was spoiling for a fight. Dirty, disheveled, and cranky is not what most men want to get themselves a little piece of.

"The smell really is awful," I said.

"Is it? I didn't notice." He worked a second finger into my sheath and I sucked in a breath.

"So then, no point in wasting any sexy aromatherapy candles on you," I managed as he began to stroke his fingers in and out of my sex.

"Guess not." He lowered his head and drew one of my nipples into his mouth while he worked me with his hand. Preparing me, I realized. Readying me for entry, the way he'd begun readying my anal passage while he went down on me.

The implication was not lost on me. I really was going to be the filling in a Nephilim sandwich. Or rather, they were going to fill me.

FIFTEEN

While I pondered the logistics and considered potential sites for staging a full-on threesome, Dal crossed the room and claimed my other breast with his mouth.

My eyes practically crossed. Two sexy men, each ministering to my tight, aching nipples with their warm and talented mouths. Two men who were capable of feeding me more raw lust than any human. Both of whom could sustain me without weakening. My knees sagged and Dal curled an arm around me to add his support to Eli's.

Eli's hand between my legs grew more insistent, more persuasive, opening me, deepening the penetration he was giving me. While they licked and sucked my breasts, Dal began to toy with my navel ring. All the stimulation added to the effect of those invading fingers.

Eli released my nipple and kissed his way up my neck. "I want you to take both of us."

"I kind of thought that was the idea," I said in an unsteady voice.

"At the same time."

"Got that."

"We'll make sure you're ready." His hand between my legs gentled, coaxed, teased my sex and caressed my clit.

"Um. Okay." I squirmed against his fingers. Dal began to use his free hand to tug at my other nipple, now that it wasn't in Eli's mouth. I felt almost giddy with sensual greed. Two mouths, two pairs of hands, two hard cocks . . . "I'm not sure how long I can stand up," I admitted.

"Then we'll lay you down."

Well. At least I knew for sure the floor was sanitary. But when they lowered me, my back touched something soft. I blinked and turned my head, saw that we weren't in the kitchen anymore. We'd transitioned. I recognized Eli's bedroom. The soft surface under me was the bed.

"Nice," I said, relaxing into it. "You're going to deflower me on a mattress instead of a hard, cold floor."

"I want to bounce your ass on the bedsprings," Eli grated against my ear. "Besides, the floor's too hard on my knees."

I giggled. Then Dal licked down my belly and the sound turned to a gasp, then a sigh. His tongue replaced Eli's hand, licking into my folds, coaxing more lubrication to flow in response. Eli curved around my side, a possessive hand splayed over my belly.

"Spread your legs wider for him," he said. "You need to be soft and wet."

"I think I already am," I said through lips that felt two sizes too thick. But I obediently spread my thighs further apart. I'd already been slick and glistening with moisture when Eli laved me with his tongue. He'd made me come with his mouth, then he'd worked me with his fingers, and now Dal was lapping at my sex. I was wetter than I'd ever been and I could feel my own juices mixed with Dal's saliva trickling down to lubricate my anus.

That was probably the plan, I realized. Dal suckled my clit. Eli stroked me from belly to breast. I squirmed and shuddered and tried not to grind my pussy into Dal's face. He released me and raised his head. "Like that, Babe?"

Oh, yeah. I licked my lips and nodded.

Dal took my other side and both of them began to explore me with their hands. Stroking my breasts. Teasing my nipples. Flicking my navel ring. Smoothing the planes of my stomach, the rounded curves of my hips, the soft skin of my thighs. Covering my sex with their palms in turn, driving their fingers into me so that I was penetrated by first one man, then the other.

"You guys are wearing too many clothes," I finally said.

"You're right." Dal gave my pussy a slow, thorough petting. When he took his hand away, I sighed in regret. But not for long, because Eli planted his palm between my legs and cupped my sex, squeezed, and then stroked my clit with a finger. I arched up to get more pressure while Dal moved beside me and made rustling sounds that told me he was stripping. Then I felt his body return to my side, all hot, hard male flesh. His cock prodded my hip.

"My turn to keep her warm," Dal said.

Eli's hand withdrew. He got naked while Dal took over petting and stroking my sex, teasing me. And then Eli was hard against my side, too, both of them framing me with their heat. I felt nearly delirious from their proximity alone.

I turned my face to Eli's. "I want you in my mouth," I told him. He raised a brow at that, but nodded to Dal, who moved over so Eli could kneel over my chest.

Eli held his cock by the base and guided it to my lips, teased my mouth with his head. "You want to taste this?"

"Yes." I kissed the head of his cock and licked at him, inviting him to give me more, to feed the head into my waiting mouth.

I felt the bed shift as Dal moved around and settled himself between my open thighs again. His tongue invaded me while Eli thrust his engorged penis forward, fucking my mouth. I sucked greedily at his flesh, licking and kissing, urging him on while my hips began to rock, pressing my sex into Dal's mouth.

The two of them were making me crazed, dizzy with heat. My mouth on Eli's flesh was urgent. Dal's tongue thrusting into my folds grew more demanding.

Acting on some unheard signal, Eli pulled himself out of my lips, breaking the suction with a wet pop. Dal gave me a last lingering lick, and then Eli lay down beside me. Dal lifted me to lie on top of Eli. They pulled my thighs apart, settled my knees on the bed on either side of Eli's hips. My nipples grazed Eli's chest and the heat of him made them ache with need.

Dal moved around behind me and slid two fingers into my well-lubricated pussy, withdrew them, and then smoothed the liquid over my puckered anus, adding to the juices already spilled there.

Eli used his hand to guide his cock to my sex, position the head, and press forward until my softened, slick flesh began to give way. He worked the head of himself into me while Dal worked a finger into my ass. I felt stretched, pulled tight, and for a minute I wondered if I could accommodate what they wanted. My womb contracted and my inner muscles clutched at Eli's invading flesh. He groaned and thrust deeper.

"So fucking tight."

I tried to relax, to open myself to him, but my sex clenched reflexively against the unfamiliar invasion. Eli let out an animal growl and thrust hard, forcing me to take more and more of his cock until he'd seated himself fully in me. I let out a muffled shriek at the suddenness of it, my body stretching to adjust to the thickness of him, the length of him, the head of his penis pressing into the entry of my womb.

"So fucking big," I mimicked back, my breathing harsh and uneven.

"But it feels good, doesn't it?"

Oh, yeah. Since the answer was plain on my face, I didn't bother saying it.

Dal kissed my back and worked a second finger into me.

His hand and Eli's cock had me stuffed so full, stretched so tight, I found it impossible to believe I could take Dal's cock in my ass at the same time. It also felt impossibly good to be so thoroughly and doubly penetrated, to have Eli buried in my pussy and Dal's fingers buried in my anal passage. If I could manage to take him, his cock would feel even better there. . . .

Eli began a slow rhythm, withdrawing, rocking back into me, coaxing my body to adapt to his invasion, sheathing himself in my sex. Behind me, Dal matched his pace to Eli's, rhythmically plundering my ass with his fingers. His other hand wrapped around his own cock, held it against the soft flesh of my butt as he began to pleasure himself.

An almost unbearable tension began to build. Eli fucking his way in and out of my body as my sex slowly yielded to his and accepted his relentless penetration. Dal, plunging his fingers in and out of my anus, stroking himself off while the head of his cock rubbed my ass as if trying to get my attention.

Dal's rhythm grew more rapid, more insistent. I felt his cock bob and jerk, felt his fingers pull out of me, felt the rounded head of his penis positioned against the sensitive skin of my anus. Then he was coming in a thick, liquid jet, working himself with his hand while he coated my rear entry with his cream. I groaned at the sensation of having my sensitized anus bathed with the heated fluid of his orgasm.

Dal continued to masturbate behind me. I felt his head beginning to press into my ass, the opening slick from his come and softened from his fingers. He thrust forward as he continued to ejaculate, the head of him just barely entering me from behind, spurting into my anal passage.

I gasped and felt my sex clench around Eli's shaft, felt his cock throb, and then I felt his first jet of liquid deep inside me. The sensation of dual penetration, of two men coming in me, one in my ass, one in my pussy, made me wild. I ground my hips into Eli, driving his cock deeper into me. Dal thrust deeper, too, giving me another inch of his length, and I came screaming while they both fucked me full of their come.

I felt Dal withdraw first. He patted the rounded curve of my butt as he slid the head of his penis out of my tight anus. Eli lifted me up and off. I made a low sound of protest as his still-hard cock pulled free of my body. They settled me between them. I closed my eyes and enjoyed the sensations of their hands on me, soothing my well-used flesh.

"You seem to have survived that," Eli said. His hand settled between my thighs and paid homage to my sex, petting and stroking, caressing my clit.

"Um," I agreed.

"I want to take you like this. Lying on your back, legs open for me."

"Okay." That left Dal out, but I could always give him a hand. Or something.

Eli settled his body over mine. His cock probed between my legs, then thrust into my sex in a slow, steady motion until he had his shaft buried inside me all the way to his balls. I felt my flesh stretching to take him, still almost virgin-tight as he worked his cock into me as deep as it could go.

"Did you like it when I came in you?" He asked the question as he began to ride me.

"Yes." There really weren't any words to describe the liquid pleasure of being bathed internally by heated jets of come. The two of them coming inside me, joint spurts of pleasure in each passage, both of my openings stretched to full capacity by thick cocks, that was a sensation I wouldn't forget in a thousand years.

"You'll like it when I come in you again," Eli promised, deepening his thrust. "I'll cream inside you until you're so soft, so slick, so ready, I could fuck you all night."

I made a hum of agreement, drunk on pleasure and his nearness, the incredible sensation of having his body on mine, his cock plundering my sex, my ass still burning from Dal's partial entry and liquid from his come.

"Is it getting too much for her?" Dal asked. He lay beside us, watching me while Eli thrust into me again and again.

"I'm fine," I said. I twined my legs around Eli's and urged him on. I thought I was starting to get the hang of this, how to arch up into his thrusts, how to open myself so that he drove deeper, how to get more pressure against a sensitive spot deep inside where every stroke made me writhe with ecstasy.

"You're more than fine," Eli said with a guttural groan. "You're hot and slick and as tight as a fist. Making you take all of me is like fucking a glove."

"That's how it feels to come in her ass," Dal said, stroking my hair. "A hot, tight, velvet glove, squeezing my cock until I come harder."

"I'll find out," Eli promised. "When I'm finished fucking her pussy full of my come, I'll turn her over and fuck her tight little asshole."

I tightened around him, shuddered under him, and Eli

gave a soft, knowing laugh. "You like that idea, don't you? You want me to cream deep inside your ass while your pussy's still throbbing from being ridden so hard."

"What's not to like?" My voice slurred. I gripped him tighter and rocked my hips into his in an urgent motion. Eli fucked me harder, deeper, faster, while my heartbeat stumbled, then galloped. My sex clenched around his cock. His driving rhythm balanced right on the thin edge of pleasure and pain, my body unused to the demands of sex, his size and width almost more than I could handle, his erotic promises sending my imagination soaring.

My body abruptly followed my mind, tightening and twisting, jerking in release as I came. Eli sped up for a few frenzied thrusts, then slowed as he reached the peak, too.

He held me down and rode his cock in and out of my plundered sex with deliberate, measured strokes, luxuriating in drawing out his orgasm, pumping his balls empty while he pumped me full of his come. I lay spent and yielding under him, my legs splayed wide, surrendering to his use of my body.

I could feel Dal running his fingers through my hair, sharing the moment. It seemed unfair that he'd given me so much foreplay and received so little in return. The partial penetration he'd gotten as he prepared my anal passage until he could work just a little of his shaft in struck me as inadequate. He'd had to stroke himself to orgasm before he could push his cock in even that far.

I tried to turn my face to look at him, to promise I'd take care of him next, but the effort was beyond me. I couldn't seem to focus on Eli above me, either. Darkness ringed my vision, moved in, filled it. And suddenly everything went away.

The world came back in pieces. Eli's face over mine, his eyes the color of a storm at sea. Cold. A winter sky wheeling overhead, gray with clouds, dim despite the distant sun. Masculine voices, too low for me to hear. Or maybe the words escaped me because they spoke a language I didn't know.

The next time I opened my eyes, I saw nothing but white. I blinked until my vision adjusted and raised my head to verify that I was, in fact, lying face-down in snow.

Hands pressed down on my buttocks and the distinctive feel of skin on skin told me I was, in fact, still naked. "Stay down. Rest."

Dal's voice. I closed my eyes and counted to ten, dead certain that it was just the two of us. Once again, Eli had gotten his rocks off with me and left.

Of course, the two of them together had probably put me in this state, so it made sense that one had to go. But knowing it was Eli was . . . disappointing.

He was my target. Of course I wanted to be in his company. How could I seduce him if I wasn't with him? I was also bound to him, which probably made me feel a pull, an inner compulsion to seek him out and stay near. To add to these factors, the sex had been unbelievable. For the first time, I'd had the full-on real deal, actual penetration, a hot, hard, male cock thrusting into my sex, ending in mutual orgasms and exchange of bodily fluids.

He'd even fucked me a second time, come in me again. He'd taken me so thoroughly I could almost feel the imprint of him still, a ghost sensation or lingering muscle memory of being stretched and filled to capacity and beyond. As if he'd hollowed out a space for himself in my body and left an emptiness behind that hadn't existed before.

I subsided into my wintry blanket and told myself I was just tired. Rest, recover, regroup, there was a sound plan. And how long had it been since I'd fed properly? No wonder I felt weak. No wonder I'd succumbed to the joint effect of two Nephilim in close proximity.

"Are you awake?" Dal rubbed my back as he asked the question. I heard the snow crunch as he shifted beside me.

"Yes."

"Do you know who I am?"

I sighed and turned my face toward Dal. I opened one eye, squinting at him. "I don't have amnesia. I'm also not so forgetful that I can't remember whose cock was first to fuck me in the ass."

He ran a hand down my spine to tease the dimple at the base, just barely touching the curve of my buttocks. "Liked that, did you?"

I wiggled my butt to encourage further exploration. I'd liked it, yes. And so had he. And he'd demonstrated a tendency to slip into lustful thoughts, however briefly. I needed an infusion of lust, and if it came with an infusion of Dal's splendid male equipment, all the better. "I liked it, but . . ." My voice trailed away suggestively.

"But what?" Dal caressed the crease that separated the globes of my rounded cheeks.

"But it was only a taste." I gave him a seductive smile. "I was so tight, you didn't get a chance to work yourself all the way in. I think we both deserve a second chance, there."

He grinned at me, flashing his dimples. "I jack off on your backside and cram my cock far enough up your virgin ass to finish coming in you while you were busy getting fucked for the first time from the front, and you complain that it was just a taste?"

"Yes." I rolled to my side, facing him. His eyes dipped to my tits. They stayed there for a flattering length of time and darkened with male appreciation. I took that as an encouraging sign. The contact with the cold snow had my skin glowing, my nipples drawn into hard little buds. "I wasn't able to take all of you. And Eli's a little bigger. He wants rear penetration. I want you to break me in for him."

Sixteen

Break you in, huh?" Dal scooped me into his arms and gathered me close. My nipples poked into his chest and the hard ridge of his erection pressed against my belly. Until that moment I hadn't realized he was still naked, too.

"Yes." I nuzzled his throat. "Ride my ass. Make me take every inch of your porn-star dick. Show me how to accommodate rear entry. You're a teacher. Teach me to take an anal fucking."

Laughter rumbled in his chest. "Such a mouth you've got on you."

"You liked it when it was on *you*," I pointed out, reminding him of the blow job he'd had from me.

"True. You sucked me so good." He slid a hand down to cup my butt, squeezed. "I owe you for that."

"No, you don't." I hooked my upper thigh over his, making my lower body easily accessible to him. "You went down on me. Twice. I owe you, and I want you to take it out of my hide."

"Out of your delectable backside." He moved his hand lower, until his fingertips brushed the thin, sensitive skin of my anus. He stroked, circled the tight opening, then probed lightly with the pad of his finger. His sensual teasing made me shiver in reaction.

"That's the idea." I shifted so that his shaft nudged me between my legs. I was still wet and slick enough to give him a good coating of lubrication.

Dal rocked his hips forward, not needing further invitation to stroke himself along my slit. I closed my eyes at the pleasurable contact of his sex to mine, arched my pelvis, moved with him as we rocked together. He stroked and caressed my anus with his fingertip while our parts glided against each other, his head furrowing into my labia but not penetrating.

The almost-but-not-quite joining of our bodies made mine draw low and tight as tension built. I almost sighed with relief when he slowly thrust his finger into my ass, entering me with some part of himself. One finger became two, scissoring and thrusting in and out, all the while caressing my sex-softened pussy with his turgid length until I burned for more. He must have felt the same, because he altered the angle of his next stroke and the head of his cock pushed inside me. We both groaned.

"Nice," Dal said finally.

I felt his cock twitch as if eager for more and laughed. "He thinks so, too," I said, my voice husky with sex.

"It'll be easier the more turned on you are," Dal informed me. He pressed forward, giving me another inch. The angle meant he couldn't give me more than partial, shallow penetration, but he was wide enough to make up for it.

"It's going to be really easy then," I whispered, squeezing his dick with my inner muscles while he continued to work my anal opening with his fingers.

He began to fuck me in hard, shallow thrusts. My sex stretched to take his cock, my sheath clenching around him until he let out a low groan. "If I don't get inside your tight asshole right now, I'm going to push you on your back and pound my cock all the way into your sweet pussy, over and over, until you get so hot the snow melts."

And that would be a bad thing, why? I shuddered and arched to take him just a little deeper. He thrust harder, almost entering me fully, then pulled out of my sex and my anus simultaneously, leaving me abruptly and achingly empty. "Get on your knees, legs apart, tits down, ass in the air."

Right. I struggled to follow his instructions with my limbs trembling and my breath coming in sharp pants. He knelt behind me and positioned himself, gripped my hips, and pulled me back as he thrust forward.

He'd done a good job of stretching me with his fingers, and the partial penetration he'd given me earlier helped. His penis had a slick coating of my body's natural lubrication to ease his entry. It still burned as he pushed his way in, first the rounded head, then inch by deliciously agonizing inch, he worked his shaft into me until I'd taken it all.

He reached one hand around in front of me and searched out my clit to give me more stimulation. "Relax. You're doing fine."

I let out a soft laugh. "I feel like I can't take it all, like it's too much." The sensation of being overfilled, stuffed beyond capacity rode that fine edge between *stop* and *don't stop*. I wasn't sure how I could handle it when he began to thrust.

"That's what you get for asking a giant to break you in for anal sex." There was a teasing note in his voice, but I noticed he didn't offer to pull out.

Dal stroked my clit, coaxing me to respond, arousing me all over again. When my hips began to move of their own volition, he began to ride me from behind in slow, easy strokes, fucking my ass with gentle but insistent pressure.

I gave into it, surrendering to the hard cock tunneling into my anal passage, to the rhythm of Dal's fingers on my clit. I felt the beginning contraction that I was quickly learning spelled orgasm and gave a low moan.

Dal began to rock faster, giving it to me harder. The primal position encouraged him to feel lust and he did, obliging me with a wave of it that pushed me over the brink of orgasm and swept me away in spasms of pleasure that continued to ripple through me as he began to spurt deep inside me.

I came, grinding my pussy against Dal's hand while he pumped himself into my ass, fucking me deep and hard and thoroughly, lustily, giving me every inch of himself while he poured every ounce of ejaculate into me until he shuddered in a final spending, bathing my newly penetrated passage with his come.

He continued to thrust for a few furious strokes. "Feel

how easy it is now," he whispered, bending low over my back, covering me with his heat like a blanket. "Your ass is so hot and slick now that I've come in you. Your opening is stretched from taking my cock deep. You're nice and relaxed from coming while I worked you with my hand."

Dal shifted his rhythm, making his thrusts short and hard as he continued to ream me. "That feels so good, doesn't it?"

"Yes." I felt so much better. He'd given me just enough lust to sustain me before he regained control, and he'd satisfied my body thoroughly in the process. Experiencing the hot delight of his cock thrusting into the tight grip of my anus made me confident that I could take Eli this way and it would be a pleasure for both of us.

I pushed my hips back into Dal's strokes, accepting the full length and width of his sizable penis, driving him deeper. He continued to screw me in the ass as we moved together in companionable silence and watched the sky darken. I'd asked him to break me in, and he did the job with a thoroughness I found admirable.

When he finally withdrew, I made a soft sound of protest.

"No more for you just now." He slapped my bare buttocks with his open hand. The contact stung just a little, in the very nicest way. "You've had a very busy day. Eli stuffed your little pussy full of his big cock for the first time, and I gave it to you in the rear. You've been very well fucked both ways, and if you ever want to walk right again, you'll take a little rest before you spread your legs for more."

"You sound very confident that I'll spread my legs for more of you," I said, smiling even though he couldn't see my expression.

He had good reason to be confident. I wasn't cold, despite our location. Dal had kept me nicely warm. I was almost glowing, in fact. For that alone I'd be accommodating. I was also feeling inclined to be generous with him since he'd fed me a much-needed appetizer of lust. And he'd done such a lovely job of teaching me to take full anal penetration. Bending and spreading for him wasn't exactly a hardship.

"You'd take more right now." He spanked me again and I gave a happy sigh.

"Oooh. Stop that if you aren't trying to give me foreplay."

"Wicked wench."

"Bad boy. Paddle me until I cream myself."

He let out a short laugh and gave me another sharp spank. "There. Content yourself with that."

I gave a longing sigh of mock-regret. "I suppose I'll have to."

He pushed me down into the snow and then rolled me over onto my back, grinning at me. "No wonder you overheat. You're so hot to begin with."

My nipples were taut and erect, and dusted with snow that melted and ran down my breasts in tiny rivulets. Dal watched and then bent his head to lick the cold moisture away. I squirmed and wiggled to avoid his tongue, and he retaliated by pinning me down and suckling my breasts, raking my nipples with his teeth.

I giggled and sighed and surrendered, enjoying the oral attention he lavished on my breasts. He forced a knee between my legs and shoved it up until it rode against my crotch. I wiggled my hips to encourage this move. The pressure on my sex provided a measure of soothing relief.

I glanced down at his still-erect penis. "Are you sure you're finished?"

"No, but I was trying to be polite. I've had a lengthy celibacy." Dal spoke as he switched his attention from one nipple to the other, sucking until I moaned and squirmed against his knee.

"All that pent-up desire," I murmured. "Seems a shame to leave you in need when you have a chance to work some of your sexual frustration off."

"Didn't I say you'd spread your legs for more?" He raised his head and gave me an I-told-you-so look.

"Technically, *you* spread my legs," I said. "I had them closed until you pushed your way between my thighs."

"That's because you're naked and you smell like sex and I only know what it's like to come in two out of your three holes." Dal bent and licked the valley between my breasts as he spoke. "I know what it's like to come in your sweet mouth while you swallow me down. I know how it feels to come deep inside your hot, tight ass. I can't help wondering how it would feel to plow your soft little pussy until I pumped my balls dry inside you."

"You did get a taste of that," I pointed out. We'd been limited by our position, but he'd definitely gotten inside.

"I did. You wrapped around my dick so nicely, too, all snug and slick and willing to take me deeper."

I took stock of myself. I felt well-used and a little achy from servicing two large cocks. I was also still highly stimulated, a condition Dal wasn't exactly easing by drawing my nipples into his mouth, making my sex clench as he pulled on them, pressing into my soft, sensitized flesh with his knee.

"You were just in my ass," I pointed out.

"And I screwed it just the way you wanted me to." He used his hands to push my thighs wider apart so he could kneel fully between my open legs. "Now let me screw your pretty, pink pussy the way we both want."

"Pretty, hmm?" I fluttered my lashes at him, grinning at his very effective mix of sexual aggression and temptation.

"If you're worried, I cleaned up. Magic." He wrapped one hand around the base of his shaft and displayed himself to me. "You can taste for yourself."

"I thought you wanted to screw me, not get some oral." I bent my head forward, though, and he brought himself up to my lips. I licked him and found him clean and tangy with a flavor of salt.

"Well, yeah, but I don't want to pass up a chance to put my cock in your mouth."

He was so blatant, I laughed. Then I took his head into my mouth and sucked hard. Payback for the way he'd fastened his lips on my aching nipples and made me needy for more.

"You suck so good." His rough praise made me swirl my tongue around his shaft and open my throat to take him deeper. He thrust forward, then pulled back, sliding his cock from my mouth. "No more. I want you under me, with your legs spread so wide they ache, and then I want you to take every last inch of my dick."

He used his hands to spread my labia open and guide himself into position. I felt the head of him probing at my slick, swollen entry, all hard, demanding male flesh.

"Such a pretty pussy," Dal said, drawing himself down for a better angle. "Pink and puffed, all wet and willing.

Warmed up and newly broken in. Ready to take my dick for a rough ride."

I bucked my hips and squirmed against him, trying to take him inside myself and end his teasing. "Dal. More."

"Fuck, yeah." He drove into me, so deep and fast I gasped. The restraint he'd shown working himself into my anus was gone. He took me hard, and by the time he finally let himself come in a hot rush with his cock buried all the way inside until it pressed against the entrance of my womb, I was spent. He'd made me come at least twice more while he screwed me with an intensity that bordered on savagery. And all the while, he'd kept a leash on his lust.

If he ever slipped the leash, I had fair warning of what would be in store for me.

He rocked deeper into the cradle of my pelvis as he slowly pumped me full of come, grinding into me, groaning his release and gratification. Then he came to rest on me, still planted in me, and kissed me, sweet and lingering. We'd had sex every possible way, and now he kissed me.

I kissed him back, learning the taste of his mouth and the texture of his tongue as it dipped inside and twined with mine. When he lifted his lips from mine, he rubbed the tips of our noses together. "Anytime you want me to break you in or warm you up, just say the word."

"I think I'm all broken in now," I managed to say, my voice throaty from sexual excess.

"Then next time I want to ram my cock up your ass, I won't have to be so careful."

I gulped audibly and he laughed, all male confidence and smug satisfaction.

"I'll be sweet to you," Dal promised, nuzzling my neck. "I'll make sure you're hot and ready. I'll open you with my fingers and I'll work lubrication into your tight little hole. I might even spank you a few times to get you going. Then, when I've got you quivering and aching for a good, hard ass-fucking, I'll give it to you. And you'll like it."

I squeezed his penis with my vaginal muscles. "I liked this, too."

"Good. I don't expect to get many chances to nail you, so I'll take them when I get them."

"Living dangerously." I nipped at his lip, not too hard, but giving him the edge of my teeth.

"I prefer to think of it as exam preparation." He ground himself into my sex, demonstrating his study tool. "I don't have a warrior's training in control. Magic is a creative realm, more a matter of art than strict discipline. If I'm too sexually frustrated, I think my chances of slipping into lust are greater. And when it comes to my test, I don't intend to fail."

I hadn't thought about the opposite requirements of their fields of expertise, but it did explain why Eli kept himself so closed and controlled, and why Dal was so open, his lust closer to the surface and more easily stirred.

I didn't want Dal to fail, either. My thinking might have been clouded by the orgasms he'd given me, but it seemed to me that we had a mutual interest in giving him a safe outlet for his lusty drive. If he leaked a bit of lust, I got to feed the way I was designed to.

And the more he enjoyed the pleasures of my flesh, the less likely he was to blow the lid off from sheer pent-up frustration. That scenario held entirely too much risk for my comfort. I was in favor of avoiding anything that might possibly prove fatal to me.

Yep, making myself sexually available to Dal was a smart plan, and one that would benefit us both. It didn't hurt that he had fantastic equipment he knew how to use, either.

As for Eli, well, Eli had made it clear that I was to be shared between them, and I still had hopes that by complying with all of Eli's sexual wishes I'd find the key to his lust. He'd found the sight of me going down on Dal arousing, and he'd obviously enjoyed having Dal watch us while I went down on him. He'd also really liked sandwiching me between them, both of them penetrating me at the same time.

Maybe there was an element of sexual competition that he enjoyed, or maybe it was the control factor of being the owner of my body and knowing I'd do anything he commanded, with anybody he ordered me to. That could be a problem if he wanted me to perform with somebody heinous, but Dal was hung and hot, so there really wasn't a downside for me in playing Eli's sex games.

"I don't mind helping you cram for your exam." I bumped my hips into Dal's in friendly encouragement.

"Excellent. I like cramming you full of cock."

And even though the snow was beginning to feel unpleasantly cold on my ass and my inner muscles felt spent from clamping around first Eli's shaft and then Dal's, he continued to cram me full of himself, rocking into me until we came together one more time.

SEVENTEEN

How many times did he fuck you?" Eli stood over me, his face stern and hard, his arms folded across his chest. In the kitchen, his height had merely made him loom. In this tiny closet of a bathroom, his presence seemed to overflow the available space and occupy all the air.

"I kind of lost count. Although really it wasn't so much the number of times as the duration." I gave him a cheerful grin and lowered myself deeper into the tub. The heat soothed me everywhere. There was a downside to vigorous sex: it left you achy in all sorts of inconvenient places. "You should thank him. I asked him to break me in for you, so you'd have an easier time getting me to take your big, thick cock in my ass."

"Thank him?" His face turned thunderous. "I left him to watch over you."

"Did I do something you didn't want?" The unexpected possibility made a cold knot form in my stomach and wiped the smile from my face. "The binding didn't prevent it. I thought you gave permission. I thought you wanted me to have sex with both of you."

I suddenly felt very small and very naked. Vulnerable. Tears clogged the back of my throat and stung my eyes at the thought of incurring Eli's displeasure, however unwittingly. That was undoubtedly the doing of the damned binding between us. It made him my master and rendered me incapable of disobedience.

Eli shook his head, sending his warrior braids into motion. The slide of his hair against his heavily muscled, bare chest and shoulders entranced me. "I invited him into bed with us. I ordered you to service him with your mouth while I watched. I had him ream you from behind while I took your virginity."

"So, then, it was okay to let him fuck me?" I asked the question in a tiny voice.

"Fuck him any way you want to, with my blessing. But not without regard for the risks, and not to such excess that you can no longer walk." His raised voice reverberated in the small room, making me wince.

He'd been pissed from the minute Dal materialized in the kitchen with me cradled against his chest, both of us naked and reeking of sex, my legs incapable of holding me up after that final exertion.

"I'm sorry." I stared at him, wide-eyed, my lower lip trembling.

"You're sorry." He gave me an incredulous look. "I should beat him for having so little control."

"I told you, I asked him to. I couldn't take him all the way the first time, and I wasn't sure I could've taken you at all. Anal sex takes a lot of preparation and you're very well-endowed. I wanted some practice."

Eli threw his hands up in the air. "So you asked a Nephilim with a proven lack control to break in your virgin ass without me there to hold him in check if his lust overran his senses."

"Um, yes." It sounded so much stupider when he put it that way. But better than admitting I'd felt abandoned by him when I woke to find him gone, and that I'd wanted to soothe my feminine ego and feed my demonic appetite and had used his brother to achieve both ends. Not that Dal had complained.

It was a pretty fair trade, to my mind. He'd taken the edge off my hunger, and I'd taken the edge off his pent-up lust. Since he'd regained control so quickly, neither of us had been in any danger. And we'd made each other very happy with the cheerfully exuberant sharing of our bodies.

Eli took a deep breath and fell silent long enough that I wondered if he was counting to ten before speaking again. When he did speak, his question took me by surprise. "Did he make it good for you?"

I blinked at him. "Yes. He was very careful. He said it'd be easier the more excited I was, and he was right. He made sure I was ready and he used his hand to stimulate me to orgasm while he rogered me from behind."

"Good." Eli bent down and seated himself on the floor

beside the tub. "Do you think you'd enjoy taking me like that?"

"Yes." I answered without hesitation. "If I'm turned on enough and I relax while you work the head past the opening, I think getting reamed by you would make me come until my eyes crossed."

"Think you can take full double penetration?" He reached into the tub and cupped his hand over my much-abused sex.

"Both of you together?" I thought it over. "I think the first time, it had better be you in front and Dal in the rear. Like we did before, but I'm sure I can take him all the way now that we've done it solo."

"And then you'd be confident I could take my pleasure in your ass while my brother takes his pleasure in your pussy?"

"Yes." My voice sounded a little breathy. With good reason. He was making me hot for them both, just talking about it.

"Did you like having his cock in your pussy?" Eli petted my sex as he asked the question.

"Yes. He was very, um, enthusiastic." I thought of Dal between my legs, driving his dick hard and fast and deep into my tight flesh, coming in me over and over until my thighs were sticky and my sex ached from being stretched and filled by his thick, hard shaft.

Eli probed my swollen labia with his finger. "Did you like taking my cock first?"

"Yes." I swallowed and closed my eyes. "I wanted you to be first. I wouldn't have let Dal put his cock inside my pussy if I hadn't given you my virginity already."

"What if I'd ordered you to spread your legs and let him be first?"

I answered him obediently. "If that was what you wanted, I would have let him take my virginity. I'm bound to you. I'm yours to take for yourself or give away."

"But you wanted it to be me."

"Yes." I sighed and arched up, legs parting, inviting him to touch me however he wanted. "I'm glad it was you first, Eli."

He stroked my clit, gently. "I'm glad I was first, too." Then he petted me one last time, drew his hand out of the water, and stood. "Enjoy your bath. The next cock you get between your legs will be mine. And then maybe I'll order you to let Dal fuck you again while I watch."

Rowrr. Did two libidinous Nephilim know how to entertain a succubus or what?

On that happy note, he left the room and I ducked under the water to make myself as clean and enticing as possible. Then I soaked until I thought I was capable of standing and walking again. Dal and I had overdone it a tad, but I wasn't sorry. Especially now that I had Eli's assurance that I had nothing to be sorry for.

I climbed out of the tub, all rosy from the hot water with a matching glow on the inside from sexual satisfaction. I was no longer a walking supernatural joke, the sexless succubus. If my assignment ended tonight, I would at least have the memories of a real sex life instead of unsatisfied curiosity and frustration and deprivation for all eternity.

The memory of Dal's voice saying I wasn't in a hurry for it to end came back to haunt me as I toweled myself dry. No, I wasn't in a hurry for it to end, and why should I be? I was enjoying myself. Dal and Eli were enjoying me. Why rush? It wasn't like Eli's soul was going anywhere, and it didn't exactly have an expiration date. There wasn't a time limit on my assignment.

A combination DVD player and radio I hadn't noticed sitting on a shelf clicked on. Barry Manilow began to sing. I thought about dropping the unit into the half-drained bath, but it might've upset Eli to have to replace it so I unplugged it and left the room instead.

I padded naked to Eli's room and found the boxer shorts and sweatshirt I'd been wearing earlier laid out on the bed. I took that as an invitation to borrow them again and put them on. Then I headed to the kitchen. I might've had an appetizer of Nephilim lust, but I was still hungry.

Eli was serving up plates of enchiladas when I got there. "Smells delicious," I said, taking a seat at the table. And it did. A mix of spices and cheese and beef teased my nose, making my mouth water and my stomach growl.

"Eat." He set a fully loaded plate in front of me. I picked up my fork and dug in. The enchilada sauce tasted tangy and spicy and the topping of sliced olives and fresh avocado made my taste buds sing.

"This is amazing," I said when I'd swallowed the first mouthful. "Thank you."

"I thought you'd be hungry." He finished setting down two more plates and then took the chair next to mine. "Can't have you wasting away when we need you to keep up your strength."

The sexual connotation was not lost on me.

Dal was last to the table. He gave me a smug look. "Can you sit down without feeling uncomfortable?"

"If she can't, you'll get a cushion for her." Eli glared at his brother.

"I'm fine." I bounced in my chair to prove it. Since I was braless under the sweatshirt, that created an entertaining jiggle. Both pairs of male eyes watched the oscillating motion of my breasts until they settled back into place.

"You certainly are." Dal gave me a look of warm appreciation. "That is a fine set of breasts you have. Seems a shame to keep them covered."

"Naked breasts at the table would distract everybody from eating." Eli reached a hand under my shirt to caress one as he spoke. Which kind of proved his point.

"No fair. I didn't get a grope," Dal protested.

"If you didn't get any groping in while you had her alone, you were too single-minded."

I giggled.

Dal winked at me. "I'm not sure I remember groping, but I'm very clear on the part where I kissed and licked and sucked every inch of those nicely shaped but sadly no longer naked tits."

Eli gave him a look that would have made me subside into sober silence, but Dal ignored it. "I think the memory of kissing and licking and sucking her between her legs is starting to fade, though. I'd better do that again. Want me to eat you, sweet stuff?"

"Eat your dinner."

"She can be dessert."

I smiled at their sibling rivalry and applied myself to my food, slaking one appetite in order to fuel another. If Dal wanted to go down on me again, I had no objection. It was even possible Eli would want him to do it as a preliminary, to make me all soft and slick and ready for Eli to take.

When we finished eating, Dal scooted his chair back and patted his lap in invitation. "Come here."

But before I could go to him, Eli scooped me out of my chair and deposited me on his thighs. "You'll be too busy washing the dishes to fool around."

"I'm washing the dishes?" Dal asked.

"Yes. You overdid it with her, so now you can do the dishes for her."

Dal winked at me. "It was worth it." He groped my breast as he went past on his way to the sink.

Eli shifted me sideways on his lap and cradled me with one arm. He used his other hand to tug my boxers down to my knees. Very promising. I snuggled into his embrace and wondered what it was about him that made the air feel electric and made me feel a thrill of danger with an accompanying urge to get closer.

Probably it was the same combination of things that made people compulsive gamblers, the constant possibility of winning mixed with inconsistent results and rewards. I really never knew what he'd do. He'd spanked my exposed sex, then told me to go down on his brother. He kept coming up with the unexpected, then rewarding me with pleasure.

I'd had centuries of experience with men. I'd researched every sexual possibility and perversion under the sun. I'd become his lover, and still I couldn't begin to guess what Eli would choose do with me right now.

As if to prove that I'd never figure him out, he produced a container from his shirt pocket that looked about the same size and shape as chewing tobacco. Something I was certain he didn't use, since I'd had his tongue in my mouth and mine in his. I hadn't tasted the distinctive flavor of tobacco.

"What's that?"

"For you." Eli didn't elaborate. He squeezed the top off and scooped his fingers into the gel inside the container. I sniffed suspiciously. I caught the scent of roses and something more exotic. Myrrh? "Open your legs."

Well, at least I could guess where he was going to put it. I parted my thighs and watched as he applied a liberal coating of the stuff to my sex. It felt cool and soothing to the touch at first, then pleasantly warm and a little tingly.

He slicked it over my outer labia, taking his time about it, making sure not to overlook a centimeter of flesh. He dipped his fingers in a second time and continued to coat me with the gel, applying a generous layer to my clit, parting me with his fingers to continue the treatment on my inner folds.

When that was done to his satisfaction, Eli gathered a generous amount on his fingertips and then slowly pushed his fingers into my sheath, working the gel inside me. I wasn't sure what felt better, Eli's fingers exploring and penetrating my sex, or the way the lubricant made my flesh react.

"What does it do?" I asked, having given up on getting a straight answer as to what it was made of.

"It stimulates blood flow, adds extra sensation. It coats and heals any raw spots. It's a combination healing ointment and topical aphrodisiac."

I let out a laugh. "Like I need an aphrodisiac with you two."

"It wouldn't hurt." Eli's face was serious and I felt my sex clench hard around his fingers just thinking about what he could have planned for a succubus that would require an aphrodisiac treatment. "It'll help you accommodate what I want without another day of recovery time. If you hadn't let Dal screw you until you couldn't walk, you wouldn't need this, so consider it your punishment."

Yes. Because it was so unbearable to sprawl in his lap with my shorts around my knees, his very capable hand between my legs ministering to me, the gel leaving behind an enjoyable warmth and a tingling sensation. It magnified his touch, I realized after a minute, intensifying the pleasure of a caress, making me highly sensitized to his fingers thrusting into my tight sheath.

When he'd coated my sex inside and out to his satisfaction, Eli turned his attention lower, smoothing the stuff down to cover my anus and the sensitive skin around it. When he began working it into my ass I let out a low moan and arched up into his hand, encouraging him to penetrate me deeper there. When a second finger slid inside that tight opening, I moaned again. He took his time working the aromatic ointment in, his fingers swirling and stroking inside me, preparing my anal passage for more than the foreplay digital stimulation provided.

I thought about taking Eli there and shuddered with want.

He gave me a final inner caress and drew his hand away and recapped the small round container.

"Nice playing doctor with you," I said.

I waited for him to indicate whether he wanted me to pull the loose boxers back up or leave them down. I voted for leaving him with a view of my bare sex, now glistening from the application of his ointment, until he told me otherwise.

Dal turned on the faucet, rinsing the dishes he'd finished washing while Eli and I were occupied. I listened to the sounds of plates stacking in the dish drainer, silverware pieces jangling together, and wanted to laugh in disbelief at the bizarre turn my afterlife had taken.

In a million years I never would have expected to find myself holed up playing house with two supernatural studs, discovering the hedonistic joys I was so good at promising but had never fully experienced for myself. Sharing meals and chores. Sharing a bed. Not that we'd actually slept together, but we'd made good use of Eli's wide expanse of mattress.

It was almost domestic. Although most people's idea of domestic routine probably didn't include threesomes and magical aphrodisiacs.

EIGHTEEN

"What are you thinking?" Eli asked the question as he shifted my borrowed sweatshirt up to bare my belly. He toyed idly with my navel ring.

"That threesomes aren't the normal afterdinner entertainment." I grinned at him, feeling lazy and comfortable and more than a little aroused. I was enjoying the opportunity to cuddle with him and looking forward to what the close physical contact might lead to.

"I'm sure you're well acquainted with unusual entertainments." His deep voice sounded even, but I caught that glittering edge in his gaze and felt my nipples harden.

"Well, there was one guy who wanted me to go down on

him while his friend took a riding crop to my bare backside," I mused, sorting through my store of exotic on-the-job adventures.

"Did you like that?"

"It didn't really last long enough for me to find out," I said. "I got in a few licks and so did the man with the crop, and then they both got carried away with lust."

Dal laughed over his shoulder at me. "Poor Beelzababe. You're too good at your job."

"Ha ha." I scowled at him. He blew me a kiss. Eli drew my sweatshirt up higher, exposing my breasts, then pulled the loose garment up and over my head, leaving me naked except for the boxers tangled around my knees.

Things were heating up. Literally, I realized. I squirmed a little in Eli's lap, trying to relieve my arousal.

He began a leisurely exploration of my breasts, stroking, caressing, squeezing, toying with my nipples. "Finished with the dishes?" Eli asked Dal.

"Yes. Are you starting without me?" Dal dried his hands on a towel and came to stand beside us.

"It would serve you right." Eli pinched one of my nipples, just hard enough to make me suck in a breath, not hard enough for true pain.

"Those will get in the way," Dal said, indicating my boxers. He tugged them down my legs and off. I was now completely naked, and they both remained fully dressed.

"Thanks." Eli sat me upright and turned me so that my back rested against his chest, my bare butt snuggled up to his groin. He guided my thighs apart, until they rested on the outsides of his.

He cupped his big hands over my breasts and squeezed. I arched my back and pushed myself further into his palms, sighing at the sensation of pressure against my achingly aroused nipples. Just when I was really starting to enjoy it, he released his grip and settled his hands on either side of my waist. He gave me a light squeeze, and that felt good, too.

"I believe Dal wanted to have some dessert," Eli said.

I thought of Dal's tongue lapping at my sensitized folds and felt my belly quiver in anticipation.

"Of course, dessert should be on the table."

My eyes were going to roll back in my head if he kept this up, I decided. Eli lifted me up, and Dal assisted. Between the two of them they seated me on the table, my knees drawn up and my feet flat against the surface. Then they lowered me back. Eli came to stand by my head. Dal stood in front of my open thighs. And I realized I was in for a session of group oral.

Eli proved my guess right by undoing his pants, opening them so that his cock sprang free. I'd have to turn my face to the side to draw him into my mouth, but the height was right.

"How does your dessert look?" Eli asked as he closed his hand around the base of his shaft and guided himself toward my mouth. He drew the head of his cock across my lips, so that answering him meant my mouth moving against that sensitive skin in a soft caress.

"Mouthwatering," I answered.

"What do you think of yours, Dal?"

Dal put his hands on my inner thighs and pressed out and down until my knees were turned out and lowered to the

tabletop, altering the angle of my hips just a little and opening me fully to his view. "Succulent and sweet as a ripe
peach."

He lowered his head and gave my sex a long lick. I opened
my mouth and Eli thrust inside.

There was an added dimension to my play with Dal
when it included Eli. Or rather, when it was orchestrated and
decided by Eli. He was definitely the leader. Knowing that
Dal was giving me oral sex and I was to surrender to it because Eli wanted it made him as intimately involved in the
act as if he'd been between my legs, too.

In many ways, I thought hazily, Dal was a surrogate or
extension for Eli the way I was a surrogate for Dal's desires.
The complexity of our threesome, which extended to the
absent Claire, went deeper than physical delights.

It was a practical arrangement for all of us, and a very
enjoyable one, but as I lay between the two men with my
body linking them, I had the strong sense of ties connecting
us in intersecting layers.

Me, bound to Eli. Eli and Dal, sharing the bond of broth-
erhood. Dal, drawn to me as a solution for his dangerous dilemma. Eli, capitalizing on my presence to prove his control.
All of us pushed and pulled by various factors to bring us to
this place, this moment shared among the three of us.

I devoted my mouth to Eli's pleasure, and Dal did the
same for me. Giving and taking flowing between the three of
us, connecting us all. I felt bound to both of them. Dal's
tongue thrust deep into my inner folds and made heat curl
through my abdomen. My lips wrapped around Eli's shaft,

sliding up and down, my tongue dancing over his sensitive skin for added stimulation.

I felt the heightened arousal from the gel that made my body ache to be fully penetrated, fully possessed by them both, a physical echo for another ache I had no words for. The rush of blood and the highly stimulated nerve endings of my anus and my sex hungered for more contact, more touch, more penetration. I squirmed and writhed on the table as the need increased. Dalen's mouth drawing on my clit made my hips buck wildly. My mouth on Eli's cock grew frantic.

"Now," Eli said. He pulled out of my mouth. Dal gave my pussy a last lap with his tongue.

I noticed that I wasn't feeling overwhelmed by their combined effect yet. They were still clothed, and physical contact had been limited so far. That was probably deliberate, so they could prepare me for full dual penetration without sending me into a heat-drunk coma.

Eli came around to Dal's side of the table, his pants still open. Dal stepped to the side. Eli gripped my hips and pulled me forward until my butt rested on the edge of the table top. Then he positioned himself between my thighs and looked down at me. "I told you the next cock you had between your legs would be mine."

I licked my lips and nodded. "You did."

His hard flesh probed my sex. He thrust forward, and I arched up to meet him, offering myself to him. He continued to press deeper until he'd buried his shaft inside the tight clasp of my pussy. He stayed deep inside me for a minute without moving. Then he withdrew, and I let out a sound of protest.

He spanked my exposed mound, and the protest turned to pleasure. Again he thrust deep inside me. Again he withdrew and spanked my swollen sex, making my hips work in helpless, urgent rhythm as my body begged for more.

He gave me a series of deep, hard thrusts next, then varied his stroke, going slow, fast, deep, shallow, until I was wild with need.

Dal watched us, his heavily aroused state visible through the straining fabric of his pants. When Eli paused with his length buried all the way inside me, Dal leaned over to suck my nipples by turns.

The pressure of his mouth on my breasts made my womb contract. My vaginal walls clenched around Eli's shaft. He began to thrust harder, so hard my tits bounced from the force of his body ramming into mine. I made inarticulate shrieking sounds. Dal laved my swollen nipples, Eli fucked me with punishing pleasure, and the two of them pushed me over the edge. I came so hard I saw spots.

Eli pulled me into a sitting position, his cock still buried inside me, and gathered me into his arms, stroking my back. Then he withdrew and my sex instantly ached with the need to be filled again.

"Time for a more accommodating surface," Eli said. To my surprise, he lifted me up in his arms and carried me to his room, Dal following. Eli settled me on the bed, and they undressed in unison. Shirts, removed and tossed aside. Pants, stripped off and discarded. They bracketed me on the bed and turned me onto my side, facing Dal.

"Lift your leg," Eli said behind me. "Hook your thigh over his."

I did, and Dal shifted so that his hard penis probed my sex-softened pussy. The contact made me shudder and press closer, trying to gain more of him.

"Like that, do you?" Eli stroked my bare buttocks, then delved between them, searching out my anal opening. "Does Dal's cock feel good?"

"Yes." My voice sounded thick with desire.

"Do you want him to slide his cock inside you, fuck you?"

"Yes." I strained my hips forward, sliding against Dal's rigid length. I was hollow and aching and I needed to be filled. "Yes, I want Dal to fuck me."

"Fuck her," Eli said as he positioned the head of his cock and began to press forward.

Dal altered his angle and thrust into my sensitized sheath. Acting in unison, Eli penetrated my anus and pushed his shaft steadily in, filling me until I was so stretched, so stuffed, I couldn't breathe. And at the same time I burned for them to move, to thrust. For both of them to take me until I could take no more.

They weren't gentle, but they didn't have to be. Eli's perfumed concoction protected my tissues, lubricated my pussy and my ass, and he really hadn't been kidding about the aphrodisiac effect. That, combined with their unique effect on me, pretty much turned me into a nymphomaniac.

I felt drunk on sex, on the sheer bliss of physical contact. Dal faced me, one hand playing with my breasts like they were his favorite new toys, his hard length thrusting between my legs, screwing me while I squeezed his dick in the tight clasp of my inner walls. Eli curved behind me, marauder and protector all in one. His strong embrace guarded my back while he plundered my ass with his implacable cock.

They filled me by turns, they filled me with simultaneous thrusts, but over and over, they filled me. They fucked me until I lost count of the number of times they made me come, until I sobbed and pleaded and begged, and when at last they allowed themselves to come, they fucked me until they'd given me every ounce of their cream.

Nineteen

It was Dal who left, after they finally withdrew from my spent body. He kissed me and I tasted myself on his mouth. I wrapped my leg around his, hugging him to me while he ran his hands over my torso and gave my tits a last squeeze. Then he got off the bed and I was alone with Eli.

I could feel his penis nestled between the rounded cheeks of my buttocks and his long hair sliding over my bare shoulders.

"I told you you should thank him," I said throatily. I gave my butt a suggestive wiggle against his groin. "If he hadn't broken me in for you like I asked him to, I couldn't have taken you like that."

"I think the job was its own reward," Eli said. "He doesn't need to be thanked for the pleasure of giving it to you in the ass. Although if he did, you expressed sufficient gratitude by spreading your legs for him until he'd fucked you into exhaustion."

I rolled to face him, nuzzling my face into his bare chest, breathing in his scent. "I'd be happy to spread my legs for you until you fucked me into exhaustion."

"Would you?"

"Mmm." I squirmed closer, pressing my breasts into his chest. "I'm not feeling sick or passing out. You timed that just right, so you could dual-penetrate me before I had too much exposure to both of you together. Also, you smeared aphrodisiac cream all over my sex parts. I am at your disposal."

"Then lie back and spread your legs."

A thrill shot through me at his words. I obeyed without needing the compulsion of being bound to him. I arranged myself in an inviting sprawl. He rolled on top of me and settled between my open thighs.

"Did you like taking me in anally?" Eli asked. He rocked his body into mine, a delicious preliminary.

"Yes. It was very intense and primitive and raw. It made me feel . . ." I trailed off, not sure I should say more.

"What?" He kissed the line of my jaw.

"Taken," I mumbled. It was an inadequate word for the emotional and physical reality of having my most vulnerable opening aggressively and sexually claimed by a dominating male. He might have bound me before, but he owned my ass now. It was his, marked, taken. I was his to fuck, his to share, his to command. Not by any magical working, but by force of sheer sexual possession.

"I did take you," Eli pointed out. "I took your mouth. I took your pussy. I took your hot ass."

"So did Dal," I said.

"That doesn't count. I gave you to him." Eli rocked into me again and I felt his penis probing at my labia. I rubbed myself against him in blatant invitation and felt deeply grateful for magical cleansing that made interrupting the flow of the action unnecessary.

"That's what I mean. You took me." Not that I was complaining.

"And I'm going to take you again."

I tilted my pelvis to make a cradle for Eli and he settled into it as he thrust deep, filling me with his demanding length once again. I wound my arms and legs around him, urging him on, holding him close, surrendering to his possession.

He fucked me long and hard, ejaculating inside me twice more in violent spurts of spending, finally coming to rest with his penis still buried in my plundered sex as if unwilling to relinquish his physical claim of ownership.

I expected him to be gone when I woke, but I luxuriated in the sensation of being held close, my body still pinned under his and joined with his, while I drifted off to sleep.

I dreamed of fire and smelled sulfur. My dream self went looking for the source, opened a door, and stepped into a familiar room. Nick sat behind his desk as if expecting me. He waved me to a chair.

"No, thanks," I said to dream Nick. "I'd rather stand."

"Perhaps because you can't sit down." He tossed a file onto the desk and gave me a basilisk stare. "Are you enjoying being their plaything, Edana?"

"Are you criticizing my performance?" I crossed my arms over my ample chest. "I am doing everything under the sun to provoke them into fully surrendering to lust. You just neglected to mention that their species is capable of immense sexual energy without succumbing to lust. They're even powerful enough to experience lust without being controlled by it. In other words, they can screw a succubus silly while starving her. I can't help thinking you knew that would happen."

He made an impatient gesture with his hand as if waving away this insignificant detail. "There's always some pertinent information missing from your case files. That's no excuse for failure."

I gritted my teeth. "I have not failed."

"You haven't succeeded, either."

"I'm trying."

"Try harder." He shot flame across the room, hitting me between my navel and the rise of my mound. I clutched at my abdomen, seared with pain, crying out in shock. "Remember who you belong to."

I woke gasping and curled my body into a defensive ball. My belly twisted and burned and I whimpered at the pain that was no phantom remnant of a nightmare.

Eli stirred behind me. At some point he'd moved off me, but he'd stayed close. My back pressed into his side as I scrunched up tighter. He rolled toward me and curled his body around mine. "What is it?"

"Stomach," I gasped out. "Hurts."

"Cramp?" He slid his hand over my belly and I flinched from the contact.

"No." I started to cry, helpless tears of pain and anger. That was no dream. Nick had hurt me.

"Shhh." Eli gathered me into his arms, hugging me closer. His warmth enfolded me, soothed me. His nearness was a comfort, all the more precious for being unexpected. I'd been prepared for him to leave me after he'd finished with me. But he'd stayed. "Let me feel."

I forced myself not to pull away as his large hand searched out the source of agony that twisted my insides. He pressed his palm hard against the spot and it felt like he'd stabbed me. A hot rush of tears spilled down my cheeks, but I made myself hold still for him. He spoke low, an incantation in that ancient language lost to men but still known to angels.

The pain eased by stages until it was gone, but the memory of it stayed. I'd been warned. Nick wouldn't tolerate my failure, and if my performance didn't satisfy, I'd be punished again.

"That shouldn't have happened," Eli said finally. "I left some opening in our defenses. Dalen's the better sorcerer, I'll have him inspect, reinforce . . ." His voice trailed off and his hand tightened on my belly. "Nothing should be able to harm you here. We'll find the opening and we'll close it."

I shook my head. "Not your fault. Not a weakness in your defenses. He can reach me anywhere."

"Can he? We'll see about that." Eli got out of bed and retrieved his sword. He swirled it in the air, and I saw flashes of light forming lines and markings in the darkness. When he finished, he placed the sword on the bed lengthwise as if to guard me from the front and wrapped himself around me from behind.

"Thank you," I said. "It won't work, but it makes me feel better that you tried." I didn't much trust that unearthly sword, but I knew its power. So would Nick.

Eli pulled me closer, his arms tightening around me like bands. "What makes you so certain it won't work?"

"He can reach me anywhere I am, because I belong to him." My voice sounded as dull and flat as I felt.

"Do you?" Eli's voice took on a steely edge. "Have I released you?"

I blinked in the darkness. "No."

"I bound you. I claimed you. I own you. Until I release you, you belong to me."

I was pretty sure Nick would argue that a preexisting claim took precedence, but I still liked hearing the fierce, possessive tone in Eli's voice.

He stroked my torso from breast to belly in a knowledgeable caress, overlaying the memory of pain with a touch that gave pleasure. "This is mine," Eli murmured, running his hand over the round swell of my breast, stroking my nipple. "And this is mine." He squeezed my waist, smoothed his hand over my hip. "This, too."

He palmed the naked curve of my butt. "This belongs to me." He slid his hand over my belly, rubbed the site of injury in a gentle circle, then moved down to take my sex in a possessive hold. "This is mine." He probed between my legs, drove a finger into my tight, unprepared flesh. My unready state magnified the sensation of being penetrated and claimed by him.

"Who owns you?" Eli's voice was a rough challenge in the night.

"You do." I raised one knee to open myself to him, ac-quiescing to the demand of his hand.

He drove a second finger into me, hard. "That's right. Me. I own you."

My body was already softening for him, responding to his claim, accepting the invasion of his fingers. Eli's hand between my legs gentled, his fingers stroking instead of spear-ing inside me, then withdrawing to caress my outer labia, petting and soothing the tender flesh. "Mine." He breathed the word against my ear.

"Yours," I agreed.

His strength made me feel safe. Even if that sense of safety was an illusion, it was a comforting one. I relaxed in his protective hold and slid into a dreamless sleep with his hand still cupped between my legs.

The warmth of sunlight on my face woke me. It was a much nicer sensation than searing flame across my abdo-men. I blinked my eyes open and saw the indentation on the bed where the sword's weight had rested. It was gone now, and I wondered where it went when it wasn't in use. Into a dimensional fold?

I knew without looking that Eli was also gone. I was be-coming very attuned to his absence. When Eli was near, I could feel his pull. Sort of like the moon and the tides. When he was gone, it was like a vacuum.

Stockholm syndrome, for sure. Or possibly sex addiction. Codependency. Whatever it was, it wasn't right. I was a de-mon. He was the sworn enemy of demonkind, upholding the balance and wielding the sword of justice. I shouldn't lose sight of that just because he liked to wield a fleshly sword between my legs and a few other choice places.

He parked you in the void, I reminded myself. *He made you wash dishes.*

He'd also utterly delighted my body, ravished me with awesome thoroughness and creativity, given me the blissful experience of taking two men at once in varied combinations. I was a creature of desire who had never known satisfaction, and now I was getting it in spades.

In other words, Eli had found my vulnerability, and he was exploiting it to the max. If this went on much longer, I might become too sex-drunk to even protest when he decided to banish me because he no longer needed me.

And there would come a time when he no longer needed me, when I'd outlasted my usefulness. When he'd proven himself the master of his lust, when Dal had perfected his control and no longer slipped up no matter what we did together, they weren't going to keep me around as a pet.

Did you imagine anything else? a cruel voice whispered in my head. *Did you think he might be the one to ransom you, merely because you were good in bed?*

The inner jibe turned me stone-cold sober faster than rolling naked in snow. My out-clause had never seemed more like a piece of fine print added to the contract merely to amplify the agony. It was cruel to have hope. I'd never really believed it was possible until now. Now I saw the possibility.

Eli and Dalen were both possessed of half-human souls, both protected from my demonic temptation by their half-angel natures. For the first time in my existence, I'd encountered men who could come close enough to touch me, to know me, without succumbing to me and falling victim to my demon nature.

And when they were done with me, I wouldn't just get sent back to hell with a black mark for failure on my performance record. This assignment would only end one of two ways: when I drove Eli to lust and drained him, or when he banished me after he'd withstood every temptation I could offer him.

Such cheerful morning-after thoughts. Well, at least I'd had the pleasure of the night before.

I sat up and then groaned as my body responded with a thousand complaints. I understood, too late, why Eli had told me the aphrodisiac was a punishment. I'd been a willing and enthusiastic participant in debauchery, begging for more while the two of them fucked me without limits. Now I got to pay the price.

TWENTY

I didn't want to wear Eli's borrowed boxers and sweatshirt again. They'd only serve as constant, concrete reminders of how it had felt when Eli took them off me, and what he'd done with me once they were out of the way. The very idea depressed me.

But that left me limited options. The clothes I'd arrived in had vanished, never to reappear. Which was too bad, because I looked really hot in black leather. I felt sorely in need of the boost in confidence that came from wearing a great outfit, too.

The bathtub offered an interim solution, so I soaked under a mountain of foamy bubbles and contemplated staying in there all day, or wearing a towel.

The door opened while I was staring moodily at the remnants of my dissolving cover. Dal walked in and stood by the tub, taking in the unobstructed view of my breasts. "Nice tits. Do you want breakfast?"

"They're world-class tits," I corrected, still staring at the traces of soap left floating on the water. A thin layer covered my sex. If I didn't disturb it, I had a temporary monokini. That would delay the getting dressed dilemma for a few more minutes.

"I know. I've had my hands all over them." Dal gave one a squeeze. "Bring your naked world-class tits to the table and let me look at them while I have breakfast."

"I might as well. I don't have anything to wear."

The sulky tone of my voice didn't seem to put Dal off at all. "What's wrong with what you're wearing now?"

"The bathtub isn't very portable."

Dal laughed and reached in to pull me out. He stood me on the floor facing him, wet and dripping, water streaming from me.

He bent his head to lick droplets off my nipple. I batted him away. Instead of taking that as discouragement, he grabbed my ass and pulled my body into his. He gripped and kneaded my bare buttocks while he nuzzled my neck and bumped his pelvis into mine. "If I give you something to wear, will you take it off for me later?"

That sounded like an interesting opening. "Maybe."

"Only maybe?"

I felt a smile pulling at my mouth despite myself. It was hard not to respond to Dal's good-natured teasing. "Maybe. What's in it for me if I take it off for you?"

"Well, this, for starters." Dal pressed his groin into me, letting me feel the blatant evidence of his arousal through the fabric of his pants. "I'll let you have a nice, hard cock to play with."

"Hmm." I leaned into him, my body reacting to the seductive heat of his nearness with interest. My nipples swelled.

He felt the tight buds poking against the thin fabric of his shirt and gave me a triumphant look. "Bet you'd like me to suck those now."

"Maybe."

"Ask me nicely."

"No."

Dal gave my ass a sensual squeeze and pulled me tighter into his embrace. "You know you want me to. You love it when I put my mouth on your tits."

In fact, I did. He gave me a coaxing kiss, running his tongue along the seam of my lips until I opened for him. He let go of my buttocks and reached up to fill his hands with my breasts, cupping and squeezing them, rubbing his thumbs over my nipples until I squirmed.

"Ask me nicely." He spoke against my lips, then thrust his tongue into my mouth again and pinched my nipples between his thumbs and forefingers.

Oh, what the hell. "Please."

By the time he lifted his mouth from my breasts, I was feeling a little more enthusiastic about the day ahead. Dal deserved my gratitude for that. Sinking into despondency wasn't the answer, and neither was hiding in the bathtub.

"Now your nipples are so swollen, they'll stand out no

matter what you wear," Dal informed me. "You'll look like a wet dream."

He gave me a brisk toweling, patted my ass when he was finished, and led me naked into the hall.

"Hey. What about getting me something to wear?"

Dal looked me over. "Do you really need clothes?"

"Yes."

"Okay." He traced a pattern with his hand and I was wearing a pair of very low-rise jeans that showed off my navel ring and left the dimples at the base of my spine bare.

"I think you can see the crack of my ass in these," I said. I turned around and bent over. "Well, can you?"

"Yep." He poked a finger under the waistband and toyed with the cleft between my buttocks. "I can also tell you're not wearing any underwear."

"That's because you left them off." I turned back around and gestured at my bare chest. My breasts seemed even more prominent now that my bottom half was covered. With my nipples all dark and distended from the ministrations of his hands and mouth, the effect was nearly pornographic. "What about a shirt?"

Dal grinned. "I left that off, too."

I put my hands on my hips and scowled. "Topless does not count as dressed."

"You want me to cover those up? What's in it for me?" Dal turned my earlier question back on me.

I gave him a sultry smile. "You give me something to wear, I take it off for you. Wasn't that the deal you offered?"

A black, lacy low-cut bra appeared, spilling out as much cleavage as it contained.

I raised a brow at him. "You can see my nipples."

"I know. They're all rosy and erect. Want me to suck on them some more?"

I made an exasperated sound and headed for the kitchen. At least I had something on.

When I walked in, Eli's eyes swung to me, then to my chest. "Since when does wearing a bra constitute being dressed?"

"Since the eighties," I said. "Blame Madonna. Or you could blame your brother's fashion sense."

Eli unbuttoned the denim shirt he had on, stripped it off, and handed it to me. "Put that on."

So much for finding an alternative to wearing Eli's borrowed clothes.

Well, at least I was up and dressed and ready to face the day. The tub had soothed away most of my aches, and only a few twinges of discomfort remained. I wasn't in any condition for a repeat performance, but I could manage to sit and eat breakfast. Dal had cajoled me into a brighter mood, and despite my complaints about his taste in clothes, the jeans and peek-a-boo bra did actually make me feel more confident in my sex appeal.

Also, now that I was wearing Eli's shirt, he wasn't. This meant I'd get to look at his magnificent physique while I ate. I suddenly felt more sympathetic to Dal's wishes. The sight of a bare-to-the-waist Eli was better than food.

A new empathy for Dal's desire to view naked breasts over breakfast put me in the mood to be more accommodating, but Eli had told me to put his shirt on. I couldn't disobey. I solved the dilemma by fastening only one button, the one that nestled between my breasts. Eli got me properly dressed, Dal got improper peeks at my peaks, I got to drool over Eli's six-pack. One big happy family.

"You know she looks better without the shirt," Dal said to Eli.

"Eat." Eli thumped plates down.

To my surprise he picked me up and sat with me sideways in his lap. I realized it was motivated by more than the urge to cuddle when he leaned me back and pushed the shirt aside to inspect my abdomen.

That was something I hadn't done in the tub. I'd been too busy sulking. And, well, I didn't want to think too much about it. I could joke about being between a rock and a hard-on, but I didn't want to contemplate the consequences I'd face for either success or failure. No wonder I'd wanted to enjoy the moment.

If I lost and the Nephilim banished me or sent me back to an angry Nick, I lost. If I won and brought back Eli and Dal's souls, I lost in the long term because if Dal was right, demons had become too numerous. Which meant the world needed two Nephilim more than it needed one succubus.

Up until now, I'd more or less accepted my role in the bigger picture of things because it was sort of like being a hit man. If I showed up at a man's door, he'd done something to bring me there.

The souls I'd collected at the ill-fated dogging event on my last assignment had been a targeted group of men responsible for the disappearance of at least two women. My main target would set up the events, the group of followers would show up, the video would run on the Internet from some international site, and the female costar would turn out to have served her final purpose.

What had Dalen and Eli done to deserve me? Dalen was so tied up in knots from his self-denial that he was screwing me sideways in order to keep himself from possibly hurting the human woman he wanted. Meanwhile, he kept his hands off her and nurtured her magic and trained her to use her art for the greater good.

He'd shown up in the bathroom, coaxed me out of a foul mood, and restored my confidence before I faced Eli for the day. Coincidence? Or a good deed, done deliberately? For this, he deserved to lose his soul?

And Eli. Warrior, protector. He'd even protected me, because his sense of honor wouldn't let him do anything else. He'd drawn his sword to defend me from any further threat Nick might pose. Why? He'd bound me, therefore I was his responsibility. I didn't kid myself that it was personal, but Eli had decent instincts, so he did the decent thing.

The two of them could have used me without regard for my enjoyment or well-being, but they chose to be generous lovers. Eli could have had what he wanted from me last night without the healing aphrodisiac balm he'd applied with such thorough care. Instead, he'd made sure I was in good shape to enjoy full dual-penetration.

Their personalities couldn't be more different, and those differences were reflected in the way they approached sex. Dal was fun in the sack and enjoyed giving as good as he got. Eli was more intense, more into the control aspect, but that only served to heighten my response. More intense sex led to a more intense orgasm.

Eli might have bound me much against my wishes, but I really couldn't complain about the treatment I received at his hands. For an enemy, he was a remarkably honorable one.

Honorable enemies, all three of us. And temporary lovers. So where did that leave me? Besides doubly screwed.

The answer hit hard. *It leaves you right here. Do your damned job.*

Maybe my introduction to great sex was clouding my thinking, because I kept forgetting these two were dangerous. Nick had been ruthless in his choice of method, but he hadn't been wrong to get my attention. I'd known from the beginning this could well be my last assignment, and I was here for a reason.

Eli needed to be tested. Even he understood that and consented to it voluntarily. So did Dal. They had a built-in natural attraction that might be powerful enough to act as the supernatural equivalent to a date-rape drug. It was hard to imagine any human woman withstanding determined sexual pursuit from either of them. If they were ruled by lust, they could do a great deal of damage with their overwhelming physical appeal combined with superior strength and sorcery skills.

If I couldn't lead them into temptation they'd have long and happy lives, assuming they continued to defeat all the demons sent against them. I'd go to my banishment knowing I'd done both them and the world a favor.

If I could lead them into surrendering to lust, then they were too dangerous and too undisciplined to be left unchecked.

Message received and understood, I thought, as Eli finished prodding at me and righted me on his lap. I undid the center button holding the shirt closed and flashed him the full visual effect of my breasts showcased by Dal's naughty bra at point-blank range. "You missed a spot."

"Did I?" He took in the picture I made on his lap, my body displayed to advantage by the low, tight jeans and the barely-there lacy excuse for lingerie that only served to accentuate the swells of my breasts and the rosy peaks of my nipples. "Show me."

"Right here." I touched the valley between the twin mounds that strained against the flimsy lace.

Eli lifted me up and turned me to face him, my legs straddling him, then leaned forward to press a hot kiss on the point I'd indicated. I touched one nipple. "And here."

His mouth followed, closed over my lace-covered aureole, teased me through the scant protection the bra pretended to provide. He released my nipple and kissed the bare flesh just above the edge of the low-cut cup. "Seems fine to me."

"What about here?" I indicated my other nipple, stroking over it with my fingertip. Eli gave it the same treatment as its twin before licking the sensitive valley between my breasts.

"Not seeing a problem," Eli murmured.

"I am. Breakfast is getting cold, and her back's to me so I'm missing the show," Dal complained.

"You saw plenty when you put it on her." Eli ran his fingers along the edge of the bra cups, teasing me, and I sucked in a breath, wondering who was tempting who. I wanted to tighten my legs, press myself forward so that the inner seam of my jeans rubbed against the bulge in his, invite him to rock into the receptive embrace of my open thighs, my pelvis tipped up to meet his . . .

Eli looked into my eyes, the glittering heat in his gaze matching the languid provocation that glimmered in mine. He ran a finger from the center point just below the bra down to my navel ring and gave it a sensual tug. "He's right. Breakfast is getting cold."

Forget breakfast, I wanted to say. The food might be cooling off, but I was heating up.

My unspoken wish was overruled, however. Eli settled me back in my chair, and the two of them went on with the meal. I took a minute to recover. And wondered how I could keep my mind on anything when one look, one touch from Eli sent everything else spinning away.

I wanted him. Maybe because he'd bound me and I was subject to his will, but then again, I'd been attracted to him when he was nothing but a picture in a file. And when he'd put his hand on my bare flesh for the first time, I hadn't exactly been running away. I'd been hoping he'd slide his hand higher under my skirt.

Dal slid his foot against mine under the table, winked at me, and then settled his gaze on my chest in blatant enjoyment. My nipples tightened in response to the attention. He grinned and ran his foot up the inside of my leg in a teasing caress. Eli reached out and pulled the shirt closed, making a show of touching my breasts while he covered them up and redid the center button.

"Spoilsport," Dal said.

Temporary lovers. Honorable enemies. One wickedly hot ménage à trois. If this was the last assignment I ever had, at least I was going to go out with a bang.

TWENTY-ONE

After the two brothers finished eating and headed out to their respective destinations, I piled dishes in the sink and wondered why Eli had stuck me with domestic duties.

Maybe it amused him. Maybe he really was just tired of washing the dishes himself. Hard to guess at Eli's motives. His ways were mysterious.

A claw at the kitchen door told me the dragon was back. I wasn't surprised. I turned my head and mouthed, *Be right there.*

I finished washing the dishes, and I didn't hurry. I made sure I completed my task thoroughly. If Nick had to wait, it served him right. When I'd dried my hands, I walked to the door and opened it.

Multifaceted eyes glared. "You took long enough."

"If you were selling Girl Scout cookies, I would have been faster. I like the coconut, caramel, and chocolate kind." I leaned my hip into the doorframe in a pose of casual unconcern. If Nick had come planning to tear a strip off my hide, he'd do it. But I wasn't going to invite further punishment by acting guilty if he thought he'd already made his point.

"Are you angry because I reminded you of unpleasant truths?"

"No. I'm pissed off because you fucking burned me." I glared at him, fury resonating in my tone. "That wasn't necessary."

"Wasn't it?" Smoke curled from the dragon's nostrils. The effect was suitably hellish.

"No. It wasn't. You wanted me here, here I am. You wanted me to stop Eli from banishing demons. I'm doing my best to keep him busy. You wanted him seduced, I'm granting his every sexual desire, including his wishes to watch me perform with another man and to do both of them at the same time. So far he's proven challenging, but I'm doing my best to wear him down."

"You keep saying you're doing your best, but you haven't brought me his soul. I'm disappointed in you."

I rolled my eyes. "Yeah, and I've failed you for the last time. Go ahead, flame me. See if Eli gets turned on by charred succubus. Maybe that'll be the thing that gets his gonads in a lustful grip."

My sarcasm wasn't lost on Nick, but neither was my point.

He really didn't have a better succubus to replace me with, and unless he was ready to abandon that line of attack altogether, it wasn't in his best interest to render me unappealing to visually stimulated males.

"Why were you washing dishes?"

His apparent change in topic threw me. I blinked in confusion. "Eli ordered me to."

"Ordered you? To wash dishes?"

"Yes." I shrugged. "I'm a demon. He bound me. I have to obey him."

"By washing dishes."

I narrowed my eyes. "That's right."

A puff of smoke escaped, followed by a sulfurous rumble, then a full belly-laugh. Nick was laughing his ass off.

"It's not that funny."

He collapsed on the porch and belched flame as he roared with laughter.

"Are you done?" I asked.

"Yes," Nick wheezed. "Your punishment for failing to complete your assignment in a timely matter is hereby noted as adequate."

I left him rolling in dragonish hilarity and shut the door with a bang.

A couple of hours later I'd run out of things to dust or clean. Boredom drove me outside. I wasn't hoping to catch sight of Eli, I told myself. I just needed to get out of the house before I started climbing the walls.

The quiet still struck me as creepy, but I was kind of getting used to it. The air was cool and misty and filled with the scent of forest. A light rain gave everything a soft-focus blur, ferns and bushes and evergreen trees blending together. It would be easy to get lost here, deep in the woods with the heights of the trees blocking the sky and confusing all sense of direction.

Not that I worried for myself. Eli or Dal would retrieve me if I wandered too far.

I gave myself up to the rhythm of walking, falling into an easy stride, occasionally shortening or lengthening my step to pick the easiest path around or over some obstacle. Tree roots, fallen branches, rocks, and low points in the ground pooled with rainwater all kept my attention carefully trained on watching where I stepped.

The thick trunk of a large fallen tree brought me to a halt. I shoved my hands into my back pockets while I debated whether to go over or around it. The trunk rose almost chest-high. I'd have to climb up on top of it to go over. I wasn't sure my tight jeans would allow that much freedom of movement. The tree extended too far in both directions to walk around it easily.

More trouble than it was worth. I turned around and headed back the way I'd come, but after I'd walked what I thought was the same amount of time, the house still wasn't in sight.

Oh, hell. If I got lost, I might miss lunch.

My stomach growled as if on cue, and I realized I should've brought a snack with me. I wanted a snack. Some of those sweet, crunchy cookies I'd mentioned to Nick. Maybe an apple. Maybe a large cheeseburger with bacon and a side of fries. If I wasn't feeding on lust, I needed to compensate with calories or I'd run out of energy. Get weak.

Like now. I wanted to rest, but there weren't any dry places to sit so I kept trudging forward. The rain began to fall in earnest, heavy torrents of it that soaked me to the skin. I clutched Eli's shirt around me and huddled into it. I broke through to a stand of trees and almost tripped on familiar-looking shards of plastic. The radio I'd broken. I was almost home.

I started to run, and ran headlong into an immovable obstacle. The obstacle gave off a familiar and very welcome heat signature. I sighed in relief and wrapped myself around Eli. "Mmm. Hello."

Then I backed up and did a little jump to gain altitude. Eli caught me, either a gesture of welcome or reflex. I didn't care which. I was just glad he hadn't let me slide back down. I hooked my legs around his hips in case he decided to let go.

On the theory that skin-to-skin contact would warm me up faster, I yanked my borrowed shirt open, hauled up the sweater Eli was now wearing, and plastered my bare torso against his.

"I take it you're happy to see me." His voice held a hint of amusement.

"You have no idea." I held on with all the strength my arms and legs could muster and buried my face in his neck. My nipples were tight and puckered from rain and cold under the lacy bra. I crushed my breasts into his chest and sighed at the welcome warmth and pressure. "It's dark and wet in the woods, and everything looks the same. I couldn't find the house."

"You found me."

"Mmm, I know." I nuzzled his throat and kissed my way

up to his jawline. He tilted his head down to meet me and our mouths met, then clung. I opened my lips for him, and he took over, turning the kiss deep, dark, and demanding. I clung to him while he tightened his arms around me and devoured me. Our tongues tangled, and his began a slow, thrusting slide along mine, in and out of my mouth.

"Aw. You're going to do it out here in the rain?" Dal's voice broke in.

Eli ended the kiss with hard, hot open-mouthed pressure that sent heat curling all the way to my toes. I blinked, then gave Dal a sultry look over Eli's shoulder.

"Why? Did you want to sell tickets?"

"Hell, no, I want to get in line." He came up to stand behind Eli. "Keep going. I can wait my turn."

"You can both wait. Lunch is ready."

I laughed at the prosaic declaration and snuggled into Eli, who turned toward the house without making a move to put me down. Instead, he slid his hands down to cup my ass, holding me more securely as he walked. The motion made for some nice pelvis-bumping.

"Would you really have waited?" I asked Dal. "Or just joined in?"

"Depends," he said, pretending to give it serious thought. "It's good sweaty fun to watch you in action, but it doesn't beat making you the hot center filling of a sex sandwich."

"It's polite to wait until you're invited," Eli said.

"You invited me." Dal grinned at him and reached over to tug at my jeans. "Babe, you're going to need help getting these wet clothes off."

"I think I'll have all the help I need," I said.

Eli shifted his grip on me to one hand, leaving the other free to strip off my sodden shirt. He passed it to Dal, who took it with a shrug. Then he undid the back clasp of my bra with expert fingers. I leaned away from Eli to allow enough space between our bodies for him to peel away the black lace clinging wetly to my breasts.

Eli tossed that to Dal, too, who caught it and twirled it around one finger. By that time, we'd reached the back porch. Dal went in first and held the door. Eli carried me through and set me on a kitchen chair.

Dal hung the wet shirt and bra over the back of an empty chair and took the opportunity to tweak one of my nipples.

"You look cold." He promptly covered my bare breasts with his palms in mock concern, squeezing my soft flesh in a cheerfully lecherous grip.

Eli knelt in front of me and undid my jeans, then stood me up to work them down my hips. It wasn't easy to peel me out of the tight, wet denim, but he managed it. I stepped out of the cold folds of fabric once he had them down to my ankles.

Then I was standing naked between two men for a dizzying moment. Eli picked up my jeans and hung them with the shirt and bra, leaving me with my back to Dal, his hands making free with me.

He watched us, and I leaned into Dal, my eyes on Eli. Dal kneaded and stroked the full curves of my breasts, massaged my nipples, then slid one arm down to my belly and pulled me tighter into his embrace. I wiggled my butt against his groin in invitation. He let his hand slide lower, until it nestled between my thighs and cupped my sex. I tilted my pelvis forward, pushing myself into his hand, then rocked back, pressing my ass against his cock.

I wondered how we looked to Eli. Me, fully naked, skin slick from rain, nipples pebbled into tight rosy buds. Dal, fully dressed, holding me close with his hand covering my mound and his free hand caressing my bare breasts. My hips gently moving back and forth, alternately offering Dal my ass and arching into the intimate clasp of his hand.

"Come here." Eli held a hand out to me. Dal loosed me and I walked to Eli, reaching out to take his hand. He cupped his other hand between my legs and gave me a testing squeeze. I made a soft sound of encouragement. He gave me another pleasurable squeeze and drew his hand away, giving my clit a stroke in the process.

Then he turned me around and gave me a little push accompanied by a light slap on my bare ass. "Go put on something warm."

"Ah, there goes my view," Dal complained. He caught me around the waist as I passed and pulled me in for a quick grope and a brief kiss, then added his own swat to my buttocks. "Soft and spankable."

I giggled and went on my way to get dressed with an extra bounce in my walk. I could almost feel Eli's eyes on my bare ass.

I retrieved the sweatshirt and boxers I'd passed up in my early-morning mope and burrowed into them. Then I rummaged in Eli's drawer until I found a pair of thick wool socks. They went almost up to my knees. I didn't care how ridiculous I looked. I wanted to chase away the damp chill from being outside in the rain.

I closed my eyes and replayed the moment when my body had connected with Eli's, the sense of recognition and the way I'd wrapped myself around him. He'd held me, kissed me, carried me. Stripped me naked. Watched me enjoy another man's hands on the body he'd bared. Sent me to change into dry clothes.

His hand between my legs after Dal had touched me there had felt possessive, branding me with his touch. I felt warmer all over just thinking about it. I'd been cold and lost, and then I'd been held by both of them in turns. Offered heat, comfort, and a little sex play.

I didn't realize Eli had come in until I felt his hands on my shoulders. I closed my eyes and savored the warmth of his touch. He ran his hands down my sides, shaped themselves over my hips, drew me back until my butt nestled into his groin.

He didn't speak. Neither did I. He kissed the side of my neck and gave a soft laugh when I trembled in reaction.

I stood in his embrace, submissive, quiescent, his to command.

"If I told you to get on your knees right now, you'd do it," he murmured just below my ear.

"Yes."

"You'd let me slide these boxers down and stroke your pussy or spank your inviting ass. Maybe both. You'd wait to see if I'd open my pants, and then you'd let me fuck whatever hole I'd choose to take. Wouldn't you?"

"Yes." I arched my neck as I answered, baring the vulnerable curve, offering it to him. He nuzzled the soft expanse of skin.

"If I slid my hand between your legs and filled you with my fingers until you were soft and wet and open and then gave you to Dal to fuck, you'd spread your legs for him and obey me. And as a reward, maybe I'd give your sweet ass a reaming while you did it."

I made a soft moaning sound.

"Or maybe I'd order you to take Dal in your tight ass while I plunged my cock into your waiting pussy."

He teased the hollow of my collarbone with feather-soft kisses. "Maybe I'd tell you to get on your back, and spread your legs. Then the two of us would take turns settling on top of you and thrusting into you until you were almost ready to come, then pulling out and trading places. Making you wild for cock. Wild to come."

"Eli." I reached down and covered his hands with mine. "I'll do anything you want."

He raked the curve of my neck with his teeth. "Come and eat."

I clenched my jaw so I wouldn't scream in frustration, nodded, and wondered if he was deliberately trying to drive me insane or if that was just a fringe benefit.

TWENTY-TWO

How come you two weren't soaked to the skin?" I asked Dal. I still didn't trust myself to speak to Eli.

"We came inside before the rain really started to come down," Dal answered.

The implication that I didn't know enough to come in from the rain danced in his eyes. I stuck my tongue out at him. He just grinned. "Come closer and say that."

"I'm not trading tonsils with you when you have no sympathy for a girl who got stuck in a torrential downpour."

"Babe, this is a rainforest." Dal was openly laughing at me now. "What did you expect?"

I narrowed my eyes at him. "I don't know, but if it keeps raining that hard, I hope you're building a boat."

He winked. "I'll just hold onto you. You can be my flotation device."

I scowled at him. "My tits are not that big."

"Why are you so cranky? Didn't Eli give you any when he followed you into the bedroom?"

My face must've said volumes, because Dal scooted back and patted his lap. "Aw. Come here. I'll give you some."

"I don't want any," I grumbled. "Are you done with that plate? I need to start the dishes."

"You do too want some." Dal stood up with his plate and carried it over to the sink. He waited until I joined him with my plate and took it out of my hands. Then he crowded me against the counter and ran his hands under my sweatshirt.

"Do not." My voice was surly.

"Do, too." Dal searched out my breasts and ran his hands over them. My nipples hardened, and he grinned at me. "See?"

"It's a reflex." I glared at him.

"Oh, yeah? Then you won't mind if I check to see if you're getting wet." He worked a hand into my boxers while I wiggled and twisted in his hold. He was bigger and stronger, and in the end he had me pinned easily with one hand while he slid the other between my legs.

Dal gave me a triumphant look as he felt the evidence that proved him right. I ground my teeth. He laughed softly and slid a finger into my slick sheath. Then back out. Then in again, finger-fucking me while I tried and failed to break loose.

"Quit fighting me, or I'll have to spank you." I bucked and writhed and almost got free. Dal slipped his hand out of my shorts, yanked them down, and turned me to face the sink while he gave my bare ass a swat that made my sex clench. Then he pushed his body into mine as he worked his hand down my front and began to stroke my clit. "There. Isn't it better when you just stand there and take it?"

"No."

"Liar." Dal rocked his pelvis into my butt, letting me feel the hard ridge of his engorged cock, reminding me how good it had felt to take him anally while he worked my clit. "You want to come so bad."

"Do not." But my voice was breathy and I squirmed into him instead of away. I needed lust. I'd gotten weak walking too far, and that had sounded a warning in my head. Food was sustaining me, but it wasn't a complete replacement, and I wanted to feed on Dal's lust while he satisfied mine.

And perversely I wanted Dal to make me come while Eli sat watching us. I shifted my feet a little apart, making it easier for Dal to touch me.

"Your body says you do." Dal pushed a finger into me, then a second.

"I don't want you." I rocked into his hand.

"Wrong answer." He slid his hand out from between my legs, leaving my sex empty and burning to be filled. He pushed me down onto my knees on the floor, kneeled behind me and spanked me twice more. It only increased the state of my arousal, and we both knew it.

Then I heard him unzip and closed my eyes, waiting, my ass turned up in invitation, my sex swollen and slick. His hands closed on my hips, pulling me close. I felt his cock probe for entry and fought to evade him, knowing he'd overpower me and ride me down. Wanting him to. Needing him to.

My hips bucked and he wrestled me down until his body covered mine, pressing me into the floor. He forced my legs apart and got his hands under my hips, raising me up just enough to make the angle accommodating. While I tried to squirm away, he pinned me and drove inside in one deep, forceful thrust. A hot rush of lust accompanied the sensation of Dal's cock pushing into my sex harder and faster than I could comfortably accommodate.

I cried out, and rose up, and found Eli's eyes fixed on mine. Burning into mine.

He watched as Dal took me, fucking me hard and fast, and I started to come almost instantly.

Dal laughed low in triumph, feeling the telltale spasms gripping his invading penis. "That's what you wanted."

Yes. It was. He gave me just enough lust to strengthen me, and then he was coming, too, his cock jerking inside me, my inner muscles clenching around his shaft and milking it, prolonging the pleasure for both of us.

We collapsed together in a boneless heap, his cock still buried inside me. Dal crooned, "Good girl," and I laughed.

Eli clapped in sardonic appreciation for our performance and we both grinned up at him, sweaty and satisfied.

Then Dal pulled out of me, helped me stand up, and gave me a deep, tongue-tangling kiss. When he raised his head, he grinned into my flushed face. "Isn't that better?"

"Yes."

"*Yes* is the right word. Remember to say that next time and I won't have to spank you."

He pulled my boxers back up and patted my ass. Then I went to wash the dishes. Dal left. Eli brought his plate over to the counter and stood close enough behind me that I could feel the heat of his body.

"You pushed him into losing control for a minute."

I'd wondered if he could tell. Now I knew. "Am I going to be in trouble for that?"

"No. But he will be if he can't learn to remain in command of himself."

"If he can't learn to remain in command of himself, I'm the least of his worries," I pointed out.

Eli slid his hands around the front of me, cupping the weight of my breasts in his palms through the bulky material of the sweatshirt I wore. "I'm not worried about what you'll do to him, as long as I'm in command of you."

As if I needed a reminder. I arched into his hold, fully aware that he'd aroused me to begin with and then stepped back to watch the drama play out as Dal stepped in to give me what Eli withheld.

"Do you enjoy watching me?" I asked him.

"Yes. I like the way you look when you come. I like the way you surrender to sex." He pulled my back against his chest as he spoke.

I snuggled into him, then turned in his arms and wrapped mine around his waist, making it a full embrace.

"I like knowing that even though you just finished taking another cock between your legs, you'd spread them for mine."

I felt the hard evidence that told me he really did like that. "I think you're a control freak."

"You like it." Eli's knowing voice made me shiver. Yes, I did like it. I liked this odd connection between us. I liked my response to him. I wanted him to take me now, after he'd watched Dalen take me, watched me take my pleasure with another lover.

I tipped my face up for a kiss, and he took my mouth, claiming it until every breath was Eli. Then he lifted me onto the counter, tore away the boxers, spread my thighs wide, and took me until my body knew nothing else.

I woke up naked from the waist down, my thighs sticky from sex, and a smile on my face. Eli had carried me to his room and put me to bed when he'd finished screwing me mindless, and as far as I knew, the dishes were still piled in the sink, left undone while other matters took precedence.

I was fed, rested, and had an infusion of lust to fend off the treacherous weakness that had threatened me at the end of my walk. Dal had given me a fun and mutually satisfying round of pretend forced seduction. Eli had given me, well, something. Dominance. Intensity. When I had sex with Dal, it was about sex, and I could take the lead. When I opened my body to Eli, it was to be taken over and molded to his will. Him, I couldn't lead anywhere. At least, not so far.

A smart woman would prefer Dal's lighthearted sexual romping to Eli's focused assault on every barrier I might have until he'd won my complete surrender. But maybe I was a little on the dark side myself.

Maybe? A little? Try a lot, demon.

Okay, so no big surprise that Eli got my panties wet. He was dark and dangerous, and while Dal would hesitate to banish me, Eli wouldn't. What did it say about me that I liked giving it up for a man I knew would end me if he thought I posed a threat?

It wasn't low self-esteem. It was, in a twisty way, the opposite. Eli was a match for me, and I respected him for it. I also knew he wouldn't make me suffer. If my honorable enemy thought I represented a threat to the balance, he'd act to eliminate that threat, but he wouldn't be cruel.

Neither of them was cruel, in fact. Their personalities seemed unmarked by any tendency to use their strength or skill for sadistic ends.

Which didn't mean they couldn't do plenty of harm from good motives. That was the first step onto a well-worn road to hell: the sincere belief that the ends justified the means.

I liked them, both of them, and for a minute I didn't like myself very much for being the one to tempt them. But what options did I have? I couldn't just quit. Even if I could, Eli would still have to release me.

And then something else would take my place. I'd told Eli the truth—better the demon he knew. Especially since he had the upper hand with me. Did I want to risk Nick's sending in bigger guns?

No. I didn't.

Well, then, I'd just have to suffer being their sexually sated shared bedmate and trust Dal to learn better control with practice. Eli's control, I was beginning to believe, wouldn't break under nuclear attack. As for me, apparently I had no control, so it was a good thing they did.

Of course, I was a soulless succubus. I wasn't supposed to have control. I was supposed to be sex on two legs.

I rolled over onto my stomach and hugged the pillow that held Eli's scent and hoped that I could be his a little longer. It seemed like such a small thing, but it wasn't, and I knew it. How much time could I have left? A day, two?

I thought of the comfort of his arms around me in the rain, his warmth, his body imprinted in mine. Belonging to Eli, however temporarily, was an event I'd never experienced before and never would again. My enemy, my lover. The immovable object to my irresistible force.

Well, now I knew what happened when the two met. I wasn't able to move him. Maybe I wasn't all that irresistible.

Try harder, Nick had said. How? What tactic could I apply?

Since lying there wasn't bringing any deep insights, I got up and found the boxers lying at the foot of the bed. Eli must have put them there when he tucked me in. The sight made me smile.

I retrieved them and went to clean myself up. I washed my face and found a comb for my hair while I was at it. Then, composed and clothed, I went to clean up the kitchen on the theory that dull scrubbing would lead to brilliant thinking. Or if not, at least I'd be fulfilling my duties as pet demon in residence.

The problem, I decided when I'd stacked the last dish in the drainer and started to attack the counters and tabletop with my excess energy, was that it was hard to find answers when I didn't know the right questions.

If Eli was really incorruptible, I was wasting my time.

But everybody wanted something. He had to want something for himself, something besides doing his duty.

"What's your secret weakness?" I asked out loud. I knew from the contents of the freezer that it wasn't ice cream. In fact, there didn't seem to be evidence of any of the deadly sins cluttering up the house.

If either of them had a porn collection, I would have found it on my dusting and cleaning spree. The food choices didn't exactly appeal to gluttony. No bags of chips, no boxes of snack cakes. Everything was far too well maintained to indicate sloth, and as far as I could tell, Dal and Eli devoted more hours to working than most wage slaves.

The lack of perks and conveniences and the aged house in what had to be the direct opposite of a hot location for real estate said no to greed. Neither brother seemed envious of the other's abilities, and they openly enjoyed sharing me as their sex partner. No signs of anger-management issues that would lead to wrath.

Which left pride.

That one had real potential. Although how a demon who specialized in arousing lust was supposed to capitalize on it escaped me. Subtly attack his masculine pride as a lover? That was likely to turn him off, not turn him on.

Besides, how could I tell him he didn't do it for me when we both knew what a big fat lie that was?

I could see the scenario playing out like a bad movie. Me, dressed in a short plaid skirt, argyle socks and loafers and prim white blouse and nothing else. I frowned at the mental image and edited in a bra so my nipples weren't so visible.

Then I took it off again and wavered over the possible effect the outfit would have on Eli. Too obvious?

I decided there was no point in getting hung up on details and moved forward. I would be wearing an outfit designed to make him instantly hard. Eli would come in and see me and want me. He would slide his hand up under my skirt, but I would pull away. "Not tonight. I'm not in the mood."

At which point he would either laugh at me, give me an aspirin for the headache we both knew didn't exist, or simply spread a liberal coating of aphrodisiac over my sex and proceed to shag me rotten. While I moaned and came repeatedly.

Yeah, that would work. Not.

Eli was too practical to fall for that ploy, even if I could attempt it with a straight face. Telling him I wasn't interested was not the key to his pride.

This line of thinking seemed fruitless.

Except . . . maybe he prided himself overly much on his self-control.

TWENTY-THREE

I made it through the rest of the day without being laughed at by a dragon, drenched to the skin, or getting lost in the woods. That alone felt like progress. I did wander outside again, but I borrowed a rain slicker and stayed within sight of the house this time.

There was a whole lot of nature outside, I discovered, and a lot of it was disgusting. Snails. Slugs. Mud. Giant spots of mold creating polka-dot patterns of holes in plate-sized maple leaves that had fallen to the ground.

Okay, maybe I was just cranky. Maybe nature grew on you, like the moss that seemed to cover every surface that would hold still for it and a few that wouldn't.

I slouched into the rain slicker and kicked at a fallen fir cone. I wasn't incapable of amusing myself. I wasn't dependent on the presence of my captor to feel complete or calm.

Not that I felt all that calm when Eli was around. Crazed and heated and mindless with pleasure didn't really add up to calm. He wasn't exactly soothing company. He provided a whole lot of stimulation.

So then, I was feeling the absence of that stimulation. That made sense. All that intensity, and then it was just me and the snails. How could I adjust from having the dial turned all the way up to high and then shut off? No wonder I felt at a loose end.

Besides, how could I do what I was there to do if he kept disappearing? I even had a plan, sort of. Well, not so much a plan as a line of approach. Still, it was something, but I couldn't implement it because Eli was off doing . . . whatever he did.

Slaughtering demons, maybe.

That thought made me shiver. I really hated the idea of being one of the enemy.

What if, I thought, circling a tree trunk. What if there weren't so many complications surrounding us?

I mentally pictured the two of us naked in a large, comfortable bed. In my complication-free fantasy, Dal joined us. Eli stretched out on his back, I stretched out on him, face to face, and Dal came behind me. They filled me.

The three of us would probably look damn silly from the viewpoint of an outside observer. All those body parts straining to fit together. Naked butts making humping motions.

I laughed out loud.

"What's so funny?"

I turned toward the sound of Dal's voice and grinned at him. "Sex."

"Not if you're doing it right." He walked up beside me and kept pace with me as I circled the tree trunk again.

"We've laughed a time or two, and I think we did it right," I pointed out.

Dal hooked an arm around my waist and pulled me into his side. "You have to keep a sense of humor about sex, sure. Like everything else in life. Make it too serious and it gets out of perspective, until it appears distorted and you can't see it clearly."

Maybe that explained my lack of perspective when it came to Eli. I'd wondered what it would be like to be with him without all the complications, but without those complications our paths would never have crossed. I sighed.

"Buck up, Beelzebabe. I have something you'll like." Dal kissed the top of my head and pulled me toward the house. I went with him. I'd had enough of communing with nature, and besides, if Dal thought I'd like something he was probably right.

"Do I get a hint?" I asked, matching my steps to his. Dal shortened his stride to make it easy for me, and I thought of Eli, who made me work to keep up. Even a simple thing like walking side by side revealed their differences.

"Yes. Chocolate."

My mouth watered. "What kind?"

"What if I said the edible body paint kind?" Dal waggled his brows at me.

I blinked at him. "Is it?"

"No, but if it was, would you let me lick it off you?"

We'd reached the door by then, and Dal dropped back a step to let me go inside first.

I turned to grin at him over my shoulder. "No. I'd lick it off you."

· It turned out to be chocolate-chip cookies, and he was right. I did like them. Soft, chewy, warm from the oven. They smelled incredible and tasted even better. Rich, dark chocolate melting on my tongue. Bliss.

"Did you make these?" I asked Dal after I'd swallowed.

"Not in the traditional way, but yes."

I assumed the nontraditional way involved chants and incantations. If magic could produce cookies like these, I fully agreed that the world was in sore need of more magic.

And really, did it matter how they got here? I decided that it was best not to look a gift cookie in the mouth and ate another one. Dal poured a glass of milk and handed it to me, and I gave him a you-have-to-be-kidding look.

"You dip the cookie in the milk," he said, demonstrating with his own.

I followed suit and wasn't sure if it was truly better that way or not, so we began to implement a systematic test approach, where we ate cookies singly followed by drinks of milk, dunked cookies, alternated undunked bites with dunked, and by the time I'd polished off half a dozen cookies my stomach was full and sore from laughing.

"So tell me why sex is funny," Dal prodded when I finished my milk and leaned back.

"No. The moment is lost," I said.

"Chicken."

"Ba-gock," I agreed, mimicking barnyard fowl. "Although you really can't say I'm yellow now that I've taken that rain slicker off."

He gave me an affronted look. "That was my rain slicker. I'll thank you to not attach any suggestion of cowardice to the color."

I turned to face him and propped my feet in his lap, so I could get more comfortable. "It was a brave slicker and it kept me very dry. Have you built the boat yet?"

Dal shook his head at me as he captured my feet in his hands. "If a little rain worries you, it's a good thing we're not having any wind along with it. You'd be hiding under the bed." He tickled my arches, but I was too relaxed to fight it.

"I would not. I'd be hiding in the bed, under you."

"Would you be facing me, or on your tummy under me?" Dal asked, giving me a hot look.

"Both are equally nice."

"Nice." He looked disgruntled. "I dragged you down on the kitchen floor and nailed you while you tried to get away. Was that nice?"

"Very." I smiled in remembered satisfaction.

"Women."

I stirred myself enough to climb over into his lap, straddling him so we were face to face. "I'm a demon. Remember?"

"I remember."

I leaned against his shoulder and he ran an idle hand under my sweatshirt. I shifted to make it easy for his hand to fit itself over my breast. I liked his good-natured teasing and groping. His cookies were good, too. I'd miss him, and not just because he made sex fun. I hated the thought of never seeing him again, losing both of them when it was over.

I cuddled into him and sighed. He rubbed his chin against the top of my head. "He'll be back soon," Dal murmured.

"I wasn't sighing for Eli," I said.

"Ah. That was for me?" He thumbed my nipple and snuggled me closer.

"Yes." I pressed into his hand, and said, "You lusted earlier. That worries me."

"You're a succubus. You like lust."

I leaned back so I could look into his eyes. "Of course I like it. I subsist on it. I need it. But I don't like it if it leads to losing your soul. You need your soul."

He frowned at me. "Aren't you playing for the wrong team to give that speech?"

"If anybody is entitled to give this speech, it's me. I screwed up and I've been paying for my mistake since the Norman invasion." I blew out a breath. "Look, you're a bonus, you're not my assignment, so it's not a direct conflict of interest for me to be blunt. What you told me about humans needing magic—if that was right, then you're important. You have to master your lust."

"I know." He kissed the tip of my nose. "That's why I'm practicing so diligently with you."

"Practice harder," I muttered.

"Babe. You care." He grinned at me and kissed me. And because I did care, I kissed him back and his heat washed over me. Our mouths parted and tongues met. He bunched the sweatshirt up and filled his hands with my breasts. I rocked into him and felt my sex rub the hard swell of his penis through the layers of his pants and my shorts.

He caressed and stroked the sensitive undersides of my breasts, the rosy aureoles, and the hollow of my cleavage. His touch was so warm, so welcome. His liking for me was evident in the way his hands moved on me, and so was his healthy appreciation for my body.

Friends with benefits, I thought, and smiled against his lips.

"Is the sex funny now?" Dal asked, punctuating the words with kisses.

"No. Nice."

He growled and slid his hands down to cup and squeeze my buttocks, grinding me onto his cock. "I'll show you nice. I'll ream your sweet ass."

"Promises." I laughed into his open mouth, and he began a thrusting rhythm into the open cradle of my hips that made me groan and move with him.

He began working the loose boxers down my hips, baring my butt. I shifted up and off his lap, standing long enough to get free of the shorts and kick them away. I pulled off the sweatshirt and tossed that aside, too. Dal took the opportunity to get his pants open, but he left them on, tugged down far enough to be out of the way.

"Not even going to stop to take your pants off?" I asked.

"Nope. Come sit on this."

I sat with my back to his chest and my legs spread wide, my thighs to the outside of his. He adjusted my position, leaning me forward to get the angle he wanted and kissed my back as he reached around to tease my clit.

He made sure I was slick and eager, then eased his cock inside, entering me by inches, pulling me down onto his shaft in a slow slide. My sex stretched around him, enclosed him. His heat warmed me from the inside out. He began a gentle rhythm, rocking into me while his hand between my legs alternately rubbed my mound in a circle or stroked my clit.

When our bodies began to take on a more urgent motion, he put his hands on my hips and lifted me up, sliding out of me on the next downstroke. He pressed the head of his cock against my anus and pulled me down as he pushed into me, slick and warm from my body.

"Call me nice now," he challenged me, grinding against my ass once he was seated all the way inside. The chair creaked in protest but continued to support our combined weights.

"It feels so nice," I sighed, and squirmed in his lap.

"Yeah, it does." His hands roved all over my body, free to touch me easily while he took me from behind. He toyed with my breasts, pinched my nipples, tugged at my navel ring, reached down to tease my clit. "It feels damn nice to fuck your hot, tight ass."

"Really. Nice," I agreed, my breath catching.

"Fucking great." He began to thrust harder, his hand on my clit more insistent. He felt so good inside me, taking me. I felt my body seize up as I teetered on the verge of orgasm. Dal felt it and gave a sexy laugh, the sound full of masculine confidence. "You want to come now."

"No, I don't," I said, biting my lower lip.

"Do, too." He applied pressure with his hand and began to thrust deeper and I came. A few strokes later, he swelled inside me, filling my ass even tighter, reaming it harder, and then his cock was jerking as he came in a series of hard spurts.

He hadn't slipped once, I realized as he continued to cuddle me in his lap. He'd taken me two ways and even the primal pleasure of anal sex hadn't made him leak lust.

Practice was making perfect, but I hoped selfishly that he wasn't quite done practicing yet. Meanwhile, it was just us in the kitchen redolent with the warm vanilla scent of freshly baked cookies, our bodies still joined, Dal's hands on me in lazy afterplay.

I felt his lips on my cheek and turned to angle my head into his kiss that tasted as sweet and rich as chocolate.

TWENTY-FOUR

By the time Eli came in, Dal and I had moved to the living room so I could be closer to the source of heat. Dal had a fire crackling in the woodstove. I stretched in front of it on my belly. Dal sat crosslegged on the floor. Between us lay the chessboard. I played black to his white.

Dal was trying to talk me out of castling, both of us laughing over his ridiculous explanations when we both knew he just wanted to make me second-guess my strategy so he could win.

"Enjoying yourselves?"

Eli's deep, harsh voice made my head come up and turn toward him. "Yes," I said, still smiling. "Even though Dal is a sore loser."

"Finish your game." He stalked out and I blinked, all laughter gone.

"Was I supposed to make dinner or something?" I asked Dal. "Or were you, and I distracted you?"

"Why do you think Eli in a foul mood has anything to do with you?" Dal swept up my knight with his bishop and I groaned at the attack I hadn't seen coming. "Check. I told you not to castle."

"I don't know. Something about the way he came in and glowered at me gave me that idea." I stared at the board and realized that Dal had me in three more moves no matter what I did to maneuver out of it. I tipped my king over, surrendering.

"Giving up so easily?" Dal's face had gone serious and I was sure he wasn't talking about chess now.

Two sayings collided in my head. *Pride goes before a fall. The bigger they are, the harder they fall.* Eli was big and proud, but could I make him fall?

"Did something happen today?" I asked, not answering his question.

"Many things. We had sex. Maybe you've forgotten."

"Um, no. I have not forgotten that you spanked me, screwed me twice, and then gave it to me in the ass." I wiggled my butt as evidence that my memory was just fine. "I meant, did something happen today that could make Eli particularly touchy toward someone who might be, oh, a demon?"

"No more than usual."

That was helpful. I gave Dal a disgruntled look and got to my feet.

"Oh, sure. Go on, leave me," he said with a mock sigh. "Forget all about the one who fed you cookies and fucked you so nicely."

I dropped into his lap, facing him with my legs straddling his hips, and rubbed my breasts against his chest. "You do fuck so very nicely. Don't think I don't appreciate it."

"You're not bad yourself." Dal filled his hands with my butt and squeezed.

I shook my head. "I am very, very bad." I wrapped my legs around his waist and tightened them so that our masculine and feminine parts pushed together. I nipped at his earlobe with the sharp edge of my teeth and murmured, "Which is why it feels so good."

Dal laughed. I got up and headed to the kitchen, leaving him to put away the chess pieces. I had a plan to pursue, and also I was curious about what had Mr. Immovable on edge.

Eli wasn't where I expected to find him, so I checked his room next. He closed the heavy armoire just as I came in. Without turning around, he said, "Get naked."

Oookay. Not what I expected to hear, but so far my experience had proven that naked plus Eli equaled fun for everyone. Even if I hadn't been bound, I wouldn't have objected to his plan.

I got naked. Fast. Then I waited for him to turn around, look at the naked succubus in his bedroom, something. I was starting to shift my weight from foot to foot when he took off his clothes.

Promising. Although it was starting to bother me that he hadn't looked at me once.

When he turned around, I took in the view he presented

me with and appreciated every inch. "Wow. Is that for me? I didn't get you anything."

Eli didn't respond to my teasing with so much as a twitch of his lips. He walked toward me and something about his grim silence made me want to back up. I stood my ground, instead. When he reached me, he picked me up. "Wrap your legs around my waist."

I did. He turned and backed me against the closest wall. The rough surface behind me made an interesting contrast to the smooth flesh touching me in front. He stared into my face, with that dangerous edge glittering in his eyes. I felt my mouth go dry and for a minute I was more than a little afraid. "Eli?"

He shifted and I felt his cock probing at my sex. "What?" His voice sounded harsh and guttural.

I swallowed and tried to make my body relax, but being nervous made me tighten up. At the same time, the close physical contact had me reacting to the heat of his skin and the scent of him. His broad head pushed between my legs, and the visceral memory of pleasure coaxed a response.

"Kiss me," I whispered.

His eyes turned darker, and his mouth came down on mine in a hard, bruising demand. I clung to him and surrendered to the kiss, to the taste and feel of him. I felt my body softening for his, my nipples tightening and my breasts swelling as they were crushed against his chest.

The punishing pressure of his mouth on mine eased a little, turning by degrees into something more sensual, more an exchange than the one-sided taking it started as.

"Eli," I breathed against his mouth. My throat caught. My

legs tightened around him, urging him closer. He began to thrust into me, working his length in by inches, rocking back and forth in hard, urgent movements that drove him deeper and deeper until I was stretched and filled to capacity.

He lifted his head and stared into my eyes in silence as he fucked me against the wall. His cock pounded into me and I held on, straining to accept him as hard and fast as he wanted to take me. The position gave him all the control and made me helplessly receptive.

It was primal and exciting, with a little thrill of uncertainty. I couldn't read him to begin with, and in this mood I was even more clueless than usual.

He pulled out so suddenly the shock was almost pain.

I stared at him, stunned and confused. "What?"

He let me slide down the wall and let go of me when my feet touched the floor and turned his back on me again. He started to walk away.

Walking away? As in, leaving me to suffer? I narrowed my eyes at the wall of his back and practically shouted, "Oh, hell, no."

He paused and looked back over his shoulder. "Stay naked. I may want you again."

I picked up the nearest projectile, which turned out to be the sweatshirt I'd borrowed from him. I wadded it up and hurled it at his back. It was too soft to be very effective, but it was what I had within reach. "You may want me again? What if I don't want you, you prick?"

I realized too late that I'd lost my temper, but it was truly lost, so even though I knew I was going to regret it, I searched for something else to throw.

"You're angry." Eli's hands closed on my wrists, keeping me from grabbing a book to hurl at him next.

"No," I snarled, sarcasm dripping from my voice. "I always yell and throw things when I'm happy."

"You're mine to treat as I will." He sounded hard and cold, and it hurt me to hear that tone from him. The hurt made me want to react defensively, offensively, to hurt him back.

I closed my eyes and clenched my jaw. *Breathe. Breathe. Don't hit him, you might break your hand.* I finally said through grinding teeth, "Let. Go. Of. Me."

"I will touch you when and where and how I wish. And I will set you aside when it suits me."

I saw red. I'd always thought it was a figure of speech, but a scarlet haze filled my vision and for a minute I was so furious I couldn't even breathe. I twisted free and probably succeeded only because he wasn't expecting it, then drove my fist into his belly.

It hurt. As I'd already warned myself it would.

Pain had a way of clearing my head, and the first thing I realized was that there was more to this than met the eye.

"Sorry," I said, rubbing my aching hand. "Just a little frustrated, here. I imagine you are, too."

"Not really." Eli released me and turned away from me again.

Fine. I'd talk to his back. "Maybe you want something other than sex from me right now."

"Sex is what you're for." He started to dress again, every movement utterly controlled and even. Dismissive.

A minute earlier I would've tried to separate his head

from his shoulders for saying that. Even if it was true, there was no need to be rude. Good thing he hadn't said it a minute earlier.

"Sex is more than fucking," I pointed out. "Sex is inseparable from life. It's a basic need, a basic drive. Something you might have a particularly strong need for after a bad day. You reached for me, so if sex is what I'm for, what do you want, Eli?"

"Nothing. Go play chess with Dalen."

The compulsion to obey him pushed me toward the door. I didn't want to go. Especially not now, when I might actually be seeing a crack in his self-control. "Don't send me away, Eli. You want me for something, or you wouldn't have held me against the wall and rammed your cock into me."

He turned to give me an unreadable look. "Are you refusing to go when I say I don't want you?"

I'd reached the doorway by now, but I was dragging my feet and going as slowly as I could. "You do want me. Let me stay."

He crossed his arms over his chest. "I gave you an order." His voice was so full of lethal threat that it sent chills down my spine.

It clicked, then. "You're trying to protect me. From yourself." I shook my head at him. "I don't need protecting, Eli. Let me stay."

"Stay, then." His voice and his expression were entirely unwelcoming.

I came back into the bedroom and closed the door. "Don't mind if I do."

"You may wish you'd gone." Eli stared at me and I saw a muscle work in his jaw.

"Can I make a suggestion?" I tried to make my tone mild, not exasperated.

"It would seem I can't stop you unless I order you to silence."

I couldn't prevent the smile that provoked. "I won't annoy you with a lot of chatter. But maybe you'd like me to give you a back rub."

That actually struck him speechless. The silence dragged on until I walked up to him and laid my hand on his folded arms. "Come on, Eli. What could it hurt?"

He uncrossed his arms, dislodging my hand. "Not five minutes ago you were violently angry with me, and now you want to give me a back rub."

I shrugged. "I have a short attention span."

Eli didn't exactly smile, but his expression softened infinitesimally. I took it as a hopeful sign.

He stretched out on the bed, and I claimed a spot beside him. I put my hand between his shoulders and stroked down the line of his spine, glided back up, down, smoothed gradually widening circles along his shoulders. The tension in his body eased by degrees.

"I shouldn't have called you a prick," I said as I tried to soothe him with touch.

"Why not? You meant it." Eli didn't sound upset about that, just matter of fact.

"No, I didn't. Not really. You're a lot of things, Eli, but you aren't a prick. At least, not on purpose."

"Damned with faint praise."

I sighed and laid my cheek on his upper arm, feeling like I was taking a daring liberty. "I was frustrated because you started something and then you stopped. And yes, you have the right to change your mind. Yes, I am bound to you. If you tell me to get naked one minute and to get lost the next, I have to obey. Although that doesn't mean I'll go quietly."

"You haven't gone at all." Eli's sardonic tone made me grin.

"Because you didn't really want me to leave." I rubbed my cheek against his bare skin, enjoying the intimacy of pillowing my head on his biceps, having the freedom to explore the broad, muscled expanse of his back.

I cuddled up to his side, pressing into him to warm myself with his body heat, and he permitted it. I enjoyed the luxury of touching him at my leisure, the simple pleasure of feeling him under my hand.

He rolled onto his back after a few minutes and pulled me onto his chest with one arm. "You should have gone."

I nuzzled his chest and kissed him over his heart. "Why? Would you really rather have a session with Mr. Hand than me?"

"Mr. Hand doesn't talk."

I took the hint and fell silent. I reached down and wrapped my hand around his engorged shaft. He didn't tell me to stop, so I stroked him, moving my hand up and down, exerting firm, steady pressure. If he wanted manual release, I didn't mind giving it to him.

"Put your mouth on me." Eli's voice was low and rough, and it sent a sensual shiver through me.

I slid down to pillow my head on the muscled wall of his stomach and took the head of his cock into my mouth. I tasted myself on him blended with his own salty, musky flavor. The intimacy pleased me. I wanted him to taste of me, to carry some trace of me on his body. He'd imprinted himself on mine. It seemed only fair that I should mark him in some way, too.

I licked and sucked him while I worked him with my hand. I cupped his balls with the other, feeling the heaviness of them in my palm. Filling my mouth and my hands with him sent waves of heat rolling through me.

Eli slid his hands into my hair and wound his fingers through the strands, tugging. Not hard enough to hurt, but exerting pressure I couldn't ignore. I let him urge my head up, away.

"On your back. Now."

Ah, such sweet talk. I rolled onto my back and opened my legs. Eli was inside me before I finished getting into position. He fisted his hands in my hair, pinned me with his weight, penetrated me with rough force. "I want to make it hurt," he growled.

"Kinky." I moved under him, urging him on.

He gave a short, hard laugh. "You have the survival instinct of a lemming."

"Yeah, but going over that cliff can be a real adrenaline rush."

And when we finally went over it together, it was.

TWENTY-FIVE

I sat on Eli's lap while we ate dinner. My chair was too hard. Not that I was complaining. He'd made it hurt so good, I didn't mind paying the price afterward.

He'd dressed me in a Betty Boop T-shirt that came down to my hips and soft white cotton underwear, both magicked up for the occasion. I'd raised my brows at him while I stood there wearing nothing but the white briefs, but he'd just smiled and looked at me with enough heat to curl my toes. So I wore them.

The fabric felt comfortable on my skin, which Eli had abraded in various places. I was pretty sure a bra would be unbearable right now. Still, it had been worth it.

He kept me close, his touch possessive and something else. I wasn't sure what, but since he'd worked his mood off getting sweaty with me there was some shift in equilibrium. Maybe he felt guilty about the hard use he'd given my body. Not that I'd given him cause to feel anything but smug. The way I'd come screaming should've told him how much I'd enjoyed myself.

His self-control had not cracked, although I'd certainly encouraged him to surrender to lust. He'd remained completely and absolutely in command despite my efforts.

I should've been depressed about that, but I figured I'd given it my best shot. I'd stuck to him when I thought he might be vulnerable to a little pressure, but Eli was immune to the dark side, evidently. Not that I wanted him to lose his soul. Still, it did underscore the distance between us. I was on the dark side and I had no immunity to him at all.

I toyed with my food but didn't have much appetite. Too many cookies. Too much milk. Too much awareness of time running out. I'd been with Eli much, much longer than any assignment ever lasted. I'd been with both of them long enough to grow attached, to imagine what it would be like to belong somewhere, to somebody, and not always alone. Always on the job.

Maybe it didn't have to be that way, though. Maybe after this I could hook up with a nice incubus. We could meet whenever our schedules meshed. Assuming I survived.

But I hated that idea. I didn't want a demon. I wanted Eli the way a three-year-old wants a cookie, and knowing I couldn't have him did not make me feel less like throwing myself on the ground sobbing and kicking.

Maybe we'd both survive. I contemplated that thought as
I leaned my cheek against his shoulder. The cage match of Eli
the immovable and Edana the formerly irresistible had to end
at some point, but what if he survived and didn't banish me?
What if he just . . . didn't release me?

Keep me, I wanted to say. *I won't be any trouble.*

There would be trouble, though. Nick wouldn't just
shrug and say, "Oh, well, it's hard to keep good help." I didn't
want to bring more trouble on Dalen and Eli's heads. They
didn't deserve that.

Eli shifted me on his lap and tightened his arm around
me. "You're not eating."

"I guess I'm not very hungry." I leaned forward and took
another bite. Then I started pushing the food around on my
plate again.

"Demons are always hungry."

Oh, wasn't that the truth. I hungered. But what I hungered for wasn't food, and my appetite for lust could never be
sated.

"Excuse us." Eli scooted back and stood with me cradled
against his chest.

Dal gave us a look that was hard to read. "Should I be
concerned?"

"This doesn't concern you."

That seemed a little rude to me. I winked at Dal and
blew him a kiss to let him know he didn't need to worry as
Eli carried me off.

He took me into the bedroom again and sat with me still
in his arms, in his lap. "I'm not proud of my behavior," he
finally said. "You may be a demon. Nevertheless, you were

an innocent when you came to me and I made you my whore."

Whatever I'd thought he might say, that wasn't it. Surprise robbed me of speech for a minute. Where had this come from?

I remembered him being disturbed by hearing that I'd never known a man in either form that first time he'd touched me. He'd said he wouldn't release me. As if he should've been expected to?

"Exaggerate much?" I finally said. "You didn't put me out on a mattress with my legs open while you charged admission to the general public. You did not make me a whore. You made me your lover, and you asked me to take Dal as my lover, too. I agreed. And, by the way, I think that's worked out really well."

"The fact that you enjoy fucking him doesn't exonerate me."

Wow. If only I were a guilt demon, his ass would be mine. Unfortunately, this guilt trip was of no benefit to me whatsoever, and it stood to carry him off on a wave of noble self-sacrifice that would guarantee I'd never get close enough to tempt him again. No lust. No sex. No Eli. If he released me, my punishment for failure could start immediately.

"The fact that I enjoy fucking him means I am grateful to you for being thoughtful enough to share," I said in a mild tone. "Demons have insatiable appetites. For everything. Trust me, being asked to do two men has not been a hardship for me."

I sat up and pushed back so that I could look him in the eye. "I do think you owe me an apology, though. I like having sex with you. I like having sex with Dalen. I like having sex with both of you together at the same time. I like it rough, I like it straight, I like it in the ass, I like giving head. In what way does any of that make me your whore?"

"I left you no choice." Eli's face was hard and closed, and dammit, if I couldn't break through to him, this was going to be it. The end. I could feel it.

"The hell you didn't. You asked me. I consented. Willingly. Damn near gleefully, to be honest. A choice I have not for one minute regretted." Frustration boiled up and I found myself waving my hands, trying to emphasize my point.

"Dammit, Eli, you're acting like I came to you as some naïve, sheltered maiden. Did you forget I'm a succubus? I've been a sex expert for centuries. There is no kink or variation under the sun I'm not familiar with. And the implication that you're some loathsome monster forcing me into sexual servitude is insulting to both of us. To all three of us, in fact."

He stared at me in silence for a long moment. Finally he said, "You're right, I do owe you an apology."

"Apology accepted." I snuggled into him and said, "I know what this is really about. You think you were too rough with me. So let me remind you that you tried to send me away and I wouldn't go. Also remember that I am not some fragile human."

He touched my hair with an almost tentative hand, then cupped the back of my head in an intimate, protective gesture that twisted my heart. "I was too rough with you. And I enjoyed it."

I shook my head at his stark admission. "I enjoyed it, too. And since you didn't put a ball-gag in my mouth, I was perfectly capable of telling you to ease up or be more gentle if it got to be too much."

"Would you have said anything?" He slid his hand down to cup my chin and tilted my face up to his.

I rolled my eyes at him. "When you deprived me of rough, up-against-the-wall sex, I threw things and yelled. Have I ever done anything to make you think I have trouble expressing myself?"

Eli's mouth twitched. "You are expressive."

"There, see?" I kissed the corner of his mouth. "Eli, maybe I'm a little bit of a nympho with you two, but I've been deprived for so long. Don't think less of me for wanting to take all I can get."

That seemed to surprise him. "I don't think less of you. I thought less of myself for abusing my position of power."

I let out a breath at that unexpected hit and put my head back on his shoulder. "Ouch. From the beginning you paid me the supreme compliment of treating me like an equal. You thought I was a serious problem when your brother thought I was a joke. Please don't insult me by thinking of me as a powerless victim now."

He was silent for a minute. "I don't know how to think of you," he finally said. "You defy classification."

"Ah. That I like." I put my hand against his and our fingers interlocked. His was so much larger and stronger, but I liked the way we fit together.

"Look at your hand. So tiny." Eli brought our linked hands to his mouth and kissed mine. The softest caress, a butterfly brush of his lips on the delicate skin covering the back of my hand, and I felt it to the depths of my being.

"Look at yours," I said. "So masculine and powerful. Able to wield a sword or cast a spell or give me unspeakable pleasure." I tugged it toward me, until I could press a kiss to his knuckles. Emotion clogged my throat. I wanted to rain kisses over every part of him, before it was too late and I was gone.

"Unspeakable, hmm?"

"Mmm." I smiled against his skin and hoped he couldn't feel the tremor in it.

I closed my eyes against the sting of tears and tried to memorize everything about this moment. The sound of his heartbeat, the heat of him, our hands joined together. The way his body surrounded mine, his legs under me, arms around me, his chest bracing me. I could hear rain falling on the roof in a distant drumming. A simple moment, but I would have given anything to make it last.

It couldn't last, though, and knowing that made my chest ache.

"We should go finish dinner," I said, trying to sound lighter than I felt. "If we stay in here much longer, Dal might not leave us anything."

"If we stay in here, I might not leave Dal anything." The sexual promise in Eli's voice sent a shimmer of heated anticipation through me.

He kissed the top of my head and then stood with me still in his arms and carried me back to the kitchen. I leaned in, determined to enjoy the ride.

Dal was waiting at the table. His eyes fixed on mine and whatever he saw in my face must have satisfied him, because he went from an alert posture to relaxing back with an easy smile.

"You couldn't get through a meal without having to stop for a quickie? And you didn't even let me watch. I'm hurt."

I smiled back. "What can I say? I'm insatiable."

"Good thing there's two of us, then." Dal winked at me. "We'll keep you satisfied."

I was counting on it. I wanted both of them, for as long as I could handle the two of them together. I wanted them individually. I wanted to take everything they could give me tonight.

Meanwhile, it felt good just to be with them. The two brothers talking, Dal teasing, forks clinking on plates. I looked around the outdated kitchen and thought how different it looked to me now. I'd become familiar with every surface of this room during my bad-mood-inspired cleaning. Which had ended on such a high note when Eli came in and re-claimed his boxers before claiming me.

The chair Dal sat in had held both of us earlier while we gave it a good stress-test.

Dal caught my eye across the table. My thoughts must've shown in my expression, because I saw a knowing glint there. He creaked the chair, repeating the sound it had made while he held me on his lap and thrust into me. I laughed.

"What?" Eli asked.

"The chair creaks," Dal said. His eyes were still holding mine, and the shared look was enough to convey the shared memory even without the smiles.

I'd had a lot of good times in this room. I'd also pissed off a witch, nearly been decapitated by an angel, strained my eyes finding all of Eli's buttons after I'd popped them off his shirt, and answered the door for a dragon.

The kitchen saw a lot of action. No wonder people called it the center of the home.

"He did you in that chair, didn't he?" Eli murmured against my ear.

"Mmm-hmm." I tilted my head to encourage the attentions of his mouth. He nibbled at the curve of my neck just below my ear. "Two ways." Not that I was bragging. Much.

"Did he tie you to it?" Eli's whisper was dark and deep and unreadable, but his words gave me a thrill.

"No. Are you going to?"

"I'm considering it. I'd have you naked and spread-eagled, your ankles tied to the chair legs. Your arms tied behind you. Maybe I'd blindfold you so you wouldn't know which one of us was touching you, or whose cock you were tasting."

His low, growling voice sent a charge down my spine that ended between my legs. Or maybe that was the touch of his lips along the cord of my neck.

"I'd know," I told him on a breath of sound. My imagination was caught by the idea of identifying my lovers by their taste and texture, their shape and their scent, the way they moved.

"Would you?" Eli captured my earlobe with his teeth and gave a sharp tug before he released the soft skin. "Do you want to put that to the test?"

Yes, I did. It'd be far too easy to be a real challenge and fun enough that it wouldn't matter; playing the game would be its own reward. Although one possibility crossed my mind that could make it very difficult for me to win. The brothers had an unfair advantage.

"You couldn't use magic tricks to disguise yourselves,"

I said. "No changing shape or anything like that. It'd be cheating."

"No tricks," Eli agreed. He raked his teeth down the curve of my neck, then kissed my nape. A soft, chaste touch of his lips, in contrast to the erotic game he described.

I shifted in his lap as a twinge of discomfort made itself felt. "Um. I might need that rose scented stuff again if we're going to play blind man in the buff. We were very energetic about working up an appetite for dinner."

"Blind man's bluff," Dal corrected me. "Are we going to play a game?"

"I knew that. I meant to say it my way." I winked at Dal. "Eli wants to play a game that sounds hotter than naked Twister. One blindfolded blonde tied to a chair. Two mystery men. Blind man's bluff, the sex-rated version."

"Are you up to it after being so energetic?" Dal asked.

"I will be, with a little help from some healing balm—slash—aphrodisiac." I gave him a naughty smile. "Want to play?"

He pretended to consider it. "Would there be naked breasts?"

"Yes." My nipples perked up just thinking about what he was likely to do to them.

"Possible blow job?"

"Mm, yes. I've sucked and swallowed you both. I should be able to tell the difference between you by taste." I was getting hot just thinking about running my tongue along the sensitive ridge of one head, then another, licking two shafts, taking two cocks into my mouth by turns.

"Anything off limits?"

I turned to look up at Eli for the answer to Dal's question. I was curious about the answer, too.

"She'll be tied sitting down, so no anal," Eli said. "Although we can always move her from the chair to my bed if she wants to try to identify us that way."

I squirmed in Eli's lap as I imagined being taken by them from behind, one by one, with only the shape and feel of the penis penetrating me and each man's technique to tell me who was riding my ass.

"I'd be willing," I said, trying to look demure. As if I wasn't sitting there squirming against the dampening crotch of my briefs with my hard nipples clearly outlined against the thin cotton T-shirt I wore.

"Babe, you're practically coming in your panties already," Dal teased. "You'll be too busy moaning and getting off to keep your mind on the game."

"I can get off and keep my mind on the game, too. It's called multitasking." I grinned at him and wiggled my butt against the hard swell of Eli's cock. I couldn't wait to lick it again and again like an X-rated lollipop while I pretended not to be sure who the owner was.

TWENTY-SIX

Eli decided to blindfold me and tie me to the chair first. Then they'd apply the magical balm that would enable the three of us to make like minks without my getting inconveniently sore and having to declare some section of the playground off-limits.

I didn't mind. That made the treatment part of the game instead of a delaying factor.

But with the decision to play made, the men weren't in a rush to begin. We decided to move to the living room with the chair near the woodstove for warmth. In the process of rearranging things, both of them found excuses to pat my butt or brush my breast.

Maybe I wasn't seducing them and reducing them to a state of mindless lust, but they certainly did it to me with ease. Dal's hand sliding over my erect nipple made me wiggle like a puppy anticipating a walk, and Eli's possessive hand on my ass made my knees weak. When he ran a finger along the lower curve of my butt, following the edge of the cotton panties, I closed my eyes and bit my lip to keep from groaning.

Dal came up beside me while I clutched the chair's back for balance as Eli moved away again. "You really are going to come before we even get you naked."

He wrapped an arm around my waist and hugged me, then shaped his hand to the curve of my hip and used his hold to urge me to turn toward him. My breasts brushed his chest as he bent his head to mine. He kissed me while his hands wandered from my hips to my waist and then up my ribcage.

Mmm. I closed my eyes and melted into the welcome warmth of his lips tasting mine like I was a treat he wanted to savor. His touch reinforced the message, teasing and hinting at things to come. Dal wasn't rushing to a goal. He was settling in to enjoy the journey.

"My turn." Eli's voice came from behind me. Dal ended the kiss and gave my waist a little squeeze. Then he stepped back, freeing me.

I turned and offered my mouth to Eli. He was thorough, and by the time he slid his tongue free of mine, I was flushed and breathing too fast. He'd only pressed his hands against the lower curve of my back to urge me closer while we kissed, but he might as well have ravished me on the spot.

I wanted another kiss, but I knew if he kissed me one more time it wouldn't stop there. Since he was going to make me wait for it while our game played out, I didn't try to bring his head down to mine again.

I couldn't help contrasting his you-are-mine-and-soon-I-will-have-you-again kiss with the take-no-prisoners oral assault he'd challenged me to lay on him. He hadn't asked me if I could do better since. My lips quirked up at the thought.

"Something funny?" Eli asked.

"She thinks sex is funny," Dal volunteered.

"I was just remembering the first time we kissed," I said. "You asked if it was the best I could do."

"I knew you could do better." Eli's mouth curved in a sensual half-smile. "You didn't disappoint me."

"Good to know," I mumbled. The shape of his mouth distracted me, drew me. I wanted to feel it on mine again. Looking at it, thinking about what he could do with that mouth, about all the things he had done and might do again soon, made my head spin and my knees weak.

Eli still had his arms around me, his hands at my back keeping me close and giving me light support. I sagged against that support and Eli tightened his arms, pulling me closer. "You won't disappoint me tonight, either."

The masculine assurance in his voice didn't exactly put steel into my bones. Although this close to him, I could feel something hard as steel that I was pretty sure Eli planned to put in me soon. The demon in me hungered and the rest of me softened in giddy delight.

"You look warm." He pretended to study my face with concern.

"It is getting hot in here," I agreed, following his lead. I knew exactly where he was going with that, and my hard nipples were eager for him to get there. I wanted to be bare to his sight, bare to his touch.

I imagined myself bare to both of them, and reveling in the touch of two pairs of hands, the attentions of two tongues, two mouths fastening on my breasts while a blindfold hid their identities.

Good thing I was going to be sitting down and tied in position. Otherwise I'd fall over.

Eli curled his hands into the hem of my T-shirt and I said a mental good-bye to Betty. He drew the shirt up, exposing my panties, my midriff, my ribcage. He made undressing me a caress and a tease, drawing it out, dragging the soft fabric over my swollen nipples. I focused on staying upright while he pulled the T-shirt all the way off.

Cool air touched my heated skin. Eli took a good look at his handiwork and gave me a satisfied smile. "There. Isn't that better?"

Oh, yeah. And the best was yet to come. "Much better," I said out loud. My voice had dropped into a lower register and the throaty sound imbued those innocent words with carnal invitation. I blinked heavy lids and felt my breasts swelling in anticipation.

"I'm glad it feels better. But you still look flushed." His smile grew positively wicked. His hands hooked into the sides of my panties and tugged, peeling them down my hips, exposing the round curves of my ass and the mound of my sex.

Eli bent down and touched his mouth to the soft skin of

my lower abdomen, just above that mound. Close enough that I felt the heat of his breath there and ached for his mouth to move lower. He drew my panties down my legs in an unhurried glide to my feet. The firm strength of his hands and the soft fabric gave me contrasting sensations all the way from hip to ankles.

Undressing as foreplay. I'd thought of disrobing in sexual terms before, as stripping to tease a visually stimulated audience. I'd never thought of it as a seduction of the senses for the female being undressed with earthy intent.

Actually, everything I knew about sex I knew from the perspective of arousing the male. Until I'd come here and found myself on the fast track to undiscovered territory. I'd known how to turn a man on. I hadn't known how it felt to be on the receiving end of focused sexual attention.

Maybe I was more of a sheltered maiden than I'd imagined. Okay, not sheltered, that was too laughable. But there was so much I hadn't known. I hadn't known the soft brush of cotton panties rolled down by my lover's hands would make my legs tremble in anticipation of more direct caresses.

"Step out." Eli's voice was low but clear and his breath teased my pubic curls.

I obeyed, knowing the movement would give him glimpses of my vulva, visibly aroused and darkened to a deep pink. I wanted him to look. I wanted him to touch. Taste. Take.

But he only finished removing my underwear and stood to set the T-shirt and panties aside. I tried not to bite my lip and groan in frustration. Eli saw the struggle on my face and the green of his eyes deepened. "Walk over to the chair and sit down."

He pointed to the chair he'd carried in for me. His. I found that interesting. It struck me as territorial. Dal had taken me in his chair, so Eli would do the same? Not use my chair, neutral turf? Of course, it wasn't actually mine. Just the one I'd claimed for myself while I was here. Still, part of me really liked Eli's choice.

Maybe I was reaching for some sign that he had any degree of feeling for me, but it seemed significant. Eli had kept me in his bed. Dal had come to join us there; I'd never been in Dal's bed, although he'd had me everywhere else. I'd thought that was because in Dal's mind his bed was reserved for another woman, but maybe there was another reason.

Tenuous, fragile possibility tugged at my mind as I walked to the chair Eli wanted me to take. I knew they were both watching me, so I put a little sway in my hips. I bent to brush my hand over the seat as if making sure it was clear to sit on. Really I just wanted them to look at my ass. I grinned since my back was to them and they couldn't see my face. Then I put on a more neutral expression as I turned around and took my seat.

I wanted to at least pretend to be compliant and obedient, patient. What I really wanted to do was, well, not. But this game would be fun for all three of us, and I wanted to play with them. As much as I wanted to touch and be touched by them, I wanted this for us. A little time for lighthearted dalliance, an entertaining diversion.

This wasn't about me trying to trip them into lust. It was the two of them giving me a healthy dose of my own medicine. And maybe a tiny bit of it was Eli wanting to do something to me in a kitchen chair that would overwhelm any lesser memory. Pride? Maybe. I didn't see it sending him into a lust-driven frenzy, but I wanted to believe that he desired me enough to want to one-up the sexual experience I'd shared with Dal.

"Spread your thighs, and hook your ankles around the chair legs," Eli said.

Game on. I took my time about it, but when I was in position I realized exactly how submissive I would look to them. A naked, willing, sexual offering. Tied. Blindfolded. Theirs to do with as they pleased.

If either of them lost his head, this game could turn deadly. I felt a pang of misgiving and didn't know who I was concerned for, them or me. The answer should have been me, but my priorities weren't nearly as clear-cut as they used to be.

I looked into Eli's eyes and found them unwavering, full of heat and promise, and felt the tension that had crept over me relax. Eli wouldn't let anything go wrong. He was in control of himself and this erotic performance. It was safe to surrender to the experience, to put myself in their hands.

Dal was the one who applied my restraints, taking liberties and stealing touches in the process. He made certain I was secured but not too tightly for comfort. Eli placed a padded mask over my eyes after Dal stepped away and assured himself that it wouldn't slip.

It amused me that they'd used magic to produce the proper equipment instead of making do with things they had around the house. One of the benefits of sorcerous sex partners: they could summon up any accessories or toys we desired.

I tensed again as I realized what that could mean. They were both capable of bringing more than themselves into play without violating the rules. "Wait," I said. "We didn't talk about magic for purposes other than disguise."

"Too late." Eli sounded immovable. As always. "Wouldn't you say it's too late for our naked prisoner to negotiate terms, Dalen?"

"Yep." Dal sounded like he was enjoying himself thoroughly. "Her ass is ours."

"Her ass is under her, but we can fix that any time we desire," Eli mused. "I might like to have that tight ass under me."

"Ha, ha," I muttered. "If either of you takes a riding crop to my ass, I'll . . ." I ground to a halt as I realized I had no idea what I'd do. I was naked, blindfolded, and tied to a chair with my wrists bound together behind me.

"You'll come?" Dal finished for me.

Oh, hell, if they did it, I probably would. When had either of them ever done anything to me I didn't like, sexually?

"I'll trust you," I said.

"That's the right answer." Eli's voice held approval and dark promise, and I knew there really were no limits. Except one. Eli's unshakable honor would keep the game within bounds.

Eli might be capable of banishing me, but he'd never hurt me. He might break my heart. It might even now be cracking, forming interstices too tiny to measure, ready to shatter when the final stress came. But Eli wouldn't betray my trust.

That left a world of possibilities for them to explore.

I waited to see how the game would begin. After a minute, I realized it already had.

This was seduction, being on display for their eyes, naked and open to their touch, blind to their intentions until they revealed themselves. Waiting. Wondering if Dal was going to fill his hands with my breasts and rub my nipples until I squirmed in my seat. Wondering if Eli was looking at the exposed crescent of my sex.

I didn't know which of them would touch me first, or where, or how. Or with what. A hand? Lips? The smooth crown of a hard cock pressing against my mouth? A feather along the inside of my thigh, or a flogger?

The answer finally came, and it wasn't anything I'd imagined. Nothing overt. No direct sexual contact. Fingertips traced the outline of the restraint on my ankle. Drawing them again on my skin, underscoring the fact that I was bound with both ankles encircled and secured to chair legs. The touch was warm and possessive and Eli's.

After tracing the bands around each ankle, those hands next touched my wrists. They followed the line made by the restraint I wore there, imprisoning my arms behind my back. I made a mental prediction and felt pleased with myself a second later when his fingertips drew the outline of my mask on my face.

I felt certain it was Eli, not because I was so good I could tell the difference between their fingertips, but because Eli would be affected by the fact that I wore nothing but bindings and a blindfold in a way Dal wouldn't.

He liked the control. He liked to play power games. He

liked knowing I trusted him enough to put myself completely in his hands. I'd agreed to play this game for my own selfish reasons, but it hadn't really occurred to me until this moment that it was also an act of giving.

My lover wanted me subject to his will and whim, and I wanted to please him as much as I knew he would please me. I moved my head back a tiny bit, raising my face to his touch, exposing the vulnerable curve of my throat.

His fingertips trailed down my cheekbones, followed the line of my jaw, touched the sensitive skin behind my ears, moved down to my collarbone to lightly explore the hollows there.

I breathed a sigh, lost in the sheer delight of his hands on me and the knowledge that I was his to touch anywhere. For this moment at least, I wasn't his enemy. I was simply his.

TWENTY-SEVEN

Eli bent to kiss my forehead and I felt the sweep of his warrior braids on my shoulders. "I love your long hair," I said.

"I should tie it back so you don't have such an obvious clue." His lips were gentle on my skin. His voice sounded deep and rough. The sexual tone sent a shiver through me.

"I knew it was you the second you touched me." I grinned at him, feeling triumphant.

"Then why didn't you say anything until you felt my hair?"

"Why do you think? Because I was enjoying myself too much to say anything that might make you stop."

"It's still an unfair advantage for you. I'll tie my hair back." He straightened and moved away. I didn't have to see to know that he was doing exactly what he'd said. Me and my big mouth. Now I wouldn't get the sensual caress of his hair trailing along my body in the wake of his lips.

A few seconds later I heard a soft sound and inhaled the distinctive scent of roses and myrrh. Ah. Time to take my medicine.

I thought Eli would apply the healing balm, since he'd felt so guilty about riding me hard. And he did. His hands were gentle, smoothing the insides of my thighs with his palms to prepare me for a more intimate touch before he stroked my sex with coated fingers. I appreciated the warning, especially since it felt cool at first.

Eli took his time with the task, spreading a good layer over my vulva before working the scented mixture into all my folds. Then he very gently inserted two fingers into my sheath to administer the treatment internally. I drew in a breath when he penetrated me. The lubricating ointment heightened the sensation of his fingers inside me, stroking my vaginal walls, moving in and out.

When he withdrew his hand, my sex felt empty and aching to be filled. I wanted him back. Instead, he reached back with a fingertip to coat my anus.

I fought a smile at the telling gesture. They were going to have me between them again. I'd have the mind-bending pleasure of being sandwiched between their heated bodies, stretched and filled to capacity by their simultaneous penetration. I shifted in anticipation. The tiny movement pushed Eli's fingertip into my ass.

Bliss. I was a total slut for anal stimulation. Who would have guessed? He gave me a few cheap thrills while ensuring I wouldn't feel any pain when one or the other of them finally spread my cheeks and pushed deep inside, and I loved every second of it.

He kissed a spot on the inside of my thigh, then moved away again. I was now ready for action. In every possible sense. My nipples tightened, my sex felt slick and swollen, and my anus tingled with pleasurable heat from the aphrodisiac's effect. I was positioned and prepared for my two lovers and I couldn't wait for them to touch me.

Dal took his turn next. He toyed with my navel ring, tickled my waist until I squirmed from one side to the other, then rolled my nipples between his thumb and forefinger in each hand. Before I was ready for him to stop, he let go and went back to my navel ring.

"Dal," I protested. "More."

"More what?" He pretended to have no idea what I wanted, squeezing my hips, massaging my outer thighs, dropping a kiss on my shoulder while my nipples pouted for his attention.

"More you know perfectly well what. Pinch them. Suck them."

"Pinch what? Your hips? That sounds painful." Dal knelt in front of me and ran his hands over my hips as if he intended to nip them between his fingers. I groaned.

"Dal. Please."

"Aw. I can't resist when you ask me nicely." He cupped his hands over my breasts and squeezed them. The welcome pressure relieved the ache for touch, and when he pinched the tight buds that seemed to tempt his hands continually, I made a low sound of encouragement.

"That's enough for now, you greedy wench." He released me and moved away, leaving me with a smile on my face.

I was greedy and I knew it. Greedy for every touch, every kiss, every shiver of pleasure. Each one might be my last. Each one was a feast to my starved senses.

After centuries of denial and deprivation, hungering continually for what I could never have, I finally had not one lover but two. Yes, I was greedy. I didn't care. I gave as good as I got, and neither of them had cause to complain about my performance.

Although really if I wanted to categorize the brothers Nephilim, I counted Eli as my lover and Dal as my friend with benefits.

Dal *was* my friend, despite my earlier mistrust of his motives. And while we enjoyed each other's bodies without inhibition, I knew where his heart lay. I was rooting for him to get his heart's desire, and hopeful that I could help by enabling him to master his control.

Eli had his reasons for sharing me with his brother. One of them may not have been altruistic. He might have wanted to keep distance between us, to keep me from becoming a threat to the tight leash he kept on himself. It seemed like a logical way for him to put me in my place, prove that while he might be fucking me it didn't mean that I had any hold on him.

Although in that case who was he trying to prove it to, me or himself?

Oh, quit analyzing, I told myself. Be greedy. Be selfish.

Be happy right now because now is all there is. Take two men and call your logic in the morning.

Two pairs of hands settled on my shoulders and I wanted to sing hallelujah. One man on each side of me. They massaged the back of my neck, the slope of my shoulders, and worked down my upper back as far as the chair would allow. Then they kneaded my arms into bliss.

Dal was on my right, Eli on my left. The difference in the way they touched me spoke clearly.

Dal's touch was affectionate, his hands strong and sure. Eli was more complicated, even when I was only dealing with his hands. He found more little spots to press and dig into, verging on painful and melting into ecstasy as muscles eased and nerve endings were stimulated. He was thorough and exacting and maybe a hair on the obsessive-compulsive side, but the result was a massage that felt like he was awakening my body on a cellular level.

The way Dal rubbed me felt good, and that was all. Enjoyable, absolutely. Dal did know what to do with his hands, and he used them to good effect whenever he put them on me. But he didn't have Eli's intensity. Or if he did, that side of him hid under the playful exterior he wore like a mask. I did know that there was more to him than he showed, a hidden depth. But I also knew I wasn't the one with the key to his deepest passions.

And that was okay with me, because while Eli might be unmovable, Dal could be hurt. I didn't want to be the one to hurt him, not even in a small way.

"Um. Not quite so deep, Eli," I said when he found a

pressure point that was more sensitive. He eased back and the intense touch became blissful. "Ah. Perfect. Thank you."

"She nailed you," Dal said. He worked his way back up my arm, rolling his palms in a side to side motion that made me want to melt.

"I nailed you, too," I said, my tone light and teasing. "I'm very familiar with your hands."

Eli dug in a touch harder. I wondered if it was on purpose, or a tiny slip that betrayed an emotion he didn't want me to suspect. Punishing me in a subtle way for welcoming and enjoying Dal's familiarity with my body? Or an unconscious reaction from his possessive nature? I knew he was territorial, and no matter how he rationalized it, I was his territory.

They finished their tandem massage and moved on to cupping and stroking my breasts. I groaned and arched my back to thrust myself into their hands. "That feels so good," I told them.

"That's what I like to hear," Dal said. "I want you grateful and accommodating when it's my turn."

Eli's fingers on my nipple sent a wave of need straight to my sex. "I am feeling pretty accommodating right now," I said, my voice thick with desire.

"Good. Then you'll be ready when it's time to accommodate us both," Eli said.

My sex clenched and my belly tightened. I could feel a hum of anticipation running through my body. "Ready and willing," I assured him. The willing part wasn't lost on him, by the way his hands responded on me. I didn't want him to have any doubt that I wanted him, wanted both of them, that I desired every wicked thing they wanted to do to me.

His hands were gentle and demanding by turns, ravishing me and cherishing me. He worked my nipple until I was squirming in the chair to relieve the ache in my lower body. Dal teased and toyed with me, squeezing my breasts, thumbing the tight bud, tickling the sensitive underside.

Then as one, their hands moved down my ribs, stroked my belly, and settled on my thighs. The level of tension in my body ratcheted up a notch and I held my breath. Who would touch me there first?

It was another surprise when it came. They both moved around to face me, each on one side, and kneeled on the floor. Two sets of hands settled on either side of my knees. Four hands stroked up my inner and outer thighs and two sets of fingers brushed the exposed folds of my outer labia simultaneously.

They moved in unison, petting and exploring my vulva. When they each pressed one fingertip to my center, I sucked in a breath and let it out in a moan as they thrust into me together.

"You two are very creative," I managed to say. Then it was all incoherent gasping sounds as two men penetrated me with their fingers in perfectly timed rhythm. Then to make me completely insane, Dal kept his finger buried in my slick core while Eli withdrew. And then they took turns. Eli plunging into me while Dal toyed with my clit. Dal penetrating me while Eli found my clit and drove me wild.

If this was a hint of things to come, they were really going to send me into a meltdown when they got their pants open. I could feel pressure building in me, drawing me tight, and just when I thought I was going to reach the point of no return, they took their hands away.

Two mouths closed over my nipples and suckled until my womb clenched and I writhed in my chair. Eli grazed me with his teeth. Dal laved me with his tongue. And I wanted them both inside me.

I had to have something inside me, now, and I wanted one of them to fill my mouth. "Eli," I whispered, the raw need apparent in the way I said his name. "Let me suck you."

He released my breast and came to stand by my head. He stroked my hair and I nuzzled his hip, despite the layer of cloth that kept me from touching skin. They were both still fully clothed, I realized, which was why I wasn't being overwhelmed by both of them touching me together. I wasn't drunk on the contact. Just aroused and aching from anticipation.

"Suck Dalen's cock," Eli said. He wound his fingers in my locks and urged my face toward Dal. I heard the sound of a zipper lowering and parted my lips. "Let him fuck your mouth. Show me how you want to suck me."

What a hardship. Dal's eager member brushed my lower lip as if begging a kiss, then slid inside as I opened wide for him. I licked at him, swirled my tongue over his head, then sucked while I wrapped my lips tightly around his shaft and angled my head to take him as deep as he could go.

Dal began to thrust in and out of my mouth, and I demonstrated my enthusiasm for oral until he pulled out and stepped away.

"You do love to suck cock, don't you?" Eli asked. I heard his zipper go down and wanted to lick my lips in anticipation.

"Try me and find out," I invited.

He guided himself to my mouth, and with a sigh, I took him. I moved my head back and forth, gliding up and down his length, giving him tight suction while I teased him with my tongue. The taste of him went to my head. I wanted him to spill himself on my tongue, let me lap up every drop, and my mouth became more urgent.

"Enough." Eli thrust between my lips one last time, then withdrew.

Nothing would ever be enough, but I didn't protest. I did sigh, but I waited. I knew the time for play was nearly at an end.

"Are you getting uncomfortable in that chair?" Eli ran a hand down my body. I thought I could hear Dal getting naked nearby, the soft rustle of clothing as it was removed.

"Yes. A little." I shifted and tested the limits of my restraints.

"Maybe this will help." Eli's hand settled over my sex. I arched into his touch.

"Do you think so?" I asked, almost panting. I was trembling with need, and when he parted my folds and began to circle and stroke my clit, I knew I was going to be lost in seconds. Something smooth and hot and hard brushed my cheek. I turned my face and opened my mouth to let Dal's cock thrust inside. The delicious sensation of having one man's hand between my legs and another's organ between my lips sent me soaring.

Eli's hand became more demanding, and I broke, shuddering and gasping.

Dal slid out of my mouth again. Then I felt two pairs of hands on my ankles. A second later my legs were free. They left my blindfold on and my arms bound, and lifted me up. Dal pulled me into his arms and fondled my ass while Eli undressed. Then Eli took me away from Dal and led me to the bed.

"On top of me," I heard him say. The two of them settled us all into position. Eli on the bottom. Me astride and bent low over him so that his chest cushioned my breasts. The heat of him burned into me like a brand. Dal moved against my back, kissing down the line of my spine, his hands stroking my round buttocks and spreading them apart.

"Now. Together." I felt Eli probe between my legs, searching out the center of my sex while Dal positioned his cock against my anus. Bracketed by their heat, dizzy with desire, I gave myself up to both of them as they penetrated me until I was so stuffed I couldn't move or breathe.

I made a soft sound that Eli might have interpreted as distress. His hands wove into my hair and his lips moved over my forehead. "Shh. We've got you. Just relax."

I arched into him. "Eli." I pushed my ass back against Dal's invading cock and moaned. "Dal. Fuck me."

"Dal can fuck you when I'm done," Eli muttered. "And I'm so hard that might be never." He can began to thrust into me with fierce urgency.

I heard Dal laugh behind me as he worked his hips to keep pace. "Babe, we're going to give it to you so good." He held my hips and Eli held my arms, his fingers digging into my biceps while his cock drove into my sex.

I felt the heat and tension building, felt my orgasm spiraling close. And then all three of us were coming, shouting, moaning, an orgy of release. I felt Dal pumping himself between my ass cheeks, Eli's shaft jerking as he spent himself against my vaginal walls while my sex clenched hard around him. My hands were freed and I stretched them up over my head.

Then I collapsed on Eli. I heard Dal's voice, low and indistinct, and roused myself enough to pay attention.

"Careful," I heard him saying.

"I know what she wants," Eli answered. "I know how much she can take."

"S'okay," I informed Dal in tones of cheerful intoxication. "I'm in good hands." Then I giggled, because Eli's hands were bad, bad, bad, and so was I because I wanted them everywhere on me.

"Maybe he's worried about me, not you," Eli said in a rough voice as he rolled me underneath him. I heard the door close and knew Dal had left. "He's my brother."

"He knows you're invincible," I said, slurring a little. "He thinks I'm a girl."

"You have breasts," Eli pointed out. As if that proved something. He took the blindfold off me and tossed it aside.

I blinked at him with blurry eyes. "Was there a point to this conversation? Why are we talking?"

"Good question." Eli's mouth closed over mine and that was the end of verbal communication. Nonverbally, we proceeded to whisper, murmur, and shout until my body was too spent to hold up my end of the conversation.

One hazy thought floated through my head as I closed

my eyes and burrowed into Eli's heat, his cock still buried inside me as if he didn't want to relinquish possession.

Dal hadn't lost control when he'd taken me in the chair two ways, or when he and Eli had seduced and teased me while I sat bound and blindfolded, or when they took me together. He didn't need me anymore.

Eli had never needed me, not really. But he hadn't been overtaken with lust, either, and I'd certainly given him every provocation.

He'd passed his test. I'd failed.

I clung to Eli as sleep swallowed me, but I knew it was a useless gesture. Still, my hands clutched at his solid form as if by sheer will I could hold on a little while longer.

TWENTY-EIGHT

Morning, sunshine." Dal turned his head to grin at me over his shoulder. "Want some coffee? Or something hotter?"

I smiled back and wiggled my brows at him, determined to stay in the present instead of panicking over the future. "Do I have to choose? I want both."

Dal winked. "You're on." He pulled out a second mug, filled it for me, then turned around and opened his arms. I walked into them and he made a game of nuzzling my neck and ear until I laughed.

Then he cupped my butt with both hands to give me a double goose while he planted a kiss on my forehead. "Thanks for this." He flexed his hands to give my ass an extra squeeze in case I missed his meaning. His antics made my Betty Boop T-shirt ride up so that my lack of underwear was obvious. Not that he couldn't tell by feel already.

"All in a day's work." I gave him my best sultry look.

Dal's face turned serious. "Don't belittle yourself or what you did for me. It was brave and generous."

That caught me off guard, and I found myself at a loss for words. "Dal . . ."

"Don't let me interrupt." Eli's voice made us both turn toward the sound. His face was hard and his eyes lasered into mine. Dal kept his hands where they were. Maybe he thought letting me go now would make it seem more like Eli was interrupting something. Or maybe he just wanted to push Eli's buttons.

I ran last night back through my mind and found myself a little hazy on some key details. Had Eli disinvited Dal and kicked him out of the bedroom?

"Worried we were starting without you?" Dal raised a brow. "There's plenty to go around. I'll just get a third cup."

Eli didn't move. Dal gave my mostly-bare butt a friendly pat and turned to make it coffee for three.

I reached around him to pick up my cup. That made the T-shirt slide up even higher and probably gave Eli more of a show than he appreciated just then, but it couldn't be helped. And I didn't really think it would make his mood any worse. A little glimpse of naked female flesh cheers most men right up, especially when it's accidental and public. Not that the kitchen was Grand Central Station, but the psychology still worked. I arched my back just a little so he could see the thatch of curls between my legs if he wanted to look.

"So you're a natural blonde."

Claire's voice cut through my happy thoughts of seducing Eli and maybe getting something hotter than coffee to liven up my morning. I waved a mental good-bye to the possibility and told myself it could still happen later. I turned around, both hands holding the mug, deliberately not reaching down to tug the T-shirt's hem into a more modest position.

"Yep." I gave her a sunny smile and took a sip of hot liquid. I hadn't heard her come in, and wasn't sure how much she'd picked up on.

"Stop showing Claire your pussy." A muscle twitched in Eli's cheek. I shrugged and complied. But I took my time about it on principle.

"Spoilsport," Dal said. He passed a full mug to Eli. Eli seemed to hesitate for a beat before he accepted it.

"I'm not into girl-on-girl," Claire said. As if I'd offered. I resisted the urge to roll my eyes.

"Well, if you change your mind, I hope you let me watch." Dal gave her a wicked look. Her cheeks heated, but not with embarrassment. With anger.

"Is that what it takes to get you going, Dalen? You like to watch? You only want a partner who'll do a threesome with you?" She jerked her chin at Eli. "Do all your women have to fuck both of you? You should've said so. I don't mind doing him, too."

I bit my lip to keep my jaw closed. Now was not the time to shoot off my mouth. Dalen and Eli could handle this one. Dal especially. Claire was his business.

"You're not doing him." Dal crossed his arms over his chest and stared at Claire as if daring her to make a move toward Eli.

"Do I get a say?" Eli asked.

"No." I reached out and grabbed him by the belt loop. I tried to tug him away but it was a useless attempt.

"No?" Claire's voice rose.

"No."

Dal sounded implacable. I winced. They were heading for a showdown, and while they needed to have it out, they did not need an audience. I mouthed *Let's go* at Eli.

He glared at me. Then he reached out and grabbed the front of my T-shirt and tore it down the center. My breasts spilled out from the ripped halves. I looked down in mock regret. "I liked that shirt."

Eli set both of our coffee cups on the counter with an ominous thump that sloshed liquid over the rims. Then he picked me up and tossed me over his shoulder and walked out, leaving the two of them to come to an understanding.

"Nice move with the shirt and the caveman grab," I said when I thought we were out of earshot. "That totally distracted them."

"You think that was a diversionary tactic?" Eli sounded even and calm, except for the clipped way he ended his words.

"Wasn't it?"

We reached his bedroom. He tossed me onto the bed and stood over me as he undid his jeans with hard, jerking movements. "No," Eli bit out.

"Oh." I wasn't sure what to say to that, so I didn't say anything else. I watched as Eli spread his open jeans apart, freeing his hard cock. He wrapped a hand around the thick shaft and worked it up and down in the same angry rhythm.

"Touch yourself." Eli leaned closer, his cock aimed at my belly button.

"Okay." If he wanted company while he took himself in hand, I didn't mind. If it pleased him to watch me stroke myself, then I'd put on the best performance I could. I placed my hand over my sex like a fig leaf first, cupping and squeezing. I gave my hips a little shimmy as if I was thrusting myself into my own palm.

"Show me." Eli's hand moved up and down, rough and quick. His eyes glittered as he watched me and the muscle in his jaw jerked.

So he wanted it fast and dirty, did he? I shifted so he had a better view. While he watched, I plunged a finger in and began banging myself in the same urgent motion his hand was making. The lack of finesse made our twin actions raw and unvarnished. Sex without anything prettying the act up.

Eli jerked himself faster and I knew he was close. He shifted his aim from my belly downward so that when the first liquid jet hit it spattered my hand as I worked my sex. He continued to masturbate over me, jerking off onto me, drenching my pussy with a second and then a third helping of his seed. He reached down and yanked my hand away, then used the hand that had been wrapped around his cock to spread the hot, slick liquid he'd sprayed me with until it fully coated my sex.

If I didn't know better, I would have taken it as possessive. A visceral way of marking his territory. My breath caught in my throat as I acquiesced to his desire, waiting for my cue, ready to follow his lead when I could fathom his direction.

Eli continued to spread his cream over my pussy, then began working it into me with his fingers. His other hand went to his still-hard shaft and began stroking himself again, but this time slower.

"Eli." I rocked my hips up to meet his fingers and deepen the penetration.

"Like that?" He stared down at me, unreadable and fierce and a little frightening.

"I like what you like." I gave him honesty and spread my legs wider. He could spear me with his cock or his fingers, whatever he wanted. He could keep coming on me or in me. He could flip me over and ream me and cream me there, too. I wanted him, and I'd take him any way he wanted me.

"Would you like this?" He moved closer, so that the head of his cock nudged my opening. "Do you want to wrap your hot pussy around my cock and use it to squeeze the next load of come out of my balls?"

Heat was coming off him in waves until I was dizzy with it and then with something else. I didn't recognize it for what it was at first because it was something I hadn't come to associate with Eli. So I made a soft, pleading sound low in my throat as I arched up to offer myself to him.

My flesh stretched to take the broad, blunt head as Eli replaced his fingers with his cock. Then he thrust deep, his body still not entirely on the bed, still half-standing beside it so I couldn't have all of him and his upper body didn't touch mine. We didn't touch at all except for where we joined.

I strained to get closer, to take more. Eli let out a harsh, feral-sounding growl and covered my body with his, letting his full weight come down on me, blanketing me while he fucked his way deeper into me. It felt so good. Too good. I felt drunk and wild for more of Eli's intoxicating heat, and then it registered.

I'd won. I'd lost. Somehow I'd made Eli give in to lust. Maybe he'd been too proud of his supernatural self-control after all, because it was gone. His human side was driving him now, and Dal wasn't here to check him. Lust burned in his every movement, seared me with every thrust he made, fed me his very essence. And I was gorging on it.

I was killing him.

I froze under him, trapped between my hunger and my despair. I had to stop him, stop this. Save him. If one of us had to lose, it should be me. I was the one who had fallen from grace, who deserved to pay.

Would you give anything for him? A voice that sounded impossibly like Nick's sounded in my head.

I didn't hesitate. There was no question. There was no choice. There was only one answer. *Yes. Anything.*

I knew what I had to do. I drew breath and whispered the words that would end me. "Eli. My true name is Edana."

He stilled over me. "Edana?"

"My name." I felt something hot and liquid trace its way down my cheek. "Use it. Banish me. I'm draining you, Eli. Stop me. Send me away forever. My life for yours."

He moved away just a little so that his eyes could meet mine. His still glittered with heat and need, but they also shone with concern as clear and as deep as the sea we'd once kissed beside. "I'm hurting you," he said.

That brought him back to his senses? Not concern for his

own neck? It was so perfectly Eli that I didn't know whether to laugh or cry. "Overprotective idiot. I'm hurting *you*."

"Your life for mine. Do you think it's a fair trade?" There was something strange and unreadable in Eli's expression. After a moment I realized it was wonder.

I laughed a little and shook my head from side to side. "No. Yours is worth more."

"You think your life is worth less than mine?"

I nodded. Words spilled out to match the tears I couldn't seem to hold back. "I'm damned. I had the gift of life once, and I ended it in an act of hatred. Let me redeem myself with an act of love now."

He shifted his weight to his elbows and brought his hands up to cup my face. "Do you love me, Edana?"

"You know I do." I wanted to kiss him good-bye, but I didn't dare. It was enough to feel his touch and to look into his eyes.

"Will you share my soul?"

The words didn't make any sense. "What?"

"You have a choice. You don't have to remain a demon." Eli's eyes bored into mine, as if willing me to understand. And finally I did.

"How would that work?" I blinked to clear the well of tears blurring my vision. "You can't share your soul. I know the out-clause, but it's not really possible. It can't be." Panic clutched at me. What if he tried and it killed him? I couldn't let him take the risk. "Don't do it, Eli, let me go. I don't love you. I love your brother and he loves Claire, so there's nothing for me here."

Eli laughed, his face shining as bright as the sun. He was

so sure of me, it radiated from him. How could my love make him so happy, when it was going to kill him? "Liar. You're a really bad liar, too. I'd clean you out at poker."

"I'm not lying and it's not funny. What are you waiting for? Do you want to finish fucking me first? Go ahead, get your rocks off. Die for it and damn the world while you're at it."

I glared at him, furious with him and with the impossible situation and my own inability to do it for him. For both of us. I couldn't stand it. I felt myself shaking with helpless rage.

"Edana." He whispered my name and covered my mouth with his. I tried, but I couldn't remain unresponsive. Against my will my lips moved against his, then parted for his. A flood tide of emotion swept me away.

Everything that welled up in my heart I tried to say without words. I loved him, needed him, ached for him, wept for him. I felt the surge of his desire and a matching swell of despair inside me, certain I was sealing his doom with a treacherous, traitorous kiss.

I hated myself for the weakness that made me cling when I should be pushing him away and for the cursed nature that made me his bane and his downfall. And still we kissed, until I thought my heart would stop with his and the world would stop for us both together.

Instead, the world . . . breathed.

Eli breathed into my mouth, and I drew something hot and sweet into my lungs. It tasted purer and more life-giving than oxygen. It didn't burn, but the searing heat penetrated to the marrow of my bones and the depths of my being. I surrendered to the transformation as Eli's sorcery changed me.

The kiss was a spell, I realized. Like in a fairy tale. But it was more like falling into a dream than waking from one. The beat of Eli's heart against mine, the rhythm of his body on mine and in mine, the taste of him filling my mouth seemed surreal and unreal.

But whatever lost moment in time this might be, it was ours. I sensed it, knew it to be true, and I held onto it with all of my will. I kissed him with all my love, loved him with all of my self, mind and body and spirit, nothing held back. All that I was, all I could ever be, all of it was his. Love without reservation or self-preservation.

I might have whispered it against his lips. I wasn't sure. But whether the words were shaped and given breath or not, I told him I loved him over and over with every inch of myself, and Eli loved me with his body until both of us bowed and broke from the pleasure.

Eli's body was strong and vital over mine, his essence undimmed, nothing spent but his breath and his seed. I didn't understand at first. Then the kiss ended and I knew. We'd shared a stolen moment of love, not lust. Love offered nothing to feed a demon and posed no risk to Eli.

A beat later I realized that wasn't all we'd shared. Eli had given me more than his body and his heart. He'd given me a piece of his soul, not so much broken off as shared between us. I was now bound to him much more deeply than I'd been before. I didn't object. I didn't feel trapped. I was free.

I was crying again, silent tears of joy and wonder. My face was probably swollen, my eyes blotchy, all of me a mess. I didn't care. I was a miracle.

I was human again.

TWENTY-NINE

This changes a few things, doesn't it?" I asked Eli a long time later. We'd changed position so that he was on his back with me draped down his front, his arms wrapped around me, my hands clutching at him as if some irrational part of me feared I'd lose him if I let go.

"There are repercussions." Eli wove a hand into my hair and massaged the base of my skull. "For starters, you might have to start counting calories now that you don't have a demonic appetite to satisfy and you have a body that burns at human metabolic rate."

"Damn." I smiled into his chest. "I was planning to go

on a hot-fudge brownie sundae binge to celebrate, but if my ass gets too big you might not want it anymore."

"I'll always want it." Eli's other hand moved down my spine until it found and claimed my butt in a possessive grip. "And you'd better not keep baring it in public."

"Will you spank me if I do?" I moved my ass in a suggestive wiggle against his hand and felt happiness bubbling up inside me.

"Maybe. Would you like it if I did?" Eli gave my butt a light slap.

I laughed out loud. "I'd like anything you wanted to do to me and with me, but going around getting naked in public isn't proper human behavior." I paused as if deep in thought. "Unless I take up stripping. Even if I don't eat as much as a demon, I probably need to get a job." I figured accepting Eli's offered soul pretty much served as my formal notice to my former boss.

Eli spanked me again, for real this time, then soothed away the sting with a caress. "If you want a job, I've got one for you."

"Really?" I rocked my hips into him. "Tell me more."

Eli rolled me under him and slid his legs between mine. "I need a dishwasher."

"Bastard." I struck at his shoulder with a balled-up fist. He ignored the puny blow, lifted his hips, and thrust home, filling me to the hilt in one stroke.

I decided we could discuss the details of my new existence later. I wrapped my legs around his waist and urged him on.

A while later, I stirred and nudged him. "Eli."

"Mmm?"

"Did you kick Dal out of bed last night?" I hadn't heard their exchange clearly, and I knew I'd missed something from the byplay between them this morning.

"Yes." Eli shifted and settled us on our sides, his body behind mine, cuddling me spoon-fashion. "He didn't need you anymore, and I needed you too much. I found myself disinclined to continue sharing."

"I didn't think you needed me at all," I admitted. "Other than as a convenient and pleasurable enough way to prove your control."

"Convenient?" Eli bit at my earlobe and tugged. "You parked your ass directly in my way and flaunted it at me. I wasn't sure what to do with you. So I bound you. Then I had you here distracting me every time I turned around. Breaking my concentration. Sleeping in my bed. Turning me jealous of my own brother because he made you laugh so easily."

"Ah. So that's why the foul mood over the chess game." I mentally replayed Eli's scowling entrance and grinned.

"Yes." He settled his hand over my belly and rubbed the rough, unshaved edge of his jaw along my shoulder. "That was petty of me, I know."

"No, actually, that was perceptive. Sex does not necessarily lead to connection, but people who laugh together are bonding." I put my hand over his on my tummy and felt faintly amazed that I could, that Eli might really be mine. "Dal and I bonded as friends, by the way. We enjoyed the friendly sex, but both of us are going to be plenty busy elsewhere from now on."

"I'm still sorry I spoiled your fun. You were only playing chess. And then I worked my dark mood off between your legs." Eli's voice was quiet, serious.

"Mm. Yes. You forced me to have countless orgasms. No wonder you felt guilty, you cruel, heartless beast." I wiggled my butt into his groin. "Let me know if you ever feel jealous again. That was fun."

"I thought Dal was being more than friendly with you this morning when I came out," Eli admitted. As if I hadn't noticed.

"And look what that led to." I sounded as smug as I felt. "Tell me you love me. You haven't said the words yet."

"I gave you my body and my soul," he said, toying with my navel ring. "Doesn't that speak for itself?"

"Don't be a chicken, Eli."

He slid over a little and pushed me onto my back so he could lean over me and look into my eyes when he said it. "I love you."

I felt my breath catch. Silly tears stung the backs of my eyes. I knew it, but hearing him say it suddenly made it more real. "Oh."

"Oh?" He scowled at me. "What, that wasn't pretty enough for you? Do you want me to say I see the stars in your eyes and your smile lights up a room like the sun? Do you want me to lay everything I am at your feet and vow to be a better man?"

I smiled at him, a little tremulously. "Does my smile really light up a room?"

"Yes." He sounded sincere, which meant that either it really did, or he saw it that way. Either way, it worked for me.

"Oh," I said again. "Um, I have a temper. And sometimes I'm impulsive. I probably don't look that great first thing in the morning, and—"

"And I love you." Eli cut me off with a kiss that kept my mouth busy for a while. It was sweet and hot and full of heart, and it went on long enough to make me dizzy and pliant and hopeful.

"You don't need to be a better man," I said through swollen lips when he was finished. "I love you the way you are."

"Oh."

He said it deadpan, but I laughed. "What? Not pretty enough for you? There's a poem about loving to the depth and breadth and height a soul can reach, but I didn't memorize it. When I didn't have a soul, that was just depressing."

Eli gave me a thoughtful look that made me a little nervous. "You've memorized a lot, haven't you?"

I shrugged. "I had a lot of time on my hands. What else are you going to do with a few centuries? I studied things. Part of it was job-related. I always had to do research, keep up with new developments and cultural changes, but I liked learning."

It had also kept me from dwelling too much on my afterlife, my loneliness, things like that.

Things had definitely taken a turn for the better now. I had a lover. I had family of a sort. A place to belong. I wasn't really sure what my place was, though. Dishwasher was all well and good, everybody had to pitch in and do their part around the house. But what else was there for me to do while Dal and Claire and Eli were busy saving the world?

Eli brushed another kiss across my lips and levered himself up. "Come on. Time for a bath. Since I got you all sweaty, I'll bathe you."

"There's an offer I can't refuse." I let him lead me to the tub, but the back of my mind kept turning to the future. We got wet and soapy and slippery and there was a lot of fooling around on the way to getting clean, but Eli noticed my distraction.

"Edana."

There's power in saying a name, and when it's said by a sorcerous warrior, that's even more true. My head came up, and my eyes met his. "Yes?"

"You aren't paying attention."

I looked down. His hands were on my breasts. "I'm not paying attention? You already washed that part. A couple of times." Not that I was complaining.

Eli scooped water in his hands and let it run over my breasts, rinsing away suds. "You look worried."

I blew out a breath. "Well, yeah. Let's start with this one. I'm not a demon anymore, but you're still a Nephilim. What if I'm not woman enough for you?"

He laughed. "You are all the woman I want."

Considering the effect he still had on me, I didn't really doubt I could keep up with him in the sack. And I knew his self-control well enough to believe that he'd rein himself in if I couldn't. I thought the physical side of things would work out just fine. Which meant I had to talk about bigger concerns.

"What am I going to do as a human, Eli?" There it was on the table, the big question.

Eli kissed the corner of my mouth, his warrior braids tickling me in the process. "About that. You need to speak with my father."

Oh, shit. I went cold despite Eli's shared heat. "Your dad hates me. He tried to cut off my head, or did you forget that?"

Eli set me back a little, finished rinsing us both, and helped me out of the tub. He wrapped a towel around my back and used the ends to pull me close. "He didn't actually try to decapitate you. That was just to get your attention."

I whimpered.

"Trust me."

I looked into his eyes and saw love and confidence in equal measure. I sighed. "Okay." I'd do it. But maybe I could put it off for a decade or two.

As it turned out, though, Eli was dead set on pushing me into the path of an angel with a big sword without letting me stop to have a snack or a nervous breakdown first. He produced a replacement for my destroyed Betty Boop tee, or maybe he just repaired the one he'd torn off me, along with a pair of white jeans and sneakers. Socks and underwear to match.

I looked down at myself, all in white except for the splash of cartoon character color. "This is so wrong."

Eli kissed the top of my head. "You're a former demon. You've switched sides. If you still want to go around wearing black leather, you can, but for today this is appropriate."

"If you say so." The doubt in my voice was palpable.

Then I put my small hand in his engulfing grip and let him lead me to my doom.

We met in a circle of oak trees. Eli stayed outside the circle, sending me into it with a little push. I walked with dragging steps to the shining column of what looked like the light of creation in the center, stopping when I came close enough to talk. It was a lot closer than I thought was safe.

"Kneel." The voice boomed like thunder into the silence of the clearing. I knelt, with a silent apology to Eli for getting grass stains on the new jeans.

Something touched me on one shoulder, then the other, and all the heat drained out of me as I realized what it was. I was dead meat. I hadn't said good-bye to Dal, wished him luck with Claire, hadn't kissed Eli one last time . . . I felt tears pooling in my eyes, and sniffled. At least it would probably end quickly. One strike of that sword would do the job.

The unearthly weapon was driven into the ground in front of me, and I blinked. Now what?

"Rise. Draw your sword."

What? "No," I said before I thought. "I can't. You can't give me one of those. I'm not worthy." I'd seen *Raiders of the Lost Ark,* I knew what happened when the unworthy unleashed power not meant for them.

"Draw your sword."

Eli's dad obviously meant business. I wasn't brave enough to argue with him.

Okay, then. I stood up and closed my hand around that shining grip. I pulled, and it came up out of the ground. I stood there feeling like the actor in a play who didn't get a copy of the script and tried not to point the sharp end at anything.

"None are worthy," Eli's dad said. "And all are worthy."

Yeah, that made sense. Not. But I thought I grasped his meaning anyway. I didn't deserve it, but Eli had still shared his soul with me. Love wasn't earned, it just was. Like the sword, maybe.

"Serve with honor." With that final oblique statement, the light vanished, and I was left standing there alone with a magic sword in my hand that I had no clue how to use.

"You took the sword." Eli's voice was close behind me, and he sounded pleased.

"I don't think I had a choice," I said. I turned to him and put my free hand around his waist. My knees were shaking and I needed support. "What now?"

"Now I train you." He said it with a note of surprise in his voice, like that should have been obvious.

"Oh." I leaned into him and breathed his scent, clean male and cedar. "You're going to teach me how to be a badass like you. That should be interesting."

"Dal will teach you magic."

"Oh, good." My voice sounded about as faint as I felt. Well, I'd wanted something to do. Who would guard the guardians? The answer was us. We'd guard each other.

Thirty

Fall merged into winter and winter into spring, and I learned and trained and loved and remembered what it was to be human.

Eli made me work harder physically than I'd ever worked before. Considering I'd been born in a time when manual labor was really manual, that was saying something. There was something about our sparring sessions that had a tendency to turn into foreplay, but that only made me more enthusiastic about practicing.

Dal challenged the limits of my mind and imagination, but as it turned out, all my study and memorization over the years paid off. I'd been a perennial student for centuries.

Magic study was more demanding, but at least I was accustomed to continual learning.

I took to magic fairly well, and Claire only turned me into a newt a couple of times when Dal worked with both of us together. It was as unpleasant an experience as I'd imagined, but I couldn't really blame her.

Eli installed an automatic dishwasher for me. I loved it almost as much as the diamond ring and matching platinum band he'd put on my finger.

The physical side of things continued to go really well. My centuries as a succubus were good preparation for marriage to a Nephilim with a potent sex drive. Eli and I matched each other, in bed, out of bed. Against walls. In chairs and on tabletops and various outdoor locations.

Now that I was human, all that uninhibited activity led to an inevitable conclusion. I stopped fearing that my in-laws would blast me out of existence when my lower belly grew distinctly rounder. Although the sympathetic looks Eli's human mother gave me made me nervous for a new reason. Considering Eli's size, I was so getting an epidural when the time came.

I started taking walks by myself, sometimes standing in the oak circle because it felt peaceful there. Not exactly meditating. Just . . . being.

One chilly, wet spring day I'd just finished climbing over a fallen log when I looked up and saw Nick making his way toward me, dressed in faded jeans, sturdy boots, and a fleece vest. If I hadn't known better, I'd have taken him for a hiker out to bond with nature.

"By the pricking of my thumbs," I said, giving him a Shakespearean entry line.

"Calling me wicked?" He grinned. "I could say something about pots and kettles."

"I used to be wicked. I'm retired. Or reformed. Or something." I still wasn't really sure what.

"Redeemed." Nick came close enough to touch.

"Do you miss me?" I tilted my head to meet his eyes.

"Yes." He raised a hand and traced his fingertip in a circle on my forehead just above the center point between my eyes. It didn't burn. I felt a cool sensation instead.

"Did you know this would happen when you sent me to him?" I'd been wondering about that, and I didn't think I'd get another chance to ask the question, so I blurted it out. Had Nick known all along, planned this? Was this the outcome he'd expected?

"Do you think if I'd known, I would have been unselfish enough to send you?"

I scowled at him. "I hate when you answer a question with a question."

"That's why I do it. You're so cute when you're mad."

I snorted.

"Be happy, Edana." His lips replaced his fingertip in a good-bye kiss.

"I am," I said. Unanswered questions and all.

He gave me a last smile and headed down the trail, possibly in search of a soul to tempt in the wilderness. Not such a bad place for him to drum up business. Plenty of people who got lost would be willing to make a deal for directions.

Nick had his place in the big picture, too. As long as demons didn't overrun humans, we were all part of the balance.

I continued to make my way back to the house, wondering if Nick had left a mark like a burn on my skin again or if that was another thing that had changed.

When I opened the kitchen door, the radio was playing "Sympathy for the Devil." I shook my head. At least it wasn't Barry Manilow. I made my way to the bathroom and faced the mirror.

A flower decorated the spot just above and between my eyes, bright and colorful, like carnival face paint. As I watched it faded and vanished and my face was just my face again.

Eli's appeared over my shoulder. "Checking to see if you've gotten more beautiful?"

"No." I smiled and turned to face him, sliding my hands up his chest. "For that, I don't need a mirror. I just need to see how you look at me."

"Oh?" He settled his hands on my thickened waist and tugged me closer. "How do you look, then?"

"Really freaking hot."

Eli laughed. Then he kissed me, and the heat in it told me I was right. When he maneuvered me further into the room so he could push the door shut with his foot, I knew I was in for a very good time.

Chandra Walker isn't who she thought she was. She has a secret hidden in her genes—she's a rare female werewolf. Now that her all-male pack has located her, it's her destiny to sample each man's pleasures and choose a mate from among them—a mate who will become leader of the pack. Soon the strongest alphas are competing to bring Chandra the most ecstasy, but only one man will claim her.

Read on for a preview of Charlene Teglia's
upcoming erotic romance
Animal Attraction
Available from St. Martin's Griffin in Summer '09

It's amazing how much can change in the space of a heartbeat.

One minute I was alone in the Tysons Corner leather store organizing stock; rehanging jackets that had been tried on and decided against, or, more likely, tried on for no better reason than to get me to turn around and reach up to unhook them. It had been that kind of afternoon.

And then the hairs on the back of my neck stood up. My first thought was, *oh shit, I'm going to be robbed.* In which case I would have calmly and quietly opened up the register and let the crackheads clean it out. There are some things worth fighting for, but a minimum wage job in a mall store isn't one of them.

"I want . . . that," a voice said, far too close to my ear. The voice was deep, masculine, and sort of growly. The owner of the voice exhaled and warm breath moved over the exposed skin at the nape of my neck. I wished I hadn't cut my hair so short. A strange man's breath on my skin made me feel far too vulnerable.

I turned, putting a little space and the brown leather bomber jacket I was holding between us in the process. Now I could see who I was dealing with. His eyes were dark brown lit with amber. His hair matched his eye color and it fell just to the top of his shoulders, although the natural curl made it look shorter. He had an uncompromising expression and features that looked vaguely Slavic, and while he wasn't much over six feet, he managed to give the impression that every inch was formidable. He wore blue jeans, cowboy boots, and a white long-sleeved T-shirt with a Harley David- son logo that couldn't possibly be warm enough in the dead of winter, even in Virginia.

Maybe he really had just come in for a jacket. The hack- les he'd raised coming in didn't lay down, though, so I re- mained on guard. I have pretty good instincts for trouble, and they've saved me too often for me to ignore them.

"I don't think it's your size," I said, continuing to hold the distressed leather between us. Not that it made much of a barrier, but it was something. "There are more over there." I tilted my head to indicate the rack. My hands stayed right where they were, at about middle height, where they could block low or high without having to travel the full distance either way.

He gave me a measuring look, and then obligingly moved to the display of bomber jackets. I breathed a little easier when he put a couple of feet between us.

"Chandra," he said, drawing the word out. He lifted a sleeve for closer inspection as he said it. "That's your name?"

"Says so on my name tag," I said. I smiled, but my lips were tight over my teeth. I didn't want to encourage any familiarity. He'd come into my store while I was alone, he'd stood too close, he'd breathed on me, and now he was using my name. That was a good tactic for getting somebody to relax and trust you; use their name. It had the opposite effect on me, coming from him.

"Did you know it means 'the moon shining'?"

"No," I lied. I knew what the books said, but I was pretty sure it really meant that my birth parents were liberal arts students with more romantic ideas than money or sense. They'd put me up for adoption, and stuck me with the name as part of the adoption requirement. Although part of me had always wondered if that was so I could be tracked down eventually. There aren't a lot of redheaded American women in their early twenties with Sanskrit names.

"Do you dream of us?" He raised his head as he asked the question, his eyes intent on mine.

"I have lots of dreams. Everybody does." I shifted my feet, preparing to fight or run if I needed to. I didn't like anything about this encounter. "One of my dreams involves making sales and staying employed. Do you want to buy that?" I asked.

"I haven't tried it on yet." His lips curved in a smile I didn't like, even though I had to admit it looked good on him. He looked like he was laughing at me. Toying with me.

"I'm not sure it fits." He took the jacket off the hanger and put it on. It seemed to me that he drew the motions out deliberately, like he was putting on a show for me.

I watched the way he moved, but not because I was taken in by a nice body. I noted the harnessed power in his movements and mentally upgraded his strength significantly over my initial estimate. If it came to fight or flight, I'd run. I was too likely to lose a physical confrontation, no matter how many dirty tricks I knew. He was solid and graceful and he knew how to use his body to advantage.

"I'm Zach," he said, smoothing the front of the jacket. My eyes followed his hands. The jacket looked good on him. I suspected pretty much anything would.

"Nice to meet you." My tone was flat and unfriendly. The gleam in his eyes told me he wasn't discouraged.

"Now we're on a first-name basis." Zach the stranger took a step forward, and I stepped back to maintain our distance. He quirked a brow at me. "Running away?"

I ignored the question. "Bombers are on sale this week. Twenty percent off. Would you like to wear that out?"

"Yes." He grinned at me. "I suppose you'd like me to buy it and leave now."

"You might also want something to protect the leather." I waved at the counter by the cash register. "You should treat it before it's exposed to rain."

"The cow this came from stood outside and got wet," Zach pointed out, his lips twitching with what looked like a barely-contained urge to laugh.

"The cow wasn't a fashion garment." I walked around and behind the register, managing not to turn my back to him in the process.

"Already you're changing how I dress, and we haven't even had our first date." Zach the outrageous flirt took the jacket off and handed it to me so I could remove the security tag and scan the price. His flirting didn't reassure me at all. Everything about him screamed *stranger danger,* no matter how hot he looked in tight jeans and boots and a leather bomber.

"Then you're getting off lucky, since we aren't going to have a date." I charged him for the leather protector and told him the total. Zach gave me a gold card that didn't improve my opinion of him in the least. So he had money. That didn't make him safe. It might conceivably make him an even greater threat.

I gave him the jacket to wear out of the store and bagged the bottle of leather protector I didn't think he'd ever use. Which made me even happier about selling it to him.

"You don't trust me." Zach's smile vanished as he donned the garment.

"Mom warned me about guys like you."

"Then you should have expected me." He looked so in-tent and determined as he said it that I had to fight the urge to take a step back. "I'll be seeing you, Chandra."

After he left, I stayed still, focusing on breathing until my heart rate settled down. What was that crack about my mom? I'd meant my adoptive parent, but was he in some way connected with my mysterious all-records-sealed birth mother?

I finally went back to organizing the stock, but I couldn't shake the feeling of being watched. When two other store employees came in and my shift ended, I was glad to leave. I wandered through the large shopping center on a random route just in case I wasn't simply jumpy and paranoid after meeting Zach-I'll-Be-Seeing-You.

Most guys didn't rattle me, not even bullies. Zach had not been most guys. But I didn't see anybody who matched his height and shape, didn't glimpse a brown bomber or curling hair when I paused and turned to look around me from time to time under the guise of browsing. So I made my way to the entrance nearest my car and headed toward my parking spot. I walked quickly but steadily, head up, eyes forward, the keys ready in my hand.

A trio got out of a car near mine, two men and a woman. I didn't make eye contact, just noted their position and adjusted my angle so that our paths wouldn't intersect.

Except they did, because they moved toward me and spread out, making a sort of loose net. They were too close for me to safely get my door unlocked and inside, so I turned to put the side of my car at my back and drew my feet into the cat stance. It looked like a neutral pose to the average person. If any of these three had enough training to recognize it as a fighting stance, well, it's not like they weren't already aggressive.

The back of my neck was prickling again and goose

bumps marched up and down my skin. I ignored the distraction and kept the three of them in my field of vision.

Which is why I saw Zach before they did. He appeared behind them, seemingly out of nowhere, and maneuvered himself in front of me so fast I blinked.

"Rhonda. Wilson. Miguel." Zach nodded at the each of them in turn. "Did you want something?"

"Is she your bitch?"

The woman who I guessed to be Rhonda asked the question. I had a sudden vision of Zach and myself in orange prison garb and swallowed a laugh. His bitch? Was she kidding?

"She's my business and none of yours." Zach's answer was flat.

"She's on our territory." This from the big, bald black guy. I wasn't sure if he was Miguel or Wilson. Neither of the men looked Hispanic to me.

"She has a job in the mall."

"She should find another one. It'd be better for her health."

Oh, hell. I went cold. Had I stumbled into some sort of gang-related turf struggle? *Thanks, Zach.*

"I take her health very seriously." Zach's tone intensified with threat.

"As seriously as we take the insult of your presence here?" That came from Rhonda, followed by a roundhouse kick that proved she wasn't just a pretty face.

After that, things happened fast, and I missed most of it because Zach was hard to see around. But when it ended, the three of them were down. Zach grabbed my wrist, plucked the keys from my hand, and unlocked my car, pushing me inside and following me in one uninterrupted move.

I scooted over the gearshift and into the passenger seat, my back to the door, my fingers reaching for the handle so I could open it and jump out the other side. Zach caught the arm closest to him in a grip that was hard enough to hurt.

"Stop."

I froze. Then I saw blood on his Harley shirt that hadn't been there before. The shirt had a new rip in it, too. "You didn't zip the jacket," I said, staring. That was dumb. Leather might have protected him. "Which one of them had a knife?"

"Rhonda."

"And she called *me* a bitch." I shook my head and reached out a tentative hand, lifting the shirt to see how badly he was hurt. "Do you need a doctor?"

"No. It wasn't silver."

I frowned, unable to process why the type of metal the blade was made of would make any difference in the severity of his wound. My frown deepened when I couldn't find the wound on his perfect six-pack that should have been there to go with the cut shirt and the blood.

"I'm fine, but feel free to inspect." I looked up and found Zach's eyes on me, full of humor and a heat I didn't think the situation warranted.

I planted my hand on his bare skin and ran it slowly over every inch that wasn't covered by his jeans. Belly, ribs, chest, all of it strong and beautiful and warm to the touch, and none of it marked by any sign of injury.

"I can unzip if you want to keep going." Zach indicated

his lap. I took my hand away, let his T-shirt fall back into place, and sat back.

"No, thanks." I didn't know what to think. I still didn't trust him, but he'd defended me, fought for me. Taken a wound for me. And now it had somehow vanished? "Who the hell are you?"

"Zach." He lifted the hand he hadn't released and drew it to his lips. He pressed a warm kiss to the back of my hand. Heat shivered over me. "We have a date."

"No, we don't." The denial was automatic.

"The moon is waxing." Zach leaned toward me and brought his other hand up to cup my cheek. I didn't pull away. "It'll be full in three more nights. If you don't come to us, we'll come for you. It's time."

"What, are you in some sort of gang or cult?" I blurted out the question. "I don't want any trouble."

"Trouble wants you." Zach caressed my cheek, trailed his fingers along my jaw, and touched the racing pulse at my throat. "You'd better find another job. We've been looking out for you, but nobody likes you coming onto panther turf six days a week. Next time there might be more of them or they might be quicker."

Zach had been unbelievably fast, and he'd still been cut. They could be quicker than that? I mentally kissed my job good-bye and wondered how fast I could find another one. Maybe I should simply move on. Zach's implication that others were watching me, following me, and planning to move in on me three days from now made greener pastures seem pretty attractive.

"Don't try to run." Zach frowned at me as if he'd read

my mind. "It's dangerous for you to live apart from us, especially now. You need to come home."

"I have a home. You don't belong in it." Not that he'd be unpleasant to wake up to, but he did seem to be up to his neck in complications. Anybody sleeping next to him might be sleeping in a danger zone.

"Maybe you belong in mine." Zach's lips curved, and then his head dipped toward mine. It was more the promise of a kiss than the real thing, a brush of lips, a breath of heat. It was enough to send my heart stumbling and make my blood rush. "Come to us, Chandra. You'll find us at the place you see in your dreams."

Before I could think of a comeback, Zach was gone, and I was left wondering if I'd imagined the whole thing. Just in case I hadn't, and there were more people waiting to spring out at me, I climbed back into the driver's seat and headed for my nice safe, sane apartment, where I hoped there wouldn't be any surprises waiting.

About the Author

Charlene Teglia sold her first novel in 2004. Since then, her books have garnered several honors, including the 2005 *Romantic Times* Reviewer's Choice Award for Best Erotic Novel, a 2005 CAPA nomination for Best Erotic Anthology, and *Romantic Times* Top Pick. When she's not writing, she can be found hiking around the Olympic Peninsula with her family or opening and closing doors for cats.

To learn more, visit her on the Web at www.charleneteglia .com.